bitches & bastards angels & saints

GW00722527

Born in Northwich, Cheshire in 1959, Michael Robinson was a regular contributor to the now defunct pop music magazine, *Jamming*, and later co-founder of the music/football/everything fanzine, *The Flashing Blade*. This is his first novel.

bitches &
bastards
angels
& saints

Michael Robinson

Ringpull

First published by Ringpull Press in 1994

Copyright © Michael Robinson 1994

This book is copyright under the Berne convention
No reproduction without permission
All rights reserved

Ringpull Press Limited
Queensway House
London Road South
Poynton
Cheshire
SK12 1NJ

A CIP catalogue record for this book
is available from the British Library
ISBN 1 898051 05 4

Typeset in 12/12.5 pt Melior
Filmset by Datix International Limited, Bungay, Suffolk
Printed in England by Clays Limited, St Ives plc

To my parents

Nadene Braxton saw him coming. He was the Task Force. She was the Falklands. He had his mission. He didn't care who knew.

One woman's terrorist is another girl's freedom fighter. And Nadene Braxton was a feminist of sorts. A wilful child, her mother called her. A proper little madam. A selfish bloody bitch. Such were the brand names of ambition in Bradford. Ambition was viewed with derision and scorn. Evil southern voodoo. Not welcome here.

From a very early age Nadene was alert to the dangers of environmental suffocation, alive to the threat of community veto. A fiercely independent spirit, nurtured through school, finally blossomed on her eighteenth birthday, when she kissed good-bye to wagging tongues and bunched fists, and took a cab from the car park of the Bled Pig to the slip road of the M1, where she posed raunchily with her thumb aloft and her legs apart and a sign that read 'London . . . Fast'.

The lorry driver who picked her up, the one who won the race, said to call him Dick. The irony was not lost on Nadene. She knew where she was coming from, and what she was going to. Every ten minutes she broke into giggles. Dick thought she was crazy. Maybe Dick was right.

The Task Force commandeered a barstool and established an exclusion zone. This island's mine − negotiations are out. He was late twenties, early thirties. Tall and ruddy and running to flab. Suit well cut to accommodate dignity and easy breathing. Hair finely crimped to all but mask a bald patch. His boozy eyeballs shone, his mouth hung in a leer.

He did well in sales, Nadene tiredly deduced. Made money. Lived hard. Talked a load of shit.

'Good evening,' he said, his voice faintly slurred. 'My name is Dexter Humpage. I was sitting across the other side of the room. I couldn't help but notice you. I wondered if maybe . . .'

Her empty glass fell limp in her hand. He turned to the bar.

'Barman,' he snapped. 'Drink for the lady.'

The barman, a busy Mediterranean whose visa was good, chose to ignore the impolite intrusion.

'Hey! You work here or not? Drink for the lady.'

Gino cocked an eye.

'One minute, bigshot. You're next in line.'

Honour seemingly satisfied, Dexter Humpage swivelled on his barstool and propelled himself at Nadene, gazed intently into her tough unswooning eyes. She knew his scriptwriter. Was familiar with his works. Had studied him for O level. Hadn't been impressed.

'You know,' Dexter said. 'Some women act sexy. Some women are sexy. But you . . .'

Deliberate pause to heighten effect.

'. . . Are sex.'

Nadene blinked twice. And her lips trembled. His breath made her nauseous.

Dexter eased off, as if to weigh the impact of his opening salvo. He sipped his drink, allowed his stomach to fall. Prepared to puncture the proffered ego.

'All right,' he said, 'so a corny line like that you heard a hundred times over.'

Make that a million, Nadene thought to herself. And then he caught her with a sucker punch, the old one-two. His forehead jutted, his chest sprang.

'But of all the cheap studs who ever delivered it, I'll tell you one thing for sure. I am the best.'

Nine hours later Nadene was hurriedly fixing her hair in Dexter Humpage's bathroom. Each time she stepped back or turned sideways she knocked an

2

elbow or a knee on the wash basin or the toilet bowl. A tight little torture chamber – complete with garish grey suite and self-willed shower unit – the bathroom constituted approximately one tenth the floor space of a cramped and claustrophobic single-bedroomed flat within the boundaries of Fulham.

'Snapped up this cosy pad just days before repossession,' the drunken Dexter boasted – just seconds before dropping the coffee tray and ruining his trousers. 'The guy was really desperate. Oh shit! My pants!'

Nadene angled her head to check her reflection. The mirror was over the toilet. Just like a man. To admire himself while peeing. But despite the straining neck muscles she thought she looked OK – she passed her own test. So she put away the brush and straightened her flimsy blouse, shuffled into her brief leather skirt and smoothed her dark speckled stockings, lowered herself painfully into steep black stilettos. The worst thing about Saturday night pick-ups – one of the worst things about Saturday night pick-ups – was the struggle home Sunday in your dress-to-get-laid gear. As a general rule Nadene avoided public transport – all those probing, disapproving, insanely jealous glances. She preferred to take a cab. Cabbies are discreet. They've seen it all and more.

With everything in place she crept back to the bedroom for one last peep at big boy. And there he lay, resplendent in his odours, like a whale on a beach, a hippopotamus in dry dock. His head hogged both pillows. His lips shivered slightly as his mouth expelled wind. One bare leg dangled from the side of the bed. He had somehow managed to wrap the duvet round his belly. His hands clawed incessantly at his own breathing bulk.

And Nadene found herself miraculously transported to the assembly hall at school. Her ears filled with a rousing rendition of 'All Things Bright And

Beautiful'. And she wondered, did the Lord God really make this one, this creature both great and small? For despite his weighty presence, and barroom boasts and fanfares, poor old Dexter Humpage had singularly failed to do the business on the mat.

A night to remember? Nadene found it hard to forget.

After scalding himself with hot coffee, Dexter returned to her in bright blue towelling, a lengthy cord knotted around his waist. Now Nadene was familiar with the props of affection. So what does he want to do? Tie my arms behind my back? My ankles to the bedhead?

But for once her razor-sharp instincts for second-guessing a predator fell wide of the mark. For Dexter did no more than settle himself down in an adjacent armchair. A little chagrined, Nadene leaned across and began to tickle his chest, her fingers slipping in where the dressing gown parted.

Dexter looked at her and opened his mouth. Nadene shushed him.

'Talk is cheap. I have expensive tastes.'

He seemed a little more sober now. Less wild in his eyes. A little nervous, even. She felt what seemed like an age-old urge to lie on the carpet and massage his feet. Just to see if they were chilly or stone cold. Bark and bite, she mused angrily. Same old bloody story. This smooth-talking scumbag is no better than some blank bragster in Bradford, bemoaning brewer's droop.

Dexter spoke hesitantly.

'Uh? You go on through. I'll be along. Just need a couple of minutes . . . To prepare.'

Now what the hell does that mean? Forty press-ups? Full scale workout? Quick change into a rubber suit? Hand-job with a magazine? Nadene asked no questions. Just trooped obediently into the bathroom. From where she heard clickings and whirrings, fol-

4

lowed by a rising tumult of the orchestral kind. Wagner, if she wasn't mistaken. Dexter had Wagner on the CD. Which led to fresh speculation. He was on some kind of Nazi kick. Jackboots and slapped faces and 'You vill do as you are tolt!' Oh well. It takes all sorts. And I seem to find them.

Nadene lay in bed and waited for Adolf. In the next room Wagner raved on. Christ, she thought, does he need the whole symphony? What has he got? A regiment out there? However will I cope? Little Nadene One Crack.

And then the noise abated and he appeared in the doorway. Still in blue towelling. No SS armband.

Nadene smiled invitingly.

'I enjoyed the music,' she lied. 'It relaxed my body. Sharpened my senses. Helped my juices flow.'

Dexter swallowed hard, looked sheepish and coy. Then he padded forward, and perched on the edge of the bed, his back turned towards her. He reached for the handpull and switched off the light. Shy boy, she thought. Or teenage nostalgic. Manic masturbation, fury after dark.

She expected a long fumbling intro to the proceedings proper – a pompous pop epic prefaced by strings, an arty film in which the credits came up half way – but none of it. The shape that was Dexter shook off the dressing gown and lifted the duvet, rolled onto Nadene like a crushing machine. Strong legs weighed anchor, rough hands shuffled her pack, while his mouth came a-munching, a frenzied JCB. The bed shook like a treehouse in a tempest, the mattress squeaked like a cellarful of mice. Dexter grunted and grimaced and struggled and strained. Perspiration puddled on his brow, rolled down his nose, dripped onto Nadene's face. But for all the sweat and muscle, it soon became apparent that little of any consequence was stirring below.

Failure in the engine room. Captain concerned.

5

'I . . . Uh . . .' he began, agitated, embarrassed.

'Don't worry, baby,' she whispered, then crawled beneath the duvet to take the matter in hand. What's this? A child's portion? I'm a big girl now. So she smacked the sorry sliver, dispensed a tongue lashing too. Stroked it. Sucked it. Bit it. Blew on it. Took it and poked it at every orifice in the book, and maybe one or two more.

Nothing happened. Not a sausage. No way José.

Ever resourceful, Nadene switched tactics. She climbed on Dexter and put her mouth to his ear. Reverting to broad Yorkshire she bullied and belittled, cajoled and begged. She talked dirty, she talked filthy, she made up new words.

Much pained expression. No Battleship Potemkin.

A shade desperate now, she reverted to the physical. Jockeyed and jackknifed and swivelled and stretched. Tickled his fancy. Rubbed him up the wrong way. Rode him like a broomstick and beat him like a carpet. Finally she fell off him, weary, defeated.

'Dexter,' she said, 'you're not normal.'

His anger swelled. It was high time something did.

'You fucking bitch,' he snarled, and lunged for her throat. She rolled aside to escape him. His head hit the pillow and he crashed out, asleep. Feeling useless, superfluous, she dug his ribs with her fists and kicked his knees and shins. Then she fell asleep beside him, too exhausted even to service herself.

And now she glared at the corpse of his exertions. Rotten slob! Bastard Jimmy No Prick! What do I need with a lump like you? You've not even got one thing I can use for five minutes.

Calming herself, she opened up her handbag and looked around for souvenirs. She was not a prostitute. And she was not a thief. But, like a true Thatcher's child, she detested the notion of effort unrewarded. And she never believed that the cheque was in the post.

From the living room she took a handful of cassettes, a cut-glass ornament and a copper plate off the wall. In the kitchen she appropriated a set of silver cutlery. The bathroom offered sweet-smelling soap and a useful tub of skin lotion. And then, on the bedroom dresser, she emptied Dexter's wallet. The plastic arsenal she had no use for. But forty pounds in cash would cover cab fare, breakfast and a substantial tip.

She thought that as a parting shot she would leave him a note. She found a scrap of paper and scribbled in lipstick.

Dexter,
Didn't wait for you to wake up. After all, I spent most of last night waiting around for you. Now I know what you'll say to the boys in the bar. About what I am. And I won't contradict you. But whether I've had three or three hundred I'll tell you one thing for sure. You were the worst.
    Nadene
      X

*

Consciousness came to Dexter Humpage like a dubious friend. He knew his own name, but not that of the country he lived in, let alone the street. Life? Life? What is this life?

He coughed. God, the air in here. Gets so muggy and stuffy. He opened the window. Somewhere outside a church clock was striking noon. What does this mean? Does it hold significance?

With a dribble then a gush the world worked its way in. The world of cruelly compact but highly-priced living quarters in fashionable West London. Momentary panic. Why aren't I in work? On the phone? At the wheel? Krunt will flay me, fire me, roast me alive. And then he remembered. Sunday. Lovely Sunday. No need to shift units. To peddle hardware, software. To tot up totals and calculate commissions. To bawl out the troops and lick the general's ass. Sunday. Lovely Sunday. Better even than Saturday. No need to drink oneself stupid or blitz the body with drugs. To gorge on junk food or smoke filthy cigars. To go chasing after skirt or perform miracles in the sack. Sunday. Lovely Sunday. Nothing to do except lay back and trumpet.

To go chasing after skirt or perform miracles in the sack. One more remembrance docked safely in his brain. He recalled last night's girl. A spunky little vixen. Noreen. No, Nadene. Nadene Braxton. When I spied her in the nightclub it felt just like old times. I knew she was the one to break the blasted hoodoo. The easy way she flicked her chin, the dense inferno of her eyes. The pert protrusion of her breasts, the hungry nip of her waistline. Her slinky gift-wrapped thighs, the open secret of her snatch. And I played my part so well. Came on strong and macho. Dragged her to my lair. Made her bide my time. Then charged her like a bull. Pinned her for my pleasure.

The question could no longer be avoided. What exactly happened?

The answer was carved in stone. Nothing at all. The fading striker. The girl at his mercy. Missed again.

Dexter glowed with shame. His eyes – two sunken sockets – raked the stodgy terrain of the duvet like a pair of vengeful gunners. Undercover, his miserable member trickled into his testicles – an ostrich in sand.

Goddammit! Why? I even – and this sounds ridiculous now – but I even did what that smug swine Nuttall Mann says he does. I even listened to classical music. Bloody Wagner. Whoever he is. That sales assistant in HMV saw me coming all right. Bloody Wagner. Bloody hell.

But why am I in this ridiculous situation? Huh?

God? Tell me. Why am I humbled and humiliated so? Years and years and not a flicker of a problem. Never too soon. Never too late. A three times a night man, three times at least. Women said (and I believed them) I was the best they'd ever had. A stallion. A rooster. A ram with horns.

But now. What am I now? A fieldmouse? A hamster? May as well be a fish.

These last six months. Seven to be precise. Seven and a half.

I simply cannot make it. Cannot muster. Cannot shoot. What the hell is wrong with me? Is it the male menopause? I'm only twenty-five. So I look a little older (the belly, the hairline, the tension and worry), but that cannot be a factor (do you think?). What else though? Some psychological problem? The only one I know of is that I can't get it up. Perhaps it goes back to my childhood. But I always managed then.

Now I daren't risk sleeping with anyone I know. The whispers would sink me. The laughter down the corridor. I'd have to go abroad.

Hence the endless run of attempted one-night stands. How many willing wenches are there in London? How many left?

For the first time Dexter wondered – where is she now? Nadene Braxton? Glance to either side. No. Not in the bed. Nor anywhere else. In a place this small you can detect the breathing. Which means she's done a bunk. Just as well really. Saves the aggravation of chucking her out.

He rose slowly, like a creature from a pit, and surveyed the contents of his wallet, strewn upon the dresser. Don't remember tipping it up like that. And so little cash left. These Saturday nights are going through the roof.

He wandered into the living room. The armchairs where we sat. Forget it, forget it. Play a little music.

Not bloody Wagner. How about Madonna? Now where's that cassette? Must have left it in the car.

He raised a leg and jabbed a large oft-stubbed toe at the control panel of the TV. Blap. Some sort of gibberish for ethnic minorities. Blap. Some alternative gibberish for the indigenous population. Blap.

He looked about the room. Wasn't there a cut-glass doodah on the table there? Maybe I smashed it one night when I was pissed. What happened to that saucer thing that used to hang on the wall? The one I had in my bedroom as a kid. My mother sent it on to make me feel at home (silly cow).

Into the kitchen. Put the kettle on. Two slices in the toaster. Can't find a knife. Thought I had a few. Must be under that festering stack in the washing up bowl – the festering stack I'm going to sort out one of these weeks (can I apply for a home help? do you have to be disabled? in my current state I am).

Bathroom next. The mirror played straight man. The jokes were on Dexter. Cue for salvage operation.

The shaver screamed against his skin and rattled in his head. He stepped into the shower. Burst the banks of the Ganges. Bastard thing. Five minutes to wash yourself. An hour and a half to mop up.

He switched it off. Settled for the wash basin. Out of soap again. Where's that bloody skin cream? Hardly ever use it. Present from Alison. Alison of the old days. Alison who got hers. Alison the shrieker. Who didn't complain.

He dried himself with a hand towel and thought he'd head back to the bedroom for a serious doze. It was then he found the note. Taped to the bedroom door. He read it slowly. Once. Twice.

Why the! The little! How dare?

He glowered. Clenched his fists. Then found himself enveloped by a balmy sense of tranquillity and calm. He felt like a convert in biblical times. For his nakedness revealed a serpent of biblical proportions.

Stiffened body, gleaming head. A proud beast, which had perked and risen of its own accord.

All at once Dexter Humpage felt empathy and kinship for the eternal challenger, the mutt who learns his lesson while being counted out, who snipes for a re-match once the champ's back is turned.

Oh, spunky spunky vixen. Allow me one more shot.

Johnny Hammer loved his Mum and Dad.

He loved them for the nonchalant yet immaculate timing with which they engineered his dramatic entrance; the fortuitous combination of drunken lust, burst contraceptive, failed abortion and premature drop which saw him snatching first breath on the very afternoon his fellow countrymen stuffed the Krauts at Wembley and brought the World Cup home, in the year of Alf Ramsey, 1966. According to legend, Charlie, Johnny's Dad, was informed of the unexpectedly early event over the crackling Wembley tannoy. But what with extra time and prolonged patriotic joy and one thing and several others he somehow never made it to the hospital until teatime the next day.

'Your wife had quite a time,' the hostile sister scolded.

'So did I,' Charlie happily replied.

Johnny Hammer loved his Mum and Dad. He loved them for the right royal no nonsense moniker he was blessed with.

Charlie's first instinct, understandably, was to name his new-born after one or other hero of the hour. He scoured the match programme for suitable material. Geoffrey Hurst Hammer. Robert Moore Hammer. Anything but Nobby Stiles. But Babs, Johnny's mother, insisted upon a more formal christening, and Charlie reluctantly agreed to honour the memory of her late cousin John, an active socialist and philanthropist, who just months earlier had met an untimely death, the tragic consequence of an accident with gelignite during an ill-fated attempt at wealth redistribution inside a jeweller's shop in Canning Town.

John. Prince John. King John. Loyal John. Big John.

Hammer. Hammers. Hammering. Hammered.

Johnny Hammer loved his Mum and Dad. He loved them for the rich East End heritage into which he was born.

'One thing I'll say about Ronnie and Reggie,' Charlie often opined, 'is that they was always very fair.' His father's familiarity with the Kray twins was something Johnny doubted (everybody east of Whitechapel said that Ronnie and Reggie was always very fair), but it was certainly true that during his own infancy and adolescence the house was often frequented by such colourful lowlife characters as Fat Legs Eddie Roman, Steve the Slash, Albie Alibi and Fast Mits Finnegan. This was the early seventies, and these were second rate gangsters, and sometimes their escapades were as ridiculous as their trousers, but their cheery vernacular and indefatigable enterprise made a vivid impression on Johnny, and helped shape his attitudes towards life, work, society and the Filth.

Johnny Hammer loved his Mum and Dad. He loved them for the way they instilled in him an unbending sense of personal pride, and then took positive steps to help push out his boat.

Well Johnny recalled the warm and bloody afternoon on which he raced home in search of sympathy, having just had his eye blacked by an Irish kid on the Mile End Road. Charlie was furious, and with a short powerful jab made the other eye purple. 'Next time,' he stormed, 'you don't come home until you've proved you're the guv'nor.' So when the Irish kid – thinking he was onto a good thing – came hunting for a re-match, Johnny moved quickly and effectively, took him behind a bush and broke half his teeth, then dragged the wailing victim home with him, a prize. Charlie was delighted. He presented Johnny with a used ten pound note, then together they roughed the Irish kid a little more, finally sitting down to a special celebratory tea, over which Babs was treated to a full and graphic account of the entire heroic episode.

Later, when Johnny was twenty-one, he announced to his parents that he felt the time had come to fly the family nest and establish a place of his own, at the same time to quit his job in the scrapyard and start a little auto business, self-employed like. Sat in the kitchen, Charlie almost shone; his one-time problem child had emerged as a man. He crumpled the cigarette he was smoking, leaving a longer than usual stub, and dashed upstairs, returning five minutes later, a bulging cardboard box underneath his arm; a thing he must have dug out of a corner of a wardrobe, for Johnny had never seen it before.

'There's five grand in there,' Charlie said, 'and it's for you. Where it came from is ancient history, so feel free to spend it. All the best, my son.'

'Isn't your father good?' said Babs, a tear in her eye.

Johnny Hammer loved his Mum and Dad. He loved them for the dignified way they had settled into middle age, pulling up roots and abandoning the East End, heading up into Essex, where many of their old friends now resided.

'It just wasn't the same no more,' said Charlie, regretfully, speaking of his own and Johnny's birthplace. 'Full of niggers and Pakis and slit-eyes and spics. Gangs of kids roaming the streets and showing no respect. Come at you with a blade or a shotgun if you so much as clip their earholes. And apart from that, one or two people had the word out for me, you know what I mean?'

So now Johnny drove up when he could on a Sunday morning. Like today for instance. It was nice to leave behind the shambolic interior of his terrace in Walthamstow, to padlock the pound of Johnny's Unbeatable Bargains, to breathe the clean wholesome air of Epping Forest (it positively whooshed into the car when he wound down the window to flick out his fag), to park his wheels in the driveway behind his father's Merc.

Charlie was looking well. Happy and contented. A lovely shade of red, a big healthy paunch. He had given up cigarettes and beer, switched to cigars and whisky. Johnny still wasn't sure how he had financed the migration to the country, but he insisted everything was paid for, and the Old Bill hadn't been around. Every now and then Charlie slipped out for a night on the town – nightclub, hotel, high class prostitute – but these occasions were becoming fewer, as he found himself increasingly satisfied with a simpler way of life – satellite dish, CD player, car phone, microwave. A back to nature boy, these days, was Charlie.

And Babs too was looking a picture. She was forty-six now. But would pass for forty-three. Her long-time lover was no longer on the scene, not since Charlie and Fast Mits Finnegan deposited him on the steps of the local hospital in urgent need of a BUPA subscription. So now Babs devoted herself whole-heartedly to Charlie, and did all she could to please his bloodshot eye. Had her hair fixed once a week – she was a natural bleached blonde. Spent hours on her face (Picasso, Charlie called her). Still caused eyes to pop when she wore her necklines low. Still wobbled precariously on plucked and polished pins. I mean you'd pick her up. If you'd had a few. Take her home. Give her one. If she wasn't your mum.

'Come and get it,' she yelled now. 'Before it goes cold.'

Charlie and Johnny joined her at the table. Johnny loved eating Sunday lunch with his folks. Such a pleasant change from greasy wop takeaways and cheap frozen muck. The piping hot potatoes, rocks of

15

roast and drifts of mash. Undulating greens, so tender to the fork. Extravagant sauces, the best in the high street. And top of the bill those succulent slabs of elegantly roasted beef, hacked by Charlie, served up by Babs. They looked so good they all but mooed. And just to think that, but for human ingenuity, they would at this moment be wandering aimlessly in a field, chomping uselessly at the grass. Funny old world. Eh?

Lunchtime conversation was sporadic and largely incomprehensible, for both Charlie and Johnny spoke with their mouths full, and Babs knew better than to reprimand either of them for the crime of bad manners.

Occasionally Babs herself would address Johnny.

'Isn't it about time you made an honest woman out of Tracey? Or Julie? Or Shirley? I mean you're almost twenty-three. Ought to think about settling down.'

And Johnny would shovel a mouthful of cauliflower and say:

'Plennyochimeforratmum.'

Or Charlie would suck a roast spud off his fork and interject with:

'Levvaboyarone. Lerrimavesamefun. Oneyyoung-once.'

Pudding followed main course and coffee followed pudding. When all was demolished Charlie and Johnny observed ritual belching – Babs took it as a compliment – and then the family rose in unison. Charlie to stroll down the local. Johnny to lounge on the sofa and flick through the Sunday papers. Babs to clear the table and wash and dry the pots.

'Hey son, you want a lager?' called Charlie, before leaving.

'You got some?'

Charlie opened the fridge and took out a four-pack. He slung it at Johnny, baseball style. Johnny caught it an inch in front of his own nose.

16

'That's my boy.'

'Cheers, Dad.'

Johnny picked up the papers and carried them to the sofa. It was obvious that his family was class. They took three Sunday papers. Nothing too high-brow. No Mail or Express or nothing like that. But a nice selection, a broad spectrum of sport and scandal, tits and titillation, what with all the magazines and supplements, just the job for a lazy Sunday afternoon, especially when there's no football on the telly.

He cracked open the first can and settled himself down. As he hovered over the opening headline so Robin came bounding into the room and started sniffing Johnny's legs. Robin was a rottweiler. A bloody big one. With wild psychopathic eyes, and an enormous seemingly ever erect penis which hung from his fuselage like a vital appendage to a flying machine.

'Hey up Robin. Where've you been? In the garden? Up the woods? Killed anything? Nobbed any bitches?'

Robin was almost four years old, and the stories surrounding him were legion. He was like the third Kray twin. The time he mauled a moggy/ bit a beaver/ savaged a squirrel/ nearly took the hand off a sweet old lady who came around collecting for Dr Barnado's. Cost Charlie a fifty quid donation, that last one. It wasn't that Robin was naturally vicious or anything. He just had this territory thing. And his territory was England.

He was, however, a massive hit with the lady pooches (though not with their encumbered owners) – one look at him at any time and it was obvious why. An abundance of canine snatch queued groupie fashion at the Hammers' gatepost. And Robin wasn't too particular. Again there were stories. The dachshund was laughable. The chihuahua obscene. Leaning over, Johnny showed him a picture of a Sunday belle, human sort. Robin sniffed it, licked it, wagged his tail, swung his baseball bat.

In the kitchen Babs clattered a spoon against a freshly filled bowl of chopped juicy rabbit heads, or some such delicacy.

'Come and get it.'

Robin trotted to the kitchen in search of nourishment. As the dog's pockmarked backside swanked out of view Johnny indulged a lurid fantasy. It had crossed his mind before. A flitting vision of Robin straddling Babs. He could do it, you know. Prove his crossover potential. Rear up at her. Pin her shoulders with his paws. Rip her dress with his teeth. Mount her across the kitchen table.

Absorbed now, like a child in a fairytale, Johnny wondered whether or not his mother would cry rape. He recalled certain pointed jibes thrown his father's way at times of bitter strife. For certain Robin had no deficiencies in that direction. And she was unashamedly fond of the family beast – the tease in her eyes as she scratched behind his ears, the frolicsome way she slapped his heavy haunches. And the affection was reciprocal. In summer Robin wrapped his long pink tongue around Babs' bare calves; all year round he snuffled his cold wet one against the increasingly conspicuous tuft up the top of her skirt. But to the best of Johnny's knowledge he had not yet attempted the ultimate union. Perhaps just as well. Who wants a werewolf for a brother?

Johnny leafed through the newspapers. He took an interest in politics. 'Cabinet minister spanked my son/daughter/twins.' That sort of thing. Similarly world events. Some brothelling preacher out in California, or a rage of X-certificate genocide in a banana republic. Society gossip intrigued him too. 'Transvestite Earl scoffs oysters at Claridges.' And even pure trivia. 'My Randy was insatiable, says mother of twelve.' But what he wanted most from the press was something to take home with him. Something to scratch his crotch over. When he found himself alone. Or when Tracey-Julie-Shirley developed migraine or brain tumour (headaches? behave!).

For such a practised connoisseur it was a so-so week. He liked the look of Titi Topez, the teenage temptress. But most of the others ranged on the rough side of ropey. Babs looked better. Or would do. With her kit off.

Once more his thoughts digressed. The Robin-Babs fantasy had set him in a conjectural mood. And now he recalled that several times, over the years, his mother had paraded naked before him, dancing out of the bathroom, waltzing into his bedroom, justifying these appearances with such remarks as 'We shouldn't be ashamed' and 'If it's natural it can't be rude'. Maybe she was coming on to me. Like Oedipus's mum. Or at least letting me know that she was a fair bit of stuff, that I wasn't from the womb of some tacky old boiler. Funny old world. Eh? It's only when you're older that you realise these things.

Not that she's flashed her birthday suit in recent months. Maybe she's embarrassed. By the sags and hollows that maturity brings. The sags and hollows that haven't yet visited Tracey-Julie-Shirley. Perhaps I should hug her and kiss her and say she's still my old mum. And it doesn't bother me if she's a bit past her prime.

Browsing idly through the pages of a glossy magazine he stumbled on an article that captured his attention. The two faces of modern woman. One face was Lickie Loose, the girl of his dreams. Various photographic angles adorned most of the available wall space at Johnny's Unbeatable Bargains, edging out manufacturer's charts of detailed engine specifications. The hot crater of her mouth in very close close-up. Overripe nipples on forty-four inch boobs. Hungry buttocks chomping skimpy threads of underwear. Neck-snapping thighs poised like pliers. A forest of blowdried fuzz guarding the entrance to the pleasure dome. The sort of woman who commands respect. Who you'd hit your best mate for, leave your last pint.

Lickie left school and started stripping, maybe not in that order, worked her passage to the tabloids and centre-spreads, and now boasted promising careers in both TV and pop music. 'It's a man's world, and a girl has to cash in her assets, whatever they may be. If the feminists have a go at me, well they can get stuffed. I aim to be a millionairess before I'm twenty-five.'

The alternative face was a cool ice-maiden type by the name of Cordelia Welch. Not bad looking, but a trifle frigid, if you know what I mean. Cordelia (Johnny read) is the author of books on Joan of Arc and Simone de Beauvoir, and is currently compiling a text on the New Woman in Society. 'Women have to stand together to be counted. It simply isn't enough for each to stand alone. Left to themselves the weaker spirits will be crushed by outside elements. We need to formulate a common concern. The most difficult task is to make people aware. Once they become aware, our arguments are self-evident.'

Johnny looked at her again. Well, my love. We all know what you need. Be it from Robin or from me.

In the same magazine he found one of those double spread test-yourself features which he usually enjoyed. You know the sort of thing. Twenty questions. Constructed scenarios. What would you do? Multiple choice answer options. A, B, C or D. Note your selection. Then at the end tot up your score. Learn from this the category of contestant you naturally belong to. If you don't agree with the verdict go back and try again.

The quiz games Johnny preferred came under banners such as 'Rate yourself as a red hot lover!' and 'How do you measure up in the sack!'. This one was a little different, but Johnny was bored, so why not? eh? In many ways the interrogation was a natural sequel to the two faces of modern woman. 'Assess yourself as a citizen of today! Place your attitudes under the microscope! If you dare!'

Johnny dared. Manoeuvred warily through a mine-field of hypothetical situations. Some questions were sub-divided for male and female responses. Others for whites and blacks. And it wasn't one of those straightforward affairs where all the cool answers are As and all the dodos vote D. A case for varying your tactics. Meeting bluff and matching trickery.

Half an hour after commencing – and in the act of draining the fourth can – he marked his own score-card and checked the judgement panel (white male). If you scored 80–100 you were a fucking wanker, that was the nub of it. 50–80 and you were still a wanker but you didn't put it across quite so well. 25–50 a hopeless wanker closet case.

Johnny himself had scored nil. So he clearly fell into the final category.

'0–25. You are an outrageous bigot. A genuine throwback. Riddled with prejudice. I doubt you'd even tolerate a ticking clock. Your idea of debate is a fistfight in a bar. Romance starts and ends inside your own trousers. And what are you going to do about it? Nothing, I'll bet.'

As Johnny absorbed this, Charlie strolled in, back from the local, his features mottled further by four straight arm Scotches. Robin followed from the kitchen, darting at Charlie's shoelaces like a bird hunting worms.

'Leave it out,' snapped Charlie, digging the cold wet one with a reinforced toecap.

Johnny brandished the glossy mag and beamed at his father.

'Hey Dad. Look at this. Top of the class. That's me. You have a go.'

3

Roxanne Bliss ate a late lunch, alone. Nadene's lunch was in a binbag out the back. The cats were contesting it. Roxanne could hear them.

She finished her meal, and made the kitchen tidy. Then she settled on the sofa and thought about Nadene. They had shared the place in Clapham for just on six months now. Their relationship was like October. Ever unpredictable, often stormy. But beyond the tantrums and bust-ups and walkouts and eruptions Roxanne loved her flatmate like a surrogate sister. Roxanne was black. Nadene working-class northern. In socio-economic terms they were both of them niggers. In street fighting terms they wore blades between their teeth.

Prior to the present arrangement Roxanne had lived with Royston. In a chicken pen in Brixton. A single semi sub-let to three separate couples. Chaos in the kitchen. Queues for the loo. Always someone having a party, an orgy, a fracas or a fight. What hope for young love in an environment like that? What hope for young love when one half of it was Royston?

Royston claimed he was a victim of oppression.

'What chance did I have? Come from a broken home. Suffered racial harassment all of my life. Fifteen skinheads in my class at school. Fourteen plus the teacher, you know what I mean? And then you grow older and you go for a good job. You meet all the requirements. You got the qualifications But still they pass you over for some three-headed white slob. You walk down the street. Police block your path. Spit in your face. Plant drugs on your body. Fit you up on a mugging charge. Justice is a game. And the umpires are corrupt.'

For a long time Roxanne sympathised. For she

knew all this. About the odds stacked against. Her family and some of her friends knew it too. But in the end you have two choices. And Roxanne was working hard. To earn her just deserts. And so were others. Life is tough. But it isn't impossible. If you keep your wits about you and sharpen your claws.

Royston though was something of a wallower. He wore his bad breaks like badges. Instead of stinging his pride they merely fuelled his lazy streak. He drifted from employment to employment on a seemingly downward spiral.

As a couple they kept an account book in which they balanced incomings and outgoings. It began with equal contributions, but the balance tilted irrevocably month by month. He was draining her patience. Draining her purse. Not to mention her energies with his nocturnal appetites.

The crunch came on a crisp autumnal evening. At least Roxanne imagined it was crisp. Out in Kent and Sussex. In Brixton it was grim and ugly. She arrived there at eight o'clock, after working unpaid overtime at the office. Mean lecherous eyes trailed her as she walked briskly from the tube. And then she stepped inside to find Royston with his feet up, smoking a joint, supping from a can, laughing heartily at an Eddie Murphy video.

'Hey, you should see this guy,' he said, stretching to slap her bum. 'I mean, he sold his ass to the white man's dollar, and I despise him for that. But he sure is funny, you know?'

She glared at him. Royston. Not Eddie.

'Shouldn't you be in work? It hasn't slipped your mind?'

His new position. Evening shift at the Burger Bonanza (all your favourite grills, cooked genuine Western style). This his opening night.

He failed to meet her eye.

'Ah, baby. I stuck it for an hour and then I left

town. There ain't no dignity in that line of work. They make you dress like a cowboy and walk bow-legged. And the produce of the house is poison by numbers. Salmonella Sam – that's what they call the guv'nor. The sheriff, I should say. I don't want to be responsible for gunning no one down. 'Cause when the cops come around you know who'll get the blame.'

Roxanne experienced déjà vu. Four days ago the truck firm expected him to drive a truck with a faulty gearbox and no brakes. Pile-up Pete – that's what they called the guv'nor. Royston didn't want to be responsible for no carnage on the road. And there were countless other examples. Royston foreseeing tragedy like a doom-laden gypsy.

Roxanne was so tired she really had to sit down. But she stayed on her feet, and channelled her fury.

'Royston, what are you going to *do*?'

'Huh?'

'What *are* you going to do? This endless run of dead-end jobs. You've quit more times than Sinatra.'

He launched into a familiar tirade. She cut him short.

'All right. You won't eat shit. I get the message. Loud and clear. But we all have to do it in one form or another. The trick is to make it more palatable. In your case that probably means eating your own. You'll have to work for yourself. Go self-employed. I know lots of people who've done it. It's the eighties answer to the twist. Now, where do your abilities lie? You say you're good with your hands . . .'

He shuffled towards her.

'Yeah baby, let me show you . . .'

'No, Royston. No! You may be the hottest baddest lover in town, but that doesn't pay the rent. It doesn't even buy a sandwich. I got your kind of love coming out of my ears. Literally and figuratively.'

'So what do you want? An extra three inches?'

'I want to know what you are going to do. I want to help you. Maybe we could do something together. But I have to know what turns you on. Apart from . . .'

His expression was blank. She sketched in some outlines.

'You're a competent driver. You know London well. We could run a delivery firm. A minicab firm . . .'

Sarcasm bled from his lips. He was a talented mimic.

'You Boy, drive me to the West End. Get me there on time and I'll spare you a thrashing.'

'What then, Royston? For God's sake what?'

He swigged, inhaled, plumbed the depths of his mind.

'Well,' he said. 'I'd quite like to be a private eye.'

A week later she moved out. Bought him a video and a four-pack and sneaked her things out the back. She had already arranged the flatshare in Clapham. Another girl had done a bunk, leaving Nadene in the lurch. Roxanne answered her advertisement, and the two got on famously.

Royston staged a tenacious campaign to win back his woman. Somehow he managed to track down the address. Kept coming around. Haunting the telephone. Nadene was wonderful. Negotiating across the safety chain. Intercepting his calls. On one occasion he climbed in through the kitchen window and she slashed at him with a breadknife. Instinct told her just where to aim.

'Lady, that was close!'

'Well get the fuck out.'

They strengthened the locks and changed the number. His assaults grew fewer and eventually petered out. Though Roxanne wasn't yet convinced that he was gone for good. Sometimes, after dark, she looked out the window and saw inquisitive headlights parked across the street. All right, so there was a busy takeaway operating there, but maybe it was Royston. And then she'd detect a regular pattern of footsteps on the pavement, pacing to and fro. Not unusual on a main thoroughfare, but one never knows. And what about those occasional human smudges on the paint around the windows? The window cleaner? Perhaps.

The doorbell rang. Four sharp rings. Which meant Nadene. They changed the code religiously on the first of the month.

Roxanne unhooked the safety chain and Nadene tottered in. Roxanne hated to see her like this. An intelligent girl in the guise of a tart. And a busy tart at that. Handbag dangling from her elbow. Skirt rucked around her ass. Tits half hanging out. She looked like she'd been dragged through a rugby scrum backwards, and knowing Nadene you wouldn't bet against it.

'You're late.'

'No, I'm not. Regular as clockwork.'

Roxanne chose to humour her. Dress like a tart. Act like a tart. Hurry up and get changed.

'I mean you're late coming home.'

'I suppose,' said Nadene, looking at her watch, or rather for her watch, for it was no longer there, where it should be, on her slick skinny wrist. Dammit! Left it at Dexter's. Slipped it off in the bathroom. Never put it back. Too much of a hurry. Careless little girl.

'Where have you been?'

'Around,' she said, thinking of Mick. Around the houses, more like. Cabbies have seen it all and more. Well this particular cabbie had just expanded his experience. He picked her up outside Dexter's. All along the Fulham Road he was adjusting his mirror to catch an illicit peep at something that purred like pussy. Never one to disappoint, Nadene uncrossed her thighs and spread herself invitingly.

'You like what you see?'

'I think I'm in love,' he drooled, and promptly bounced a wheel off the kerb.

'You got something for me?'

'My boss would kill me.'

'The cause is worth dying for.'

'Can we use your place?'

'Sorry. My flatmate is there. How about yours?'

'Nothing doing. My wife.'

Mick stopped at lights. Nadene sensed indecision and threatened withdrawal of the goods. Mick revved the engine and said he knew a spot off the beaten track where they could park up the cab. He didn't say it was in Scotland. It wasn't really. But it seemed that way. The time it took to get there.

On the way Mick clouded over.

'The traffic's backed up.'

Nadene kept him ticking with some good whorey banter.

'You'd better think of a short cut before I think of my own.'

Just off the North Circular, it was – some beaten track. But the venue itself was nice and secluded. A little wooded glade. Mick parked beneath a canopy of leaves. Nadene thought they'd best get on. While the coast was clear. To her astonishment Mick lit a cigarette. Hey, you big sap. You're supposed to do that *afterwards*.

'Let's wait a while,' he said.

Here we don't go again, Nadene wistfully reflected.

'I don't want you to think that I'm just a wham bam merchant.'

Oh, for a wham bam merchant.

'Let's talk. Get to know each other.'

And so she talked. Or rather listened. It seemed to last for hours. Mick's marital hell. Made Dante's hell seemed like a house of fun.

At last she coaxed him into the back. They waited

patiently as a man in green wellies coached a golden retriever in the delicate art of crapping beneath a bush. Nadene wondered how the man knew so much.

Business settled, man and dog departed. Nadene felt a ripple of excitement. She hadn't done it in a car since she was fifteen years old. In Herbie Alcock's Beetle. He was twenty-four. He was also six foot three. Which complicated the logistics to such an extent that there was scant pleasure involved, and no little discomfort. All the same it cost Herbie fifty quid to fix the suspension, and they both won Blue Peter badges for perseverance and endeavour.

But whereas Herbie sprayed the seats with his ever willing hosepipe, Mick remained faithful to drought regulations. Are you Dexter in disguise? At first he blamed his failure on a heavy night's drinking. Then he broke down and confessed that it was guilt. His wife. The bitch. It was all her fault.

For some reason Nadene thought of big game hunters, trophies on the wall. Hers would make for a pathetic array. Here's a weasel that I frightened with a twelve-bore. Didn't even have to shoot it. It stopped breathing voluntarily.

Mick put himself together and resumed the only driving seat he was ever likely to occupy. He drove silently to Clapham and dropped her at the flat.

'I trust you won't have the impudence to ask me for the fare.'

'My boss will kill me.'

'I hope you die slowly.'

Now Roxanne was speaking to her.

'I threw your lunch in the bin.'

Nadene pondered this statement for precisely one second and then she exploded.

'You made me lunch? Why did you make me lunch? If I'm not here you shouldn't make me lunch. What do I have to do? Keep an appointments diary? Buy a mobile phone? You're not my mother, Roxanne. Now will you please not interfere in my life. Do you hear me?'

Roxanne heard her. It was difficult not to when the venom parked itself six inches from her ear.

Outburst over, Nadene spun on her stiletto heels, stumbled, nearly turned an ankle, kicked off the confounded death-traps, padded to her bedroom in her stockinged feet, and slammed the door behind her.

Roxanne poured herself a stiff whisky and took everything in her stride.

Half an hour later Nadene emerged, looking wholly apologetic.

'I'm sorry, Roxanne. What can I say? It's just that I . . .'

Roxanne smiled her forgiveness, not to say her mild inebriation.

'Don't worry, baby. I know how it is.'

They hugged, and then sat side by side. Nadene was dressed casually now, in a sweater and jeans. Roxanne preferred her this way. The natural look. For she really was an attractive girl. A natural beauty. Five foot five. Brief honey flavoured bob, now combed out. Lemonade eyes. Crystal complexion. Smooth contours. Sexy ass. Good legs. No need for a re-spray. No comment on a touch-up.

Nadene beamed, like a child with information.

'Wait there. I've got some presents.'

She dashed to the bedroom, more gracefully this time, and returned with her handbag, spilling her souvenirs out onto the table. Roxanne wanted to scold her but didn't have the heart. It was really rather cute. This rampant kleptomania.

Nadene counted off the booty.

'Couple of cassettes . . .'

'Nadene, they're compact discs. We don't have a CD player.'

'I'll get one.'

'It won't fit in your handbag.'

'I'll hire a van. Look here. Some ornament thingies . . .'

'They're nice.'

'One or two knives . . .'

'We've got plenty of cutlery.'

'Soap and skin cream for the bathroom . . .'

'Much more useful.'

'And here . . .'

Nadene peeled off two ten pound notes and pushed them at Roxanne.

'Take this. For the food that was ruined. Entirely my fault.'

'Nadene, don't be silly.'

'No. Take it. Buy us something special. We'll have a proper dinner. The two of us. One night in the week.'

Roxanne touched her friend's hand. Intelligent. Attractive. And a heart of gold. She left the money on the table. Nadene sat down.

'So what did you do last night? While Cinderella was getting balled?'

Roxanne shrugged.

'Nothing spectacular. I stayed in. Did some reading. I'm really keyed up for this interview tomorrow.'

She picked up a glossy magazine and opened it for Nadene.

'And look here. The very woman I'm going to see.'

'Lickie Loose?'

'No. Silly. Cordelia Welch. The writer. She's looking for an assistant to help out with research. Do you think I'll get it?'

Nadene looked at her. This supple slender gorgeous-looking black girl. Long straight hair festooned with beads and bangles. The world's biggest eyes. The world's whitest teeth.

31

'Of course you will. You'll get anything you want to. I've told you that.'

Roxanne blinked those eyes, flashed those teeth. Intelligent. Attractive. Kind-hearted. Loyal.

'And how about you?' she said. 'Still keeping mum about this prospect of yours?'

Nadene smiled furtively.

'That's right. Still keeping mum.'

They sat and talked. Roxanne made Nadene a sandwich. They both drank coffee. Nadene told Roxanne about Dexter and Mick. One long funny story with a stuttering punchline. Roxanne laughed, then adopted a more serious tone.

'Nadene, why do you keep this up? When they so obviously can't. I mean, when you hate men so much.'

Nadene was outraged.

'Roxanne! I do not hate men. I despise and feel nuclear contempt for just about every man I've ever encountered, and that includes my father, my four brothers, the child molester who stole my virginity and the two inept bunglers who took pot shots at me last night and this morning, but that does not mean that I hate men. It just means that I've been unlucky. Very unlucky.'

They both broke into giggles. Roxanne was the first to calm herself.

'OK. Well tell me this. Without flying off the handle. What exactly are you looking for on Saturday nights?'

'I'll tell you, Roxanne. I'm looking for IT. That which was promised me long ago. By the boys in my class. By the magazines my brothers hid beneath their beds. The Big Thrill. The unproven legend of the Cataclysmic Cock. All those panting grateful satiated women. I wanted to be one. I still do. So I follow the hapless trail of wiggling willies, limp apologies. When I fled to London it was only the excuses that changed. Executive stress. Yuppie flu. 'I'm much too concerned about the death of the planet.' So what do you get when you cross a hobby with an obsession? Add to that a spot of scientific – or is it anthropological? – research. At times it's like waiting for Santa Claus. You bake the mince pies. You pour the sherry. But he never shows. It's just your father in disguise. I don't expect the Earth to move. It would be nice if something did. In a crude masochistic way I want them to prove something to me. About themselves. About me. To justify history. To make sense of the ridiculous. I don't want a protector or defender or husband or lover. I just want to be fucked. Properly. Once. By a man.'

Eyes. Teeth. Intelligent. Attractive. Kind-hearted. Loyal. Crazy. Loveable.

'One more thing, Nadene. What happens if you achieve your objective?'

'You mean what will I do?'

'Yes.'

'Sexually?'

'If you like.'

Nadene considered for a moment, childlike again. She sucked her thumb, then spat it out.

'One of two things. Either turn dyke or join a convent.'

Roxanne draped an arm around Nadene's shoulders and gave her a squeeze.

'Do me a favour, baby?'

'What's that?'

'Turn dyke. And let me be there.'

4

Dexter Humpage pressed a clammy palm flat against the horn. The driver of the car in front poked his head out of the window and mouthed a choice selection of Anglo-Saxon oaths. Dexter wound down his own window and wagged a finger. An alert pedestrian dashed between the two vehicles, taking advantage of the temporary hold-up. He was still in the road when the line found motion. Dexter let out the clutch and jabbed the accelerator, almost caught the pedestrian a glancing blow.

The traffic poured slowly towards the West End. Dexter inched ever closer to the bumper of his enemy, jousting, needling, grinning like a devil. And then a despatch rider came shooting from a junction. Dexter swung right to avoid him. Belatedly, the despatch rider swung left. But the front wheel of the motor bike clipped the wing of the car, and the rider took a tumble. There was a sickening clunk as his helmet kissed the pavement. He rolled over once, and then lay still. A posse of commuters dispersed to avoid him. A heavy truck rolled over the fallen bike, left it mangled as a can.

Dexter turned down the stereo and slowed to survey the carnage, looking back over his shoulder, squinting for detail. The despatch rider was breathing, rising groggily to his feet. The truck driver behind blew a raspberry on his horn. Dexter swore angrily and gave his finger more air.

Sunday is dead. Welcome to the working week.

Dexter parked illegally in the narrow courtyard behind KCS. He walked around to inspect the damage to his company Granada. A cluster of deep silver scars disfiguring the paintwork. Barely noticeable alongside the smashed spotlamp, the bent boot lid and all the sundry marks of battle. They say a car lasts two years in London. But that means on average. Some last a lot less.

Dexter checked his watch. Eight twenty-five. He entered the KCS building via the already-opened loading bay, pausing to extend warm greetings to Michael and Hartley, two young blacks employed in the service department. The salesmen frequently regaled each other with sharp denunciations of the boys in service ('They know bog all about computers but we've got a hell of a cricket team,' being the kindest quip on record), but Dexter always made a point of being friendly towards them, at least to their faces. Create a vindictive mood and they can fuck up a sale, no question about it. Send out faulty equipment. Botch a demonstration. All right, so you have the consolation of seeing them hung, drawn and fired. But what is that against the misery of a commission down the drain?

He jogged up two flights of stairs to the sales floor. A brief reception area – an old settee and a pile of computer magazines – prefaced a long open-plan office, the main drag of KCS, flimsy partitions separating self-assembled desks, in-trays brimming with wads of paper, diaries open and soaked in ink, dates circled on calendars, notes pencilled in. On the walls a series of home-made signs – black felt-tipped pen on thin white cardboard – offered motivation ('LETS SELL COMPUTERS'), wisdom ('TIME IS MONEY'), and resolve ('THE ANSWER IS YES'). A fourth sign edged towards the abstract. 'DO IT NOW –BEFORE YOU GO HOME'.

He slung quick hellos to the handful of young hopefuls already in place (no need to court favour with these pimply morons – he could make or break any two of them by the mere allocation of a juicy prospect), then disappeared smartly into the citadel and refuge that bore his name on the door. He closed that door behind him, hung his jacket on a peg, opened the window, pulled back his chair, lit a cigarette. Dexter had been at KCS (Krunt Computer Systems) for three years now. And, like almost anyone who has kept the same selling job for that length of time, he was just about beginning to seriously recoup.

One. Financially. In his first year at KCS he earned a six grand basic, and lived off the loan sharks. In his second year he earned twelve, and his parents shored him up to buy the pad in Fulham. The third year brought twenty-five; he settled the sharks and met his own mortgage. If he accomplished his targets for this year he would gross maybe fifty, and be beholden to no one.

Two. In terms of respect. Those oiks out there, splattered with aftershave, in their Michael Douglas braces and their paisley patterned ties, competing for his patronage like breadline whores. Already this year he had been offered bribes and blow-jobs and booty galore. Selected lackeys cleaned his car and fetched his lunch, paid for it too. He was sometimes tempted to announce over the office pager that his shoes were faintly soiled. Watch the queue form at his door.

The last time he enjoyed such fawning subservience he was fifteen years old. Then, at a minor public school, he was declared a minor genius. Examination wiz. Captain of rugger. Captain of cricket.

At university his academic star dimmed as his social star shone. Hard to keep up in class when you're drinking and screwing and drugging and all. The end result was a 2.1 in English Lit. Par for the course.

His contemporaries set out on the interview rounds, agonised endlessly over rival opportunities, scrambled frantically from one career ladder to the next, looking for a leg-up; and then they disappeared, without very much fuss, into either the established professions or corporate management structures, some even doing charity work, such as teaching or catching criminals. Much the same was expected of Dexter. Only Dexter was in a hurry. He studied those ads that all the sensible chaps ignore.

His first selling job lasted precisely two days. Promoting imitation furniture he cold-called Habitat. His second venture was no more successful. Expounding the undoubted virtues of comprehensive life cover, he invoked so vivid and ghastly a spectre of death that one poor dear collapsed at his feet, immediately disqualifying her eligibility. The bereaved family brought a civil action against Dexter's ex-employers.

By all that is equal his third assignment should have been the one to shatter his spirit, to send him scurrying thankfully towards a life sentence in accountancy. For his third assignment was KCS. Was Krunt.

Joe Krunt was a man of indeterminate origin. If anyone dared to question his nationality he would wave an adopted passport and scream, 'I Breetish ... Yes?' Some said he was Greek. Others said Turkish. A Russian? A Slav? A Slovak? A Pole? His gritty fifty odd year old features (enough rock formations to justify a geography field trip) combined the harshest, least flattering lineaments of all those races, and added some of their own.

Similarly the early career of the man was impossible to fathom. He was in the navy. Or was it the army? A diplomatic posting? A stretch for manslaughter? The only sure thing was that Krunt Computer Systems Limited was incorporated in 1981 (it said so on a plaque on the wall), and at some time between then and now the operation successfully transported itself from a loft above a kebab shop in a North London suburb to these nearly swish premises in the heart of the West End.

As a slave driver Krunt stood comparison with any of the Pharaohs. He was a bully and a bastard, or so it was alleged on the wall of the gents. His basic strategy was to offer the moon and then pay cheese. The service staff turned over on a regular cycle. As for salesmen, they literally walked in off the street and begged him to employ them. And often he did, barely bothering to learn names and faces, so frequently did they change.

By a clause in the contract of employment the first two grand of commission earned by any one salesman was automatically swallowed by the company to repay 'training fees'. And, as the first two grand is inevitably the toughest, most aspiring bigshots departed promptly upon its confiscation, sobs and recriminations echoing down the corridor. For those who survived, Krunt invoked a further clause which allowed for a time lag of up to three months between point of sale and settlement of dues. Three months is an eternity in selling. Life can become hell. Four nervous breakdowns. Two attempted suicides. Much lost commission.

In the beginning it was odds on that Dexter would fall beneath familiar wheels. An inexperienced trier, he would bluff it out, fumble his way, then suffer heartaches untold as the cash he had sweat blood for was snatched from his hand. His world torn apart, he would get drunk with the boys. Compose an indignant English graduate's letter of resignation. Which Krunt would crumple with glee the moment the last door was slammed.

But Dexter hung in there. He stuck it out. Most crucially of all he learned the rules of the game. That the way to win in sales is to always keep smiling. Mass exodus means bonus time for those who sit it out. You inherit leads and prospects, plus existing customers. Where staff turnover is rapid seniority comes quickly. And so he endured the horrors and humiliations. Allowed Krunt to dress him down in public and appropriate his funds. All the time adhering to a long term plan.

He was lucky too, along the way. Picked up one or two breaks. Wandered into reception areas on the very day the board of directors were meeting to consider computerisation. Obtained useful leads on the old boy network, and from happy burbling bedtime conquests (those were the days). As the months passed by Krunt backed off him just a little. Afforded grudging respect. Allowed him room to function.

It had now reached the stage where Dexter believed that secretly Krunt feared him. Feared he would establish his own operation and steal the client list. Which was certainly something that Dexter had in mind. An ex-roommate, now an ACA, had promised to run up a cash flow. A major supplier had expressed willingness to sign a distribution deal. A respected maintenance firm was prepared to offer back-up. Dexter had merely to say the word. Only Dexter was baulking.

'Why?' he asked himself, as sunlight streamed through the window, and the desktop bathed in orange.

His answer was hysterical. A high-pitched shriek.

'Because I haven't had a hard on in over six months!'

The door opened and in danced Fran Lipp, Krunt's latest secretary. Dexter was briefly panic stricken. Had she heard his cry? But her face betrayed no sign of this. Just opened itself invitingly, gushing cool designer fragrance and droplets off the tongue.

'Good morning, Mr Humpage. Is there anything I can do?'

Dexter knew exactly what Fran would like to do. For Fran was the sort of working girl who sought upward mobility via the horizontal hold, who would bend over backwards just to please her boss. She had vacated her previous position following some internal scandal, and now, at twenty-three, was keen to net a biggish fish before she passed her prime.

During her first weeks at KCS she flashed her not inconsiderable ass unashamedly at Krunt, but like others before her found him utterly sexless. So now she was laying the welcome mat for Dexter. The welcome mat of willing flesh that rolled on and on into the Garden of Eden . . .

She answered her own question.

'If I could just pick up those letters . . .'

She leaned across him to reach the typing tray. Held the pose for what seemed like hours. Wisps of thick black hair tickled Dexter's forehead. A pair of heaving breasts swelled beneath his nose. One stockinged foot raised itself elegantly from the carpet. A knee in dark mesh perched on the corner of the desk. He was sure, as she lingered, that she was thinking of a way to slap her groin across his face.

She straightened slowly, held him in the vice of her big dove-like eyes.

'Is there anything else, Mr Humpage?'

So difficult to resist. A sexual McDonalds. Tasty looking goods with a minimum of fuss. Unhealthy perhaps, but from where he was sitting she looked beautifully cooked. The logical reaction was to wolf her straight down. Or at least order a takeaway for a lonely night in Fulham.

Yet he dare not risk it.

Or dare he? There was a brief moment yesterday when everything seemed restored. But that was not to be trusted. Probably no more than a temporary phenomenon, a passing fury as he digested those words. 'You were the worst.'

So the answer was no, he dare not take the chance. He shuddered to think of the potential damage to his reputation. Oh, he would have her sacked, no problem about that. But she would have her pound of flesh, one way if not the other. He read in advance the new home-made signs. 'DEXTER IS IMPOTENT'. 'HO HO HO'.

She flexed her barely covered shoulders. Succulent flesh rolled across collarbones.

'Yes,' he snapped. 'There is one thing.'

Her smile spread from earring to earring. She oozed anticipation. She practically came.

'And what would that be?'

Temptation. Temptation.

Discipline. I mean resolve.

'Get me a coffee. White. Three sugars.'

One forlorn ass waggled disconsolately from the room.

His concentration shot to pieces, Dexter took out files and shuffled papers around. Work to be done, but how do you set that against a crisis in your life? Feeling this way he hopped aboard an unscheduled thought train which whistled him back to when purgatory began.

It was late September. That night I always remember.

He was with Janie then. Practically going steady. Seeing her once or twice a week. Not cheating on her often.

A good sort, Janie. Bright. Vivacious. Particularly adept at . . . Well, let's not think of that now.

Dexter and Janie watched a French film on Channel Four. Then began to romp. Dexter grasped her in an armlift and rushed her through to the bedroom. They undressed so quickly that they almost shed skin. The bed moaned and groaned as they fell heavily upon it.

And then nothing happened. Dexter felt flustered, perplexed. Janie soothed him, reassured him. Eventually they laughed and cuddled. Marked it down as a one-off. Which then became a two-off. A three-off. A four-off. By this time Dexter was so embarrassed he had to finish with the girl. On this front he won an

Oscar nomination for his rousing performance. She was insincere. She didn't try to understand him. No wonder he couldn't make it with her. He was surprised he ever had.

Once she was gone Dexter cast aside deceit and levelled with himself. The truth was simple. She had become too familiar. She didn't stimulate him anymore. He didn't have a problem. What a ridiculous notion.

And so he set a course for pastures new. There was Carole. There was Judy. There was Jo. Still he didn't have a problem.

He sat himself down and delivered a team talk, the first in a series. Get a grip on yourself, advised the coach in his head. Go back to your roots. So he lay home at nights with dirty magazines. The ones they keep in plastic bags underneath the news-stands. But somehow he failed to recapture that youthful effervescence of bubbling head and froth. Simply ended up with print on his pecker.

And the video club he joined didn't do the trick either. Reel after reel of frenzied copulation. This hard-core porn really ought to be banned. All those long stiff thrusting penetrative rods. They make me sick. With envy.

Sat in the office around about this time he would dial those tempting telephone numbers freely advertised in the press, tune himself in to taped titillation. From the relatively tame fare of dim-witted bimbos trilling and cooing to the truly base material of salivating gobblers stringing obscenities. One such chorus girl caused his ear lobe to stiffen. His knuckles turned white as he gripped the receiver. Slowly he lowered it to just above his crotch.

'Get a load of that, you bastard. Then look me in the eye.'

In such dramatic pose – body rigid, brain afire – he felt the tide slowly turning. Then the door swung open and in burst Krunt, mouth already working, as was his wont, expecting Dexter to interpret his gist. Instead Dexter flapped ashamedly and dropped the receiver so it dangled on its wire. Still in mid-flow Krunt stooped to retrieve it. When the message reached his ear he forgot what it was he was saying. Dexter snatched the phone from him and slammed it into silence.

'My girlfriend,' he said. 'Sometimes she feels horny in the middle of the day. Better a phone call than a rash indiscretion.'

A few days later the stricken Dexter sought solace from a prostitute. It was the first time he had done such a thing since he was sixteen years old. Then he and Gregory Crust (vice-captain of rugger, vice-captain of cricket) took an evening train to London to celebrate the end of their exams.

'Rogering the local talent is all very well. But you and I, Humpers, deserve something better. Some rough-edged city snatch. What say you?'

On the inter-city express they buoyed each other's confidence. On the tube to King's Cross they smoked cigarettes. But neither Humpers nor Crustacean would renege on the dare. So they rode the escalator, handed in their tickets, and cruised uncomfortably in the seedy fog of dusk.

'I say. This business of whoring. Not nearly so straightforward as they portray it in the films. I mean who exactly is on the game and who isn't?'

After a couple of ungainly approaches to members of the general public, they stumbled on a pair of willing traders who could have been twins. The same bruised eyebrows. The same skinny punctured arms. The same facile encouragements. The same financial demands.

Crustacean made it standing up against a railway arch. He later said it was incredible. But he would, wouldn't he?

Humpers and his purchase ambled awkwardly over wasteground, until, at her bidding, he laid down his coat. At first it was difficult to feel a part of the situation – the overhanging gloom, the distant blobs that were the streetlights, the chill regular breathing of a girl who looked twenty-five yet was probably his own age – but once he unzipped and unbuckled, things soon squelched into place. Coition occurs in a vacuum. Always.

She wriggled and moaned. A result of the stones that were sticking in her back. But Humpers didn't know that. He thought she was enjoying it.

He held her in his arms and plunged deep deeper deep. He held it, held it, through agonising pain. Then he shot his greatest-ever load – sperm, the cruise missile. He lay there wheezing for a minute or so. Then peered through perspiration for something like a smile.

To his surprise the lucky recipient looked much as she had done before. Sullen. Bored.

'You finished then?' she asked.

The older wiser less potent Dexter had no heart at all for Kings Cross arches. He selected a call girl from the ads in the plastic baggies. 'Sexy Susie. You name it I do it.' It's simple, baby. Just bring me back to life.

On the telephone her voice was brittle. Dexter indulged a woolly fantasy in which a host of nubile virgins cavorted hornily around him. Maybe she's only just gone on the game (her father's dead, her mother's in debt) and I'm her first John. Well, you never know, do you?

'You'll come to my place?' he asked, hanging on the reply.

'Where is that, please?'

'Fulham.'

'Of course.'

'Excellent. Er . . . How much?'

A pause. A fumble. Maybe she was checking on union rates. 'A hundred.'

She was trying it on. The little tinker. But he readily agreed. He was eager for beaver.

A time was set. He waited anxiously, condoms at the ready. The doorbell rang. He stood face to face with a woman of forty-five, a holdall in her hand. Bloody Jehovah's Witnesses. They always call at the wrong time.

'I'm sorry. I'm expecting someone.'

'I'm Susie.'

He stepped back.

'It wasn't you I spoke to on the phone.'

'That was my daughter. My daughter my agent. We're a family concern.'

He let her in. She opened her holdall, began to unpack a negligee. In a fit of madness Dexter thought he would rape her. Get it all over quickly. Not even look at the lines on her face.

He made a grab for her shoulders. Taken aback, she ducked. His arm cuffed her head. Her wig fell off. He paid her. She left.

At the next team talk he sacked the coach and appointed a new man. Who inspired a drastic measure. For under his instruction Dexter picked up the telephone and made a date to see his doctor.

Doc Fuller. Been to see him a couple of times before. Picked up prescriptions for odd minor ailments. Decent chap. Early forties. Experienced. Unruffled. So maybe this is what I should have done right at the start. A frank chat across the desk. Man to man. In strictest confidence.

He stepped into the waiting room and glanced all about. The usual sickly mix of snuffles and splints. No one he recognised. Thank God for that.

The receptionist looked him up in the appointments register and made a tick by his name.

'Dr Fuller is on holiday this week. But we have a

locum in. Dr McKenzie. If you like you can go round and wait.'

Sat outside the surgery door he imagined the worst. Dr McKenzie. Some senile Scottish quack. Geriatric GP dragged out of retirement. Will he ever have dealt with a matter of such magnitude before? Has he once delved into the sexual psyche? (Probably try to equate me with some half-forgotten bout of sheep shagging mania up in the Highlands.) Maybe I should . . .

The light above the door flashed to summon the next patient. Dexter entered nervously, crept around the door. Dr McKenzie looked up at him and smiled.

'Hello,' she said.

Dexter froze, and then recoiled. Threw his arms across his face, backed up against the door.

'Mr Humpage, what seems to be . . .?'

He crumpled to the carpet, began to sob aloud. Five minutes passed in this way. Dr McKenzie probing gently. Dexter weeping like a child.

In the end she offered him the card of a friend of hers in psychiatry.

'He isn't cheap. But he may be what you need. There's nothing I can do.'

Out in the open air Dexter ripped the card to shreds. A head shrink? The cheek of it. What you think I am? Crazy or something?

Back at KCS Fran brought in his coffee. Since he last saw her she had doubled her lipstick quota. Her mouth was like a bitten strawberry cream.

'Strong and sweet. Just the way you like it.'

She placed the cup on his desk, beside his right hand. Then, like a puppeteer, she bobbled her breasts.

'Is there anything else?'

He blinked twice.

Dare I? Dare I?

No. No.

'No, Fran. Really. Not just now.'

Thwarted once more, she swivelled and disappeared, leaving only a fug of cool designer fragrance.

Dexter opened the window wider, then slapped his own face. Right cheek. Left cheek. Flat of the hand. Establish concentration. Focus your attention. It's Monday morning. Any moment now Krunt will hurtle through the door, an agenda on his lips.

He reshuffled the papers he had previously shuffled, arranged them now as he wished them arranged. He scanned the weekly reports filled out by the salesmen. Spelling mistakes, grammatical errors – whatever do they teach them in those comprehensives? But of greater concern was the fiction of the content. Good prospect here. Strong lead there. Who's kidding who? The charge of the Light Brigade, that's what this is. The quicksand motive. Down we go together.

What I need, Dexter thought, is to let somebody have it. Yeah.

And I know just who. Mr Smug Swine himself. Young Nuttall Mann. Nuttall 'Wagner' Mann. He was in here Friday afternoon. Being Friday afternoon we were gently winding down. I had my feet up. He stood at ease. And being both of us lads we were speaking of girls.

'I like to listen to classical music. As a prelude, you know. I find it works wonders. For performance. You should try it sometime.'

'You really think I need it?' Dexter said then, and Nuttall laughed – in homage. Now Dexter lifted the intercom and tapped out the number. There are different kinds of music, my son. When you start whimpering that's music to my ears.

Nuttall Mann was nineteen. Tall and good looking. Three months at KCS. Long hours. No reward. Hadn't sold a bean. Let alone a software package.

'Hello. Nuttall speaking.'

47

Well schooled in the basics. Ah well. Plenty more to fault him on.

'Nuttall? This is Dexter. Come in here, will you?'

Brisk and obedient, he materialised in the room. Launderette. Dry cleaners. Hot shower. Hair gel. United front against the Monday morning blues.

As an extension of his appearance the young man breezed and enthused, a puppy pleased to please. Dexter snickered silently. Rapport with your senior. Enjoy it while you can.

'How are you, Dexter? Good weekend?'

Dexter's eyes were like tarantulas. They crawled on Nuttall's skin.

'You may not know it Nuttall, but the weekend is history. What I'd like to do now is get on with some work.'

The casual bonhomie slid from Nuttall's face, dashed itself on the desk. The enthusiastic puppy looked hurt and exposed. Good. Let's dish out some more.

'I've been going through your weekly report, and quite frankly I wonder whether or not you have a future in this game. KCS has invested good money in you. Salesmanship courses. Product training. If you don't shape up then it's all for nothing. I'll tell you now that not one ink blot on this list will ever buy so much as a pocket calculator from us. Leaving your card on someone's desk does not constitute a serious prospect. Leaving fifty cards on fifty desks does not constitute a week's work. Look at these names and addresses here. Do you have any conception of your potential market? What do you do in your spare time? Offer Walkmans to the deaf?'

Ten minutes later Dexter felt much better. Like a pit-bull terrier. But the poor little puppy looked battered and bruised. So now the mauling was done he tossed half a biscuit.

'All right. That's all I have to say. Don't take it too

personally. We're on the same side. Never forget that. We have a mutual interest. All of us here. Now get out on the road and make a contribution. I'll see you tonight and go through what you've got.'

Nuttall picked his chin up off the floor.

'Thanks Dexter,' he mumbled, and left.

Right, thought Dexter. LETS SELL COMPUTERS.

He dialled Krunt's number. Pre-empt the bastard.

Engaged tone.

He opened a customer file, deal pending, and tried to reach his contact.

'I'm sorry but Mr Truscott is in a meeting just now. May I take a message?'

He hung up. Dialled Krunt again. Still engaged.

Foiled in his quest for instant activity, Dexter stood up and wandered to the window. So much ass, down there on the street. Short skirts. Long legs. Look away. Look away.

He thought once more – he couldn't help it, dammit – of that rough provocative lettering scratched out in lipstick. Goading. Challenging. Inviting. Begging.

Back to the window. Nadene Braxton. Where are you now? Out there somewhere. Hiding in the jungle. Are you the only one who can bring me a cure?

Then the door swung open and in burst Krunt.

5

Nuttall Mann sipped his milkshake slowly. Eleven a.m. A coffee bar in Soho. He was bunking off errands. Taking time out.

His company Fiesta was stashed three streets away. Two wheels raised on the pavement. Back end slewed across a double yellow line. Front end sticking out and blocking an entry. A regiment of parking meters starved of basic rations.

Nuttall smiled mirthlessly as he remembered the first time he took wheels in the name of KCS. It was on a Friday. Krunt emerged from his lair and barked the order himself. Take a pool car from the garage – he took the same one, he recalled wistfully, that he had on loan today – and sit in on a demonstration at this address on Dover Street. Good experience for you. Yes sir. Right away sir. This is my first week and I am anxious to please.

The demonstration was scheduled for two p.m. At ten to two Nuttall was sweating. He had never driven in London before. He had never kept to the left in hell. Escaped lunatics darted across him, cut him to ribbons, then turned around and made threatening gestures. Bushy-browed psychopaths pulled alongside him at lights and skinned him with their eyes. On every face a fiendish grin, on every tongue a foul denunciation. Assorted hooligans, windscreens clogged with fluffy paraphernalia, stuck so close to his bumper that he feared to touch the brake. Cabs anchored abruptly in front of him which meant that he had to.

But worse than all this he couldn't find a parking space. The car parks were all full, the legal roadside spots hogged. He circled around but the sea of tin was solid.

Two minutes to two. Nothing else for it. Have to bed down in a prohibited zone.

He spied a space, single yellow gleaming bright. Parked the car as one might plant a bomb. Watching for wardens, peeping for policemen. Then snuck away like a very timid thief. Gathering his briefcase, checking his watch. Forever glancing back at his illegal deposit.

The demonstration ran smoothly. Nuttall hovered impatiently as the service engineer ran through his paces. Dexter Humpage was there, holding the hand of his potential commission. By three fifteen the deal was wrapped up. Back on the street Nuttall broke into a run. My poor little sacrifice. Are you yet alive? My name is Abraham. How are you, son?

Rounding the last corner he saw it straightaway. Pinned behind the wiper. Little yellow judge and jury. KCS in court. The verdict – very guilty.

Back in the office he tried to mask his shame. Disgrace on the company, brought by his hand. He would tender his resignation. Agree to go quietly.

Sensing his misery, a host of salesmen gathered round.

'What's up, Nuttall? Burst your last condom?'

'It's no laughing matter. Take a look at this.'

He took it from his pocket. The badge of his dishonour. He held it at arm's length, as if avoiding a bad smell.

At first it was met with muted awe. Then, one by one, the boys opened their desk drawers. Jason had thirty-five. Julio had seventy-two. The rumour was that Dexter Humpage topped four hundred.

Sometimes, after hours, the boys played poker and used them as chips. At other times they walked around with handfuls and cracked well-practised jokes. 'I need three for the set. You got any swaps?' 'Take a ticket. Any ticket. Charlotte Street. Thursday. Tell me – am I right?'

When you're out on business you drop the wheels anywhere. Once in a blue moon they drag you off to gaol. Just like ... Well, something else that Nuttall could mention.

He bought another milkshake and returned to his table. Sat there, he indulged in a pleasant private fantasy in which the KCS building played charades and drew The Towering Inferno. He saw himself driving back to base, finding his path blocked by a glistening wagon with a beady blue eye, its ladder raised like the neck of a dinosaur, its water cannons grumbling and hissing forth their jets. He wound down the window of the Fiesta and gagged on billowing smoke. The chief of the city fire brigade emerged from the combat zone.

'You can't go through, son. Hell of a mess back there.'

He put the car into a three-point turn. Then, just as he was driving away, he saw chief ogre Krunt come staggering down the steps, a clutch of client files grasped in his arms, a bright squirrel of flame leaping and tearing at his shoulders and back.

And as for Dexter Humpage; that poor bastard had his sleeve caught in a cabinet drawer and simply could not wrench it free ...

Throughout the office just about everyone had an angle on Dexter Humpage. Or thought they did. For opinions expressed were various. Some said he was Dexter Midas, the luckiest salesman of all time, that leads fell into his lap like direct debits from heaven. Others portrayed him as an old-fashioned craftsman, who had paid his dues and knew the game inside out, whose experience and know-how comprised a vital source for any newcomer to tap. Conspiracy theorists maintained that he 'had something' on Krunt, a headlock of surreptitious knowledge, which accounted for his special privileges and preferential treatment. Mystery men merely tapped their noses and said 'I could tell you a thing or two about that Dexter Humpage ...'

Nuttall himself had never taken to Dexter. For a start, he reasoned, he looks so disgusting. Middle age come early, like Christmas in June. On top of that, so to speak, there's the legendary libido. Forced down your throat. So that in the end you swallow it. Conversation as a towel to rub the fractious royal ego. How much of it is true? Most of it, probably. Fran Lipp drools over him; spends quarter of an hour in the women's room before taking in his coffee. No doubt he is having her. He has hinted as much. And she doesn't deny it.

And then, to expand the picture, you have this morning's outburst. He does that several times a week, increasingly so just lately. Jerks himself off over some unlucky jack. Dispenses degradation in lethal doses. Then coughs a few droplets of life support solution. 'We're on the same side. We have a mutual interest.' He has a way with clichés, does Dexter.

Myself, Nuttall thought, I see him as shrink bait. I think he's in trouble, though I can't pin it down. Which is why, whenever I can, I do my utmost to humour him. Take for instance our conversation last Friday. 'I like to listen to classical music.' I feed him lies like that. 'I always do it with my socks on.' 'I chant a holy mantra and bless my private parts.' I wonder if he believes me?

Of course, there's always one thing I keep beneath my coat. Maybe I should unbutton and let it see daylight. 'You see Dexter, you and I engage in different ball games. You play with girls. I prefer boys.'

Nuttall Mann was conceived at the Isle of Wight pop festival, 1969. Rowley Mann and Cherry Orchard (formerly Alice Green) dug Dylan and each other, the former for an hour, the latter as often as was humanly possible. In a different age it might have been termed a whirlwind romance. For they only met on the ferry from Southampton. Alice said: 'Hey, man.' And Rowley Mann said: 'What?'

When Cherry announced her pregnancy Rowley said it was a sign. Cherry said that with all those chemicals inside her she didn't think it necessary to keep taking her pill. Either way, a hippie wedding was the order of the day. Rowley wore a headband and a shaggy Afghan coat. Cherry wore a daisy chain necklace and a loose-fitting smock. On the steps of the Register Office the best man lit a joint. The baby was christened Nuttall Hendrix Manfred.

Rowley and Alice (formerly Cherry) secured a semi in Guildford. Early dreams of self-sufficiency soon died a death. Like everyone else they shopped at the supermarket. The disciples they were a-changin'. The short summer of love dissolved into a long grey winter of monthly mortgage repayments. Rowley became a Quantity Surveyor. Alice a junior school teacher.

Reminders were few of their old way of life. Rowley's Lennon glasses. Alice's long hair. A shelf of tatty album covers and the time-warped grooves they contained. By the late nineteen seventies Mr and Mrs Mann were voting Conservative and constantly carping about the punks, the immigrants and the jobless, and had replaced their one-time vociferous campaign for the legalisation of cannabis with an equally vociferous new one for the restoration of the death penalty (for murderers, punks, immigrants and the jobless).

Rowley's promotion came at the right time and, when Nuttall was eleven, his parents elected to send him to a fee-paying boys' school.

'The state system is going to the dogs,' said Rowley. Quashing professional pride, Alice had to agree.

In his early years Nuttall was a contented child, largely satisfied with his own company and imagination, happy to make a wigwam out of his mother's old kaftan, to tote his father's pot pipe as a Colt 45, to playfully bowl a Jethro Tull record, propelling it with a stick. Rowley and Alice were a little concerned at how their sensitive self-contained offspring might react to the rigid codes of discipline of the selected establishment. But in the final analysis, Rowley insisted, it was bound to be 'character building'.

As it happened the first year and a half at Rumpiggots was the happiest time of young Nuttall's life. He positively revelled in a shameless uninhibited celebration of boyhood. Chaps together, scheming and romping. Fair hair. Pale complexions. Pure white shirts. Brightly coloured underpants.

A host of new activities intrigued and absorbed him. Furtive explorations of smooth and pliable thighs (practising rugger tackles was the highlight of the week). Breasts and buttocks bumping in the gym. Tickles and tortures inflicted at breaktimes. Wrestling matches in the grass. Underwater frolics. Larks in the shower.

Then, half way through the second year, the chaps seemed to change. Most of them lost their looks. And subsequently (it seemed) began to dream of girls. To express their new desires in extremes of profanity.

Nuttall felt apart from this. He was still handsome. He still lived for the joyous tingle tangle of lightly downed limbs. The others, sensing his obstinacy, began to brand him 'queer'. Nuttall was hurt, and withdrew into himself. Rowley and Alice asked him what was the matter. He said it was nothing. Later, when Nuttall was in bed, Rowley concluded decisively:

'It's just a phase he's going through!'

In Nuttall's fourth year a new gym teacher arrived at the school. His name was Steven Sparks. Twenty-five years old. Tall. Good looking. Beautifully built. But he was not like other gym teachers. Did not indulge in their coarse vulgarity or vindictive contempt, nor share their lust for self-deification and the belittlement of their charges. Some of the boys said that Sparky was 'queer'. According to whispers he liked to slap rumps and loved to stroke biceps. The legend 'Sparky – well dodgy' was plastered about the school by an anonymous hand.

Several times, in gym class, Nuttall felt that Sparky was courting his eye; offering, if not friendship, then a form of understanding. And the teacher always spared him the more rigorous physical demands, with their latent potential for public humiliation. So it came as a jolt when at the end of a lesson Sparky singled him for blame over some trivial misdemeanour, and ordered him to reappear at the gym, stripped and changed, that evening after school.

Nuttall approached his appointment in a mood of trepidation. He feared some horrid ritual punishment or demanding interrogation.

But Sparky, in shorts also, wore a friendly smile.

'Hello Nuttall. I'm sorry about this morning. I hope you realised that it was only a ruse. The truth is that I've been wanting to speak to you for quite some time. I've noticed you, Nuttall. In the gym and around the school. I think that you and I are two of a kind. There are certain telltale signs. As all the idiots say – it takes one to know one.'

Nuttall feigned bewilderment, but not very well. Sparky continued.

'I think you're special, Nuttall. You're not like other boys. For certain you won't be after tonight.'

That much was true. Sparky smiled lustfully and whipped off both pairs of shorts. Rapport was immediate. Rapture came quickly. As did Nuttall Mann. Playing his part in a workout for two. Across the vaulting horse. On the trampoline. Half way up the wall ladders.

For Nuttall it was a wonderful and liberating experience (the last time he'd used Vaseline it was for a chapped lip). Thereafter, in school, his sexuality was brazen. It earned him a couple of beatings from xenophobic heteros, but such temporary sufferance was far outweighed by the benefits secured. Before leaving Rumpiggots he coupled with Sparky several times more, with one other master, four sixth-formers, two fifth years, and one precocious second year. Willing conscripts to the enemy within.

However, it was not until he left school that he 'came clean' to his parents. By the late nineteen eighties Rowley was a Tory councillor and Alice a headmistress. The album covers remained on the shelf but no one had time to ever play the records.

The two forty-one year-olds sat transfixed as their only son spun his modern tale. He told them about Sparky (leaving out the name), but implied that passion twiddled its thumbs until after his own eighteenth birthday.

'It's still illegal! You have to be twenty-one!' screamed Alice.

Rowley was calmer.

'Let the boy finish,' he said.

Nuttall did just that. This is how I am. This is how I must be. Explaining to his parents the facts of his life.

When he was finished Rowley looked at him and said:

'You have twenty-four hours to pack your bags and leave this house.'

Nuttall looked at Alice.

'Mum?'

'I have nothing to add.'

She and Rowley began to mutter such things as 'If this should ever get out . . .' and 'Never hold my head up again . . .' Nuttall had not expected sympathy, and had drafted his own script. References to the past. 'So free love is fine so long as it flows in one direction.' And to the present. 'So the council chamber and the parent-teacher group outvote your own flesh and blood.' In the end all his lines went undelivered. He simply packed his bags and left. That very evening he took the London train, familiar express for migrating souls. He paid for a hotel room, then rented a bedsit. Signed on the dole, and then found work. Stayed in at night and basked in magazines, then exported himself to the intoxicating whirl of the capital gay scene, where every moon is a hunter's moon, and togetherness comes with the wink of an eye.

For a while it sustained him, even helped him grow. The inspirational throb of vibrant companionship, the lingering thrill of sex and affection, the addictive beat of hi-energy dance. Then, in the early hours, doubts began to flicker and home truths to gnaw. There was never any money, never any to spare. The first week of the month, when the rent became due, was a back-breaking chore, the strain of which was worsening. And where are all those bedbugs when the bailiff calls around? Performing martial arts under someone else's duvet. Rapture comes quickly but seldom hangs around.

On his back, in darkness, alone, he questioned the value of all this mutual understanding; scaled the walls of a seedy theme park ghetto. Bar jobs, shop jobs, while you wait to be 'discovered'. Marching against the law, but still subject to it. And overhanging everything, like a cold sickly fog, a deadly curse called AIDS (the trouble with waking up with strangers is that you don't know where they've been). Is nothing ever simple? The answer is no.

Thinking this way he made a tactical withdrawal; whittled his social life, planned to raise funds. He thought a job at KCS would accelerate the process. I'm a personable young man. I can sell computers. Just give me half a chance.

Now, in the coffee shop, reality mocked and sneered. Three months toil and nothing to show. A minimal basic wage. An ever-expanding overdraft. A rent book in arrears.

Krunt was a sadistic swindling bastard. Dexter Humpage a sod and a swine. Every now and then there were laughs with the boys (a sardonic gallows humour permeated the sales floor), but even with them he was living a lie. On his very first morning, before he had properly introduced himself, he overheard offhand remarks about 'fuckin' fags' and 'bleedin' queers'. And so, for the sake of harmony, he donned a false skin. Out of the closet and down the cellar steps. He even invented a girlfriend. Her name was Susan Sparks.

He drained his milkshake and stepped outside, strolled towards the street in which he had abandoned the car. The parking ticket he regarded as inevitable. It would be his thirty-seventh. When you reach fifty you have to stand drinks. Drinks for all the fag-baiters. Ah well.

More sombre than ever, he began to hope and pray that he had not been clamped. That was one wonderfully logical system. Your vehicle obstructs the carriageway – so what do they do? – they tether it fast for the rest of the day. You have to trek across to Camden to pay a twenty-five pound fine. Then hang around for hours until the relief van shows. It had happened to Nuttall twice already. They say things come in threes. Or is that only for straights?

But for all his pessimistic speculation he was hardly prepared for the sight that met his eyes. The sight of nothing. A gaping hole where his Fiesta had been. He paced the empty space and questioned his own sanity. Sprinted fifty yards to double check the street name. Convinced himself that on his return all would be restored. Only it wasn't.

He struggled to piece together an acceptable scenario. He had, after all, been parked across an entry. So someone seeking access had telephoned the police.

Who had rushed to the scene with towbar and rope. Possible. But unlikely. In the space of half an hour.

He saw across the street an old man selling newspapers. The sight was familiar from the time he parked the car.

'Oh yes,' said the old man. 'Not long after you left. Two of 'em, there was. Climbed in and drove away.'

'Definitely not . . . policemen?'

'I wouldn't say so, squire. To me they looked like car thieves.'

Johnny Hammer averted his gaze from the body of an Austin Metro – solid, dull, sonorous – to that of Lickie Loose – flowing, breathing, quivering – captured so artistically in a centrefold tacked to the wall. He was rubbing down the one but wished it were the other. Oh, she was an angel. A girl for all seasons. Football, cricket and everything else. Top of the range model, that was for sure. Velvet upholstery, every optional extra. And he loved her so.

She was popping up in the papers almost every day it seemed, and not just her 'magnificent melons', that was for sure. Numerous news items detailed her itinerary. She was dating 'Wussell' Maycock, the famous lisping DJ. Had signed a lucrative five-year promotional contract with the cosmetics firm D'U. Placed the production of her first album in the capable hands of a renowned international hit-maker. Was herself lined up to present 'Loose Fit' – an experimental fashion show on LWT. Busy little angel.

Johnny's fantasies regarding Lickie were many and varied. Old favourites bore repeats and sequels, while brand new material hatched almost every day. Much of the action occurred right here in the workshop. He would take her forcefully, without mercy; over the bonnet of a Rover, on the back seat of a Peugeot, in the boot of a BMW, beneath the jacked-up shell of a Jag. Sometimes, by way of foreplay, he would spray her with paint, soak her in motor oil, or pump her full of air. All of that stuff was pretty much old hat.

But not every main feature revolved around raw sex. There were human dramas too, and glamorous asides. Johnny saw himself fighting 'Wussell', battering the effeminate bastard to a busted bloody pulp ('I suwender – she's yours'). Next he was up on-stage, playing frenzied lead guitar to Lickie's raunchy vocal. Other times he simply brought it all back home. Johnny and Lickie sipping lager in the pub, sitting side by side in the stand at Upton Park. Lickie washing and ironing while Johnny watches TV. The perfect embodiment of contented domesticity.

His imagination rolled now for a variation on the theme. A typical Friday night – Mr and Mrs Johnny Hammer. Johnny locks up the pound and arrives home at six o'clock. Lickie is already there, having cut short a recording session to fix him his tea. He wolfs it down, grunts appreciatively, then points a finger at the door of the fridge. Lickie takes out a four-pack and tears off the ring pulls. Johnny slaps her bum and offers her a drink. Then washes and changes, ready to go out. Lickie is staying in. She has some shirts to mend.

A cheery evening with the lads in the pub. At eleven o'clock the whisper goes around and they stay on for a lock-in. There's local talent on the scene, just asking to be squeezed. The lads all fool around, but Johnny values what he has with Lickie and doesn't want to jeopardise it by an indiscretion here. Self-discipline is the key. Just a hand on a thigh; a quick embrace outside the toilets; a final goodnight grope. He is done with infidelity – it's a losers' game.

He arrives home at half past one. His key is in his pocket but he rings the doorbell anyway. The light goes on in the bedroom. He hears Lickie padding down the stairs. She opens the door on the safety chain and whispers nervously into the night.

'Who is it? Who's there?'

'It's me, you silly cow. Who d'you think it is? Jack the Ripper?'

She opens the door. She is wearing the flimsy dressing gown he bought her at cost price. And she is wearing it at cost price – with nothing underneath.

Johnny enters the house. An uneasy silence hovers between husband and wife. Lickie puts the kettle on. Still she does not speak. A steel band of tension grips Johnny's insides. He dashes upstairs and opens a pack of toilet rolls.

Ten minutes later, in the living room, the coffee goes untouched. They stand three feet apart, glaring at each other. Lickie castigates him for his drinking and the hours that he keeps. He is angry with her. This possessiveness is stifling. He locks her eyes with his. Resists a temptation to gawp only at her chest. Which is rising like a wave.

She draws breath, pauses in her onslaught. Temporarily short of words, she exclaims with her body. Like a petulant mare she shakes her shoulder-length mane. Stakes hands on hips, elbows jutting outwards.

The dressing gown parts an inch or so more.

Johnny lunges forward and cups his hands beneath her buttocks. The sensation is glorious – like dipping your fingers into big squelchy cream cakes. She wraps her arms around his neck and her legs around his back. He carries her to the armchair. They spill upon it, her body hot beneath him, her heels kicking wildly at the backs of his legs. He snatches the dressing gown from her shoulders. Her breasts swell large and creamy, inflated cushions of flesh. He can't get over them. So he bobs around the side. Sinks his teeth into her throat. Her thighs coil like springs.

With a skilful manoeuvre she manipulates herself to a seat of dominance. Momentarily his drunkenness overtakes him and makes him feel dizzy. He sprawls half on the chair, half off it; his back on the arm, blood rushing to his head. She rips apart his jeans, grasps his erection, stuffs it inside her. Then she rides unsparingly, Boadicea into battle. Her breasts are swinging now, a pair of funky zeppelins. He straightens up slightly and a nipple biffs his nose. Sobering rapidly, he wriggles underneath her, almost cripples himself in his efforts to please. But all the time he knows that this is not his natural role. That of functional junior partner. Prostrate humping machine. He has to claim for his own.

With a back-straining effort he rises to equal height and butts her squarely between the temples. For a second she forms a freeze frame of mingled shock and pleasure, then she tumbles backwards, landing conveniently spread-eagled. He throws himself upon her, enters without fuss (the doorman knows his face), and then thrusts savagely, deep into the heartland. At first she does not react and he fears she is dead. His tears splash on her shoulders and breasts. Two thirds of the land mass is covered by water.

Recovering her senses, she exhales softly. He breathes a sigh of relief, and goes back to work. Within a matter of seconds she picks up his rhythm. It's like a new wave classic. Basic and raw. A couple of choruses and she is jerking and pogoing and screaming for an encore. But he wipes his guitar and storms off stage. That'll teach the bitch to play with my emotions, to feign death like that.

Johnny finished work on the Austin Metro, and adjusted his pants. He took a stroll around the compound, to check on the other lads. Johnny employed three of them, all on government schemes. Yeah, he thought. That's one of the fings I like best about Conservative governments. There's always a helping hand for the budding entrepreneur. People like me what keep this country great.

Barry was busily re-spraying a recently stolen Golf. An urgent job that one – the thief wanted his car back later in the week. And you have to please the customer, that's what I always say (especially when the customer's listening). Meanwhile Phil was winding back the mileometers on some of the older stock. Nice for the kids to learn useful skills like that. Johnny paused. So where is Kevin, eh? Oh yes. Kevin phoned in sick. Internal memo to sack him next time he turns up.

Johnny looked out across the forecourt and spied a couple of prospective punters. Man and wife, middle aged, eyeing up a Ford Sierra. He wandered over and spoke as if he had known them all his life.

'Good morning duke, good morning duchess. Lovely day. Day off work? Very nice. Charming. Now then. I see that you're interested in the old Sierra. And, if I may say, you've made a very wise selection. Obviously know your product. So let me tell you the case history. 'Cause it makes for interesting listening. As you can see the car is four years old. And in that time just the one owner. That is absolutely kosher up front genuine. I can vouch for the geezer myself. He's a mate of my old man's. And as a result of the unprecedented care with which he handled this vehicle there are only firty-free fousand miles on the clock. Which I'm sure you'll agree is pretty well remarkable in this day and age. On top of that you've got solid bodywork and a very reliable engine. Free months road tax, four months MOT.'

'Bit of a dodgy paint job.'

Johnny looked aghast – hammed up the agony.

'Tell me sir. Would you honestly say so? Before you speak let me tell you the story. Minor accident damage. No more than a scratch. Just here on the door. But His Grace – fastidious old basket – he books it in for a total bloody re-spray. And who am I to argue? So I puts my number one lad on the job.

Now if you're dissatisfied with his work I'll call him out here and fire him on the spot. No question about it.'

'I don't think that is necessary.'

'All right sir. As long as you're happy. So how about you and your good lady step into the office and we have a cup of tea and juggle a few figures?'

The couple looked at each other as if he had just suggested wife swapping. The wife mouthed 'No!'

'No thank you,' said Sir. 'We're only browsing.'

They beat a hasty retreat.

'Fucking scumbags,' thought Johnny. 'Put their hands in their pockets and their backbones snap.'

Just then a Ford Fiesta pulled up (Screeech!!) and out jumped Fat Legs Eddie Roman and Fast Mits Finnegan. Johnny hadn't seen either of them for quite some time.

'All right Fat Legs? When did you get out?'

'All right Charlie Hammer's kid? Four weeks last Thursday.'

'All right Fast Mits? I heard you was dead.'

'Vat wasn't me. Vat was ve uvver guy.'

They all slapped shoulders and shook hands. Then Johnny parked the Fiesta out of sight and the three of them settled in the office smoking cigars and sipping whisky.

Fat Legs Eddie Roman was maybe fifty now; a squat man who wore ill-fitting suits, horrendously patterned ties and wonky platform boots with the heels worn down. Throughout his hoodlum career he had always been a co-ordinator, as opposed to any sort of specialist. He liked to bring people together and mastermind operations. The trouble was that his mind wasn't nearly masterful enough, and he had spent half his adult life as a guest in one or another of Her Majesty's hotels ('More stretches than Jane Fonda – that's our Eddie.').

Fast Mits Finnegan was a few years younger but if

anything looked older. His hooked gypsy nose bent all ways at once. His skin was sallow and hung in unhealthy pouches. In his early twenties he was southern area light-heavyweight champion, but soon after that his ring career hit the skids. He 'lost' fights for money and then he lost them anyway. He could have been a contender. Only he wasn't good enough. So he drifted into muscling for cheap crooks like Eddie; sometimes holidaying with them too.

Flushed with the whisky, Johnny probed for information.

'Ford Fiesta? Not really your line, Eddie. Thought you'd have gone for something a bit more flash.'

Eddie sat back and puffed on his cigar.

'Not this time, Johnny. Need something inconspicuous that won't turn no heads. You know what I mean?'

Johnny topped up all the glasses. More chinks than Peking.

'What you got planned then, Eddie?'

Eddie smiled wickedly.

'You know better than to ask me that. Very bad form. Didn't your old man teach you nuffink?'

Johnny laughed.

'All right, Eddie. What do you want from me?'

'The works, my son. And rapid too. Paintwork. Plates. I want it unrecognisable, impossible to trace. Check the engine too. Give it the old twice over. We'll see you right, don't worry about that.'

They sat in the office for at least another bottle. Eddie regaled them with tales of the old days. 'One fing I'll say about Ronnie and Reggie is that they was always very fair.'

Nuttall Mann telephoned the office to report the loss of property. He spoke to Fran Lipp, passed on the message. Then he cabbed to the nearest police station and endured the tiresome paperwork routine. When the last form was filled he took the tube to Goodge Street, and from there walked to KCS. He entered the back way. Michael and Hartley stopped work to greet him.

'Hey up, Nuttall. Where's your car?' Nuttall grimaced, and glowed with embarrassment. If service knew then everyone knew. He skipped up the stairs to the sales floor. It was fairly deserted, but the boys who were there looked up at him and laughed, made dramatic warning gestures, drawing fingers across throats. Dexter Humpage emerged, almost bumped into Nuttall.

'Dexter, I . . .'

'Krunt wants to see you. I mean straightaway.'

Nuttall knocked, and entered Krunt's office. Krunt looked like a gnarled and angry bull. His eyes left no doubt as to which shade they were seeing. Nuttall recalled the first time he was in here, at his interview for the job, Krunt feeding him a line on riches in store. Since then contact between the two had been rare and fleeting. Much petty brutality was now delegated to Humpage. And there had been no figures for the master swindler to swing.

'Sit down,' said Krunt.

Nuttall gulped. 'When he asks you to sit down – that's when you're for it.' So ran a familiar sales floor maxim.

He settled uncomfortably – crossed his legs, uncrossed them. He wondered who was supposed to speak first.

'I presume . . .' he began.

'The car was stolen,' Krunt said. 'Yes. I know that. What did you do? Leave behind the keys? And the door unlocked? Strike up a deal with one of your friends? You dump the car – he drives it away?'

A hissing, sneering, sinister tone. Dripping contempt, breathing malice. Nuttall was astounded. He had expected a grilling, but not a barrage of accusations.

'No. Of course not. The car was stolen. There was a witness. The police are involved.'

Krunt continued – his anglicised accent sprinting back home.

'How much you make on a deal like this? One grand? Two? You never any good. I say it early on. I say it to Humpage but he say you OK. Krunt is right. Krunt is always right. What have you achieved? Nothing. In three months? Nothing. Time and money invested in you. What do I do with an investment like that? And now. What can I say? A company car. Vanished. You and your friend. Two grand? Three?'

'I . . .'

'My hands are tied. I have no proof. You are very clever. Very clever criminal. But I tell you what I do with my useless investment. I throw it away. Before it drains all my pennies. You get out of here. This instant. Go on. Fuck off.'

Indignant emotions spiralled in Nuttall. He felt furious; righteous; grievously wronged. He threw back his chair and hovered over Krunt. He spat his words like tiny poisoned arrows.

'You're crazy – that's what you are. If you ask me you're sick.'

Krunt's face twisted.

'I'm sick? Ho, ho. Let me tell you. I have eyes in my head. And I see things maybe others do not see. I know what you are. Fag-boy. Fairyboy. Take it up the rear. Bum, bum, bum. Ho, ho, ho. Listen fag-boy. Listen to this.'

He reached across to the intercom and casually flicked a switch. There was a crackle of static, then he spoke on the pager.

'Listen. You all. This is Joe Krunt speaking. One of your colleagues, Nuttall Mann, has just been dismissed. For stealing from the company. But before he leaves my office I want to share his little secret. He doesn't want me to, but I'm doing it anyway. Nuttall is a fag-boy. How you say it? As bent as nine pins. Nuttall is a fag-boy. Watch your arses. Thank you.'

Nuttall stood by helplessly as all this was said. His brain beat a tattoo. Anger and frustration swallowed up his skin. But there was little point in striking Krunt – for the other man was stronger.

More helpless than ever, he spat at him and missed. Krunt began to laugh – wild, delirious cackles. He rocked back in his chair and slapped the barrel of his belly.

Nuttall was not sure whether the pager was on or off. Krunt was laughing at him. Maybe they all were. In a final futile gesture he lashed out with an arm and swept a stack of files from the surface of the desk. Papers scattered everywhere. Krunt's delirium steeled – rock formations threatened lava. Nuttall froze for a moment, staring at the mess, then turned around and fled.

The boys on the sales floor stood by their desks and watched him go. Dexter Humpage and Fran Lipp stood over by the photocopier. Nuttall did not bother to clear his own desk. He ran the gauntlet of glances and stormed through the door.

6

Roxanne Bliss stepped out onto the street. Instinctively checked left and right. Phew! No sign of Royston.

Ridiculous, she thought. This creeping neurosis. This galloping paranoia. And yet he's out there somewhere. Nursing a wound. Harbouring a grudge. On the other hand it's not yet noon. So he's probably still in bed.

The cab she had ordered rolled to the kerbside. Rattling and bumping and anxious to please. She gave the driver an address in South Kensington, and then did her best to settle in the back, avoiding the ash and the more unseemly-looking stains. She crossed her legs, smoothed her skirt around her knees. The cab pulled away. She glanced idly at the passing parade, transient street-life. A host of distracted thoughts vied for her attention.

Do I look OK? Yes, I think so. A modest outfit, modest but smart. Are the tights too brazen? No, don't be silly. They match the top. How about make-up? Handbag. Mirror. Too much sheen on the lips? Don't touch it now. And run the risk of smudging. Brush back the hair. Yes, that's fine.

I wonder what she's like? Cordelia? I enjoyed both her books. And the letter she wrote was lovely. But you never can tell. Oh, I'm sure she'll be all right. It's me that's the problem. What will she think of me?

And how about the job itself? I hardly know what it entails. I haven't done anything remotely like it before. Will I manage to adapt? And what about the money? What if it's less than I earn now? But chances are the situation will never arise. She won't pick me. She'll pick someone with more relevant experience.

Who says she won't pick me? I've always managed to achieve things before . . .

'Turn dyke. And let me be there.'

Did I say that? To Nadene? I know full well that I did.

Did I mean it though? In any way at all? And what did I expect from her? Did I suppose that she would laugh at me? Or respond? Or go away and think it over? Weigh the arguments for and against?

So far as I recall she flushed ever so faintly and then changed the subject. Which tells me nothing. Either way. But what is it that I want to hear? Anything at all?

Roxanne snapped out of her reverie. The cab was crossing the river. A tugboat or something, coughing and hooting. Trails of white froth gently rippling the water. The buildings on the bank, stern and outmoded.

'Beeeep!'

The cab swung viciously, then corrected itself. The driver cursed, spat out of the window, shook his head, turned around.

'Bloody Arab, that was. Nearly cut me in two.'

Roxanne composed herself. Legs. Skirt. Handbag. Mirror. Across the river now. Dirty streets. Industrial wasteground. Really should be priming myself for the meeting with Cordelia. And yet . . .

An episode from the past demanded a second hearing. Or rather a twenty-second hearing. But in the brand new light of the remark made to Nadene. It occurred fifteen months ago, and scratched at her now like a kitten at a door.

Royston was away for the weekend. Roxanne had arranged a girls' night out with some of her old friends. Kathy and Roberta, who were still at college. Bev, who was married, and couldn't stay late. And a new girl, Trixie, who was on Kathy's course.

They met at seven thirty at Kathy and Roberta's college digs. Nice to see you. It's been too long. Bev seemed a little different. But that was to be expected.

And Trixie was pleasant, outgoing, friendly. Roxanne stole furtive glances at this stranger in their midst. Small. Fair-skinned. Boyish. Attractive.

The girls embarked on a pub crawl, just like in the old days. Drank themselves giddy, ended up singing. One or two tomcats thought they sniffed supper, but were politely informed that they had misread the menu. Girls' night out. Solid wall of unity.

At ten o'clock Bev made her excuses. They walked her to the tube. At eleven the remaining four considered the option of a nightclub. But the prospect of further tomcats made this less than desirable. So they acquired a bottle of wine and reconvened at Kathy and Roberta's.

Chitter chat. Mellow album tracks. Late film flickering – sound turned down. Is it really after two? Much too late for Roxanne to journey back to Brixton.

Kathy and Roberta slept in narrow single beds. They offered Roxanne a sleeping bag and space on the floor. Trixie said that her place was close by and there was more room there. Roxanne agreed to go with Trixie. Perhaps because she liked her. Trixie was bright, witty, drunk but still sharp. Drunk and rapidly wilting, Roxanne admired that.

Trixie's bedsit was a cramped affair. There was only one bed. Three-quarter size.

'Do you have some blankets? I'll get down on the floor.'

'No need for that,' Trixie said. 'Get in here with me.'

Even then Roxanne's disconnected thoughts were all of college chumminess; two girls back to back, occasional mild annoyance as one or other shuffled or snored. A more sober frame of mind would have told a different story. A sober study of Trixie's face would have written a different book. For Trixie's eyes sparkled like angels – angels flitting on the dark side of the Lord.

In bed Roxanne took a passive role. She had very little choice. One, her head was spinning. Two, Trixie was like a hurricane – a frenzied whirling dervish dispensing magical gratification. A tongue that flicked and darted like a dancing viper. Fingertips charged with vibrant electricity. Roxanne laughed and moaned and pleaded and came. Later she slept in a silken cocoon of simmering body heat, tossing and murmuring, feverish with joy.

She awoke at eight, perfectly sober. Trixie lay beside her, sleeping like a child. Roxanne kissed Trixie's forehead and massaged her shoulders. By eight thirty Trixie was awake. By eight thirty-five they were rolling again. This time Roxanne took the lead, imitating as best she could the other girl's example. Tired, barely conscious, Trixie allowed it all to happen. Made the sounds of pleasure which brought pleasure to Roxanne.

By ten o'clock Roxanne had to leave. They kissed at the door, and vowed to be in touch, but Roxanne broke the vow. What could she do? With Royston and all? But was it only that? Or something deeper rooted? To this day she had not seen Trixie again. Nor Kathy and Roberta. Do they know what happened? Were they in on it all along? Have they too shared passionate nights with Trixie? Was it all a set-up? A sexual snowball? A pyramid sale?

The cab stopped at lights. A man crossing the road looked a lot like Royston. My God, Roxanne thought, I'm becoming like the white folks. All the black men look the same.

I'm nervous. That's all it is. About meeting Cordelia. I have this time to kill.

So let me think about Royston. Was that another of his sins? He deprived me of Trixie. Split me from my friends. Or was it perhaps his great heroic act? Saving me from myself. From a nether world of damaging dykedom; a twilight existence, at a tangent to society.

Poor Royston. Do I treat him harshly?

Royston and Roxanne grew up in roughly the same rough neighbourhood in south-west London. When he made his first advances Royston was fourteen years old, and Roxanne twelve. And he pursued his quest on up through the teen years. Launched sporadic forays aimed at lowering her drawbridge. Which in those days was never breached. Roxanne was a decent, respectable child. She kept her virginity locked away. In a box with her aspirations.

The population of the neighbourhood was constantly in flux. More white families moved away. More black and Asian families moved in. At fourteen Royston was a nervous kid, forever on the lookout for marauding racist thugs. By seventeen he had developed a strut, a stare and a defiant shoulder roll, as he hung out with the young blacks, cocks of the walk, and shared their street corner jive. But for all his macho posturing he could never avoid a tint of vulnerability, a hint of unease. Roxanne liked that.

Roxanne went to college. Sacrificed her virginity. Nurtured her aspirations. When she returned to the neighbourhood she found a rather different Royston. Off his own back he had attended night-school and scraped an education of sorts. He no longer wore jeans and sneakers and the trappings of discontent. Now he dressed smartly and took the tube to work. 'Nothing special – but it's a foothold, you know. I can move on from there.'

He asked Roxanne out. And in her own good time she rewarded his persistence. For a while life was good. Good company. Good sex. Everything ahead.

She stayed at his place for weekends and then for weeks. Moving to the house in Brixton made it somehow official. They threw a party to celebrate. With space so limited only a dozen were invited. Fifty turned up, and spilled into the street.

Royston lost his job – company rationalisation, no

fault of his own. In conjunction with an employment agency he lined up twenty interviews. Roxanne worked overtime, ironing shirts, stiffening collars. He set off each morning with a purposeful stride. Returned home each evening tired and disillusioned. Before very long he had twenty rejections. One radical interviewer even whispered in his ear.

'Dreadfully sorry, old chap. Nothing I can do. Company policy, you see. We simply don't employ you people.'

Thus began the downward spiral. A seemingly endless succession of demeaning stopgaps. A gradual return to street corner rhetoric. Arguments. Fights. Exit Roxanne.

As the cab took a left she tried to dwell on Royston's good points. He was certainly good looking. Really quite clever. Often very amusing. Sometimes considerate. And in his way he had constantly battled adversity. His childhood was tough. Much tougher than Roxanne's. He shook himself free from the grip of the ghetto. Only to see his chances so cruelly scuppered.

Roxanne's glossy lips formed a semi-nostalgic smile. When considering Royston's virtues, she reminded herself, there is of course one more thing.

Royston is the hottest baddest lover in town. You ask him. He'll tell you. Living breathing proof that in one area at least black is big and beautiful and better than whitey.

Roxanne recalled a joke that once did the rounds. That condoms come in four sizes. Small, medium, large and negro.

White men snigger unconvincingly, and insist it's all a myth.

Black men smile confidently and observe that (like Sellafield) everything is open to inspection.

Girls of rich and varied experience have no doubt at all where to place their casting vote.

Roxanne pictured the teenage Royston, sitting on his bunk, his fractured family rowing beneath him, a gang of white brigands baying in the street. That was the time, surely, when he began to count his blessing.

She recalled a gleaming smile, a bulging pouch of denim; concluded that Royston kept a penis much as other boys keep hamsters. Played with it. Protected it. Fed it. Watched it grow.

Most hamsters die before their owners reach voting age. But this beast of Royston's was made of sterner stuff. Became not just one of the family, but the head of the house. And for sure the adult Royston cherished his enduring mascot. To demonstrate this he gave it lots of exciting names. Pussysniffer I. Black Boy's Revenge. Royston's Love Rocket. Enola Gay. Babylon and After. The Ecstasy Express.

As propagandists go Royston made Goebbels look like a third rate graffitist. His celebrated organ received so tumultuous a drumroll that by the time he dropped his pants the lucky lady recipient was virtually climaxing already. The Michael Jackson effect. Keep the goods in storage while the publicity machine churns. Then open the box and have them swooning in the aisles.

But while the Prime Penetrator topped the bill the support acts themselves were not without merit. When Royston made a promise to 'lick you all over' he thereafter regarded it as a binding obligation. Not an inch went unlicked. Not a crevice between two toes. Not a crease in either ear lobe. Not even (bless him) an armpit full of stubble or the inner wall of nostril. Royston was nothing if not thorough.

Roxanne sighed, and made a silent admission. Yes, she said. Royston is the hottest baddest lover in town.

The hottest baddest male lover.

But how does he rate with Trixie? Or even Nadene?

Because, she thought, if you take away the sex, then in the long-term men and women are largely incompatible. Aren't they?

(Roxanne fantasised briefly. Herself and Cordelia, great friends as well as colleagues. Discussing such matters quite routinely.)

Oh, she thought, there are certain aspects of humdrum existence which lay themselves open to mutual exploitation. The notion of the jaded marriage trundling on as a purely business arrangement. Breadwinner and nestbuilder, that sort of thing. But such a relationship is most comparable to that between a horse and cart. Unconnected units co-opted by society for functional ends. Beyond that male and female retreat to their own kind, and share no confidences.

Which means that, in the end, it all comes down to sex. And sexual preference.

Ten minutes later Roxanne was sitting in a comfortable armchair inside a spacious utility room. Lovely house, she thought. I wonder if Cordelia has rented it for the day? To conduct the interviews? Or maybe she owns it? (Pause.) On reflection I hope she doesn't own it. I think it would devalue the books somewhat if I knew that they were written from a background of wealth and privilege. Or is that just foolish prejudice? Exactly what Royston, at his worst, would say?

The enigmatic Cordelia had already showed herself. It was she who answered the ring of the doorbell, peeping out gingerly at high noon in South Ken. Dressed in dungarees and a Marks and Sparks jumper. (Have I overdone it? The tights and all?)

'Hello, Miss Bliss. So nice to see you. I'm afraid that I'm running a little behind schedule. But if you'd like to take a seat just through here . . . Coffee? Tea?'

Roxanne, of course, declined. Because there was obviously no one else around and she didn't want to delay Cordelia any more than was necessary. So now, once again, she had a little time to kill.

She made herself promise not to think about Royston. So instead she thought about Nadene. Nadene the darling. Nadene the unfathomable. I mean, is all that really true? Is she genuinely searching for the cataclysmic cock? (Or is she just a nympho? That has crossed my mind. Screwing around merrily, attaching the rationale as an afterthought addendum?)

In all my conjectures I run into a buffer. A buffer called ambition.

My own ambition I assume is intact.

But Royston lost his. Or appeared to. It splintered into shards, which were crushed underfoot.

So how about Nadene? Is she losing hers? I mean her lifetime ambition, not her bedtime equivalent. She says that when she moved down here she brought a trunk of the stuff. The first time I met her it was evident in her face. A hungry, pinched aspect. Which to me enhanced her beauty.

The trouble with Nadene is that it's all so undefined. Like Royston she has drifted from job to job. She's worked at the health shop for a while now. But she doesn't seem to see it as a long-term career. She doesn't seem to see anything as a long-term career.

She takes days off to pursue what she calls 'prospects'.

'It's a secret, Roxanne. But if it comes off I promise I'll spill the beans.'

Only they never come off. So I'm none the wiser. I do know that she has a certain artistic leaning. She writes poetry, I think. There's a bundle of notepaper stuffed in the top drawer of her dresser. She doesn't keep it locked. But I would never pry.

I can't help thinking that this business on Saturday nights is somehow fundamental . . .

And then it struck her. Obvious in its simplicity. Why didn't she think of it before?

She ought to bring them together. Royston and Nadene. The hottest baddest lover in town. And the girl in search of the cataclysmic cock.

The idea overwhelmed her. It was brilliant. Audacious. Did she have the nerve to set the wheels in motion?

The door opened and Cordelia Welch appeared.

'Miss Bliss? I'm ready now. Sorry to have kept you all this time.'

Nadene Braxton won the race. The seat was vacated when an elderly man stumbled off at Embankment. He raised his bent back and the scrabble began. And Nadene got there first, pipping two strapping young men. In the jungle they speak respectfully of 'the law of the tube'.

Nadene's body chugged jerkily with the motion of the train. A host of distracted thoughts vied for her attention.

It's nice to be free at this time of day. To travel midmorning instead of in the rush hour. How long have I worked at the health shop now? Four? Five months? It's nice to have a day off. It'd be nice to have a lifetime off.

Not that it's the worst job I've ever had. It isn't so bad. Trussed up in a cute little apron. Skipping around in all that pristine spotlessness. But the money's no good. And I'm no sort of role model. Dispensing a bottle of spring water, then nipping into the back to crack open a can of tooth rot. Extolling the virtues of veggie burgers, then popping out at lunchtime to grab a quick beef sandwich. And according to the shop handbook my favourite brand of hairspray is single-handedly responsible for blasting away at least half of the ozone layer.

The thing about the ozone layer is this. We never heard much from it when it was doing OK. It only started squealing once its luck ran out.

79

'Turn dyke. And let me be there.'

Did Roxanne say that? To me? I know full well that she did.

Did she mean it though? In any way at all? And what did she expect from me? Did she suppose that I would laugh at her? Or respond? Or go away and think it over? Weigh the arguments for and against?

So far as I recall I flushed ever so faintly and then changed the subject. Which told her nothing. Either way.

Yeah, but who started it?

'Turn dyke. Or join a convent.'

Did I say that? To Roxanne? Oh, let's not go through that again. Let's stick with the ozone layer. It's infinitely less complicated.

It was pleasant to stroll along the leafy lanes of Hampstead, birds twittering in the tree tops, lawnmowers humming in the grass. Much different, Nadene thought, from the dilapidated council estate where I grew up. There the birds were all dead, and no one could afford a lawnmower, but there were no lawns anyway, so it didn't really matter. She smiled at the tranquil slab of suburbia now surrounding her. It's possible for a girl to travel a long way. And one day maybe I will.

She emerged onto a main thoroughfare and spied her destination. Set back from the road, guarded by a low brick wall, it looked more like a church hall or a boy scout's hut. But the sign on the gate said: 'Thespian Theatre of Hampstead. 1989/90 Season. Auditions in Progress.'

Nadene entered and gave her name to a lady behind a desk. The lady looked like a headmistress or a senior bank clerk. She was probably the queen of the local amateur dramatics, co-opted for duty by the visiting big guns. Squinting through narrow spectacles she searched a typed list, eventually making a pencil tick about half way down.

'Probably be about an hour, Ms Braxton. They're doing five minute slots. Improvisation. Dressing rooms are through there. If you need anything, ask me.'

There were two dressing rooms, one for ladies, one for gents, but both were thrown open. A gaggle of young or youngish people either sat around or lounged against walls or wandered nervously from room to room. There were maybe a dozen girls and half a dozen boys. The boys were all aged between, say, eighteen and twenty. The youngest girl was sixteen, and the oldest – what? – thirty-nine? Some read over notes, others conversed in whispers. The air was dank with stale cigarette smoke. Few of the girls wore make-up. Everyone favoured denim. Except Ms Thirty-Nine, who displayed a flowing one-piece creation, and sported flowers in her hair.

Nadene moved out into the corridor, found a spot from which she could view the stage from the rear. In charge of proceedings was one Basil Villiers, who was all of sixty, but looked even older, so contrived were his attempts to appear sprightly and young.

Nadene knew a little about this Basil Villiers. In the fifties he was a much-feted stage actor, tipped to soar. But he never took to Hollywood. And Hollywood stole his thunder. Then TV kicked him while he was down.

Bitter, inconsolable, he became a travelling mercenary of the boards, lending a faded name to this or that company, marrying and divorcing young actresses, buggering young actors, drinking a bottle and a half of whisky per day. As evidence of this latter affliction his personal acting roles had diminished greatly, and were now almost extinct. These days he claimed odd co-director credits, conducted auditions, handled the press. In another five years, Nadene thought, he'll be answering the phone.

To perform his current task he sat half way back

in the stalls, sandwiched by a man and a woman (just like in the old days). Nadene couldn't spot a drink in his hand, but every so often he would tip his head towards his knees, which suggested that either he was nursing a hangover or else he had a tumbler on the floor.

At the end of each audition the right hand man would call out the next name on his list. Sometimes there was a pause because the name had got cold feet. As soon as someone did appear Basil would boom out a brief scenario, sketch a loose outline within which the trembling hopeful had to work. Sometimes the hopeful would complete the routine of his or her own accord; other times Basil would intercede with a conclusive 'Thank you now!' Then he would confer with both attendants, his eyes hopping left and right, the others scribbling notes.

Nadene had endured similar patterns a dozen times or more. She waited patiently for her name to be called. A clock on the wall ticked away an hour and more. Her stomach began to snap, crackle and pop. Her throat felt parched.

'Thank you now!'

Another gladiator trooped off, mumbling, dissatisfied. Nadene perked – willed the man to call her.

'Miranda Tomkinson.'

Her hopes sank again. Close by her Ms Thirty-Nine extinguished a cigarette and stepped up onto the stage. Basil's seasoned tone positively sizzled with disdain.

'All right, Miranda. This is your scene. You're sixteen years old. And you're in love for the first time. And the boy of your dreams has just promised you a date. This is the moment you have longed for. The happiest single event in your life. And now you're rushing home to make yourself beautiful. You skip through the park and then run up to your bedroom. When you're ready, Miranda.'

Poor Miranda hadn't skipped in a very long time. She attempted it now like an elephant with lumbago. Her high heels clopped and played havoc with her ankles. Her knees caught in her robe and she almost fell over. But Miranda was game. She played out the charade. Let herself into the house. Dashed upstairs. Started splashing make-up.

'Thank you, Miranda.'

Basil was gloating over a public execution. When Miranda arrived backstage her face was stained with tears. Nadene moved instinctively to go across and comfort her.

'Nadene Braxton.'

Nadene hesitated. Her name was repeated. She trudged like a zombie out onto the stage. Behind her Miranda was sobbing uncontrollably. In the pale light of the theatre Basil Villiers looked like a bloated Count Dracula. And Nadene knew the name of the next blood sacrifice.

'All right, Nadene. This is for you.'

Nadene became conscious of a faint annoying echo that seemed to dodge around the rafters, to dart and disappear like a will o' the wisp. She focused on Basil and fought to absorb his words.

'It is the morning after. You have just enjoyed the most exhilarating sexual experience of your life. You were in a nightclub. You met a man. You were a little tipsy. You took him home. And he was incredible. Now you're in the kitchen. Fixing his breakfast. Which you then take up to him. Along with the newspapers. You're floating on air. Basking in the afterglow.'

Nadene walked straight past Basil and out the front door. 'Well I never,' opined the old ham. 'Shout the next one, Clarence.'

*

Nadene let herself into the flat in Clapham. Roxanne wasn't home. Just as well really. Nadene wanted to be alone.

She curled up on her bed and allowed the tears to flow. I never used to cry, she thought to herself. I'd scratch somebody's eyes out before I'd dab my own with Kleenex.

She laid her head on the pillow and dozed for half an hour. When she awoke Roxanne still wasn't home. She thought of popping out for fish and chips, maybe calling at the off-licence for a litre of wine. Pig-out. Immerse your sorrows. But in the end, feeling fragile and lethargic, she settled for a peanut butter sandwich and a cup of black coffee.

Back in her bedroom she took a batch of odd sized papers from the top drawer of her dresser and leafed through them one by one. These meandering snakes of ink comprised her collected works of poetry. She often turned to them in times of crisis. I'm a poet, she told herself. Not a bloody actress. But even in this area of natural expression the vehemence of her invective had tapered appreciably.

She considered her early work, composed in a different bedroom, on a council estate in Bradford.

> Bloody bastard, bloody bastard
> That's what Daddy says.
> Bloody bastard, bloody bastard
> That's what Daddy is.
>
> Nadene Braxton, aged 7½

I smile contentedly at the corpse of my brother
Floating dumbly in the bath.
It was an accident, Mummy, honest
The hairdryer slipped from my hand.
But don't you think it's odd, Mummy
Speaking of my brother
That all his inadequacies are so evident now?

Nadene Braxton, aged 13.

And onwards and upwards. Horrific blood rites. Sadistic sexual baptisms. Tales which now made their author tremble, like a ventriloquist whose dummy had just answered him back.

For light relief she turned to her latest lyric, drafted just the other day.

> The doorbell chimes
> I wonder who it is.
> The postman with a parcel I have ordered?
> The man to read the meter?
> The man to measure up the kitchen?
> The man to fix the TV?
> Or maybe, just maybe
> It is someone for me.

She closed the dresser drawer and lay back on the bed. Even her choice of reading matter had suffered a drastic transformation. Once upon a time it was always Dostoevsky and Nietzsche and other warriors of the night. These days she plumped for a lighter mode of typeface.

She rolled to the edge of the mattress and used her left hand to forage beneath the bed. Eventually she located a plastic bag and dragged it out into the open. It was the only item in her room which she hid from Roxanne.

She opened it now and emptied onto the bed a number of comic books – her very own collection of 'true life romances'. She selected one and began to read.

Roxanne sensed that the interview was closing. She wondered what Cordelia would do. Promise her a letter in the very near future? Or break the bad news now?

Oh, they had enjoyed a very pleasant chat. But those other applicants were doubtless much more suitably qualified . . .

'Well,' said Cordelia. 'That seems to be everything.'

Roxanne smiled weakly. Cordelia continued.

'What I was originally planning, Roxanne, was to have a good think and then contact everyone concerned in a week or so's time. However . . .'

Roxanne felt a twinge in her neck – an unwelcome shudder of guillotine anticipation.

'. . . As of this moment I feel unusually decisive, and I have made up my mind that I would like to have you as my research assistant. That is, of course, if you wish to accept. What do you think?'

Roxanne was not prepared for this. Part of her was still waiting for the blade to descend. She fought hard to come to terms, but in the jumble of her mind the pros and cons all cluttered. It's a step in the dark. It's a grand and a half less.

Cordelia tossed her a rubber ring.

'How thoughtless of me. You'd naturally like a little time to think it over. You take that time. And I'll follow up the offer in writing . . .'

'No! No!'

Cordelia looked confused.

'I'm sorry? Do you mean "no" as in "no"? You don't want the job?'

Roxanne stammered furiously.

'No. Yes. No. YES! I do want the job. Yes! Yes! Yes!'

The two women rose and embraced each other lightly.

'I'm so glad,' said Cordelia. 'I'm sure that we shall have a wonderful time.'

Out on the street Roxanne strove to analyse her own euphoria. Was it something to do with 'acceptance'? she wondered. Cordelia did own the house. Cordelia was a successful writer. And Cordelia had selected Roxanne. Ahead of all the others. Thereby conferring a grand acceptance.

She had had enough of taxicabs, took the steps down to the tube. In the bustling cavern her mood lost its footing. If it all revolved around 'acceptance' then wasn't that reprehensible? She was sure that Royston would have something to say.

Oh, sod Royston! I got the job! I'm happy!

But Royston was a ghost, and Roxanne a haunted woman. She recalled her daring plan to pair him with Nadene. Maybe she had better just forget it – shut him out completely. Or did it go deeper than that? A case of wheels within wheels? Did she need to employ Royston in order to claim Nadene?

7

Royston Bone drummed his fingers on the surface of his desk. By his right hand lay six sharpened pencils. By his left six biros full of ink. Immediately before him sprawled a large but virgin notebook. Next to this, in a pile, an unthumbed telephone directory, a bright new London A-Z, and a folded copy of today's edition of the Times. In the top right hand drawer of the desk, smirking evilly at a world it could not see, the grim persuading edge of a long-bladed knife (he hadn't yet managed to obtain a handgun).

The sign on the door said: 'Roy Bone – Private Eye'.

In a small cubicle in front of the main office sat young Sharon Cobb, Royston's only employee. She was filing her nails. She had it down to an art-form; working now, like a temperamental sculptress, perfecting finer aspects. A receptionist with no calls to answer. A secretary with no letters to type. A book-keeper with no transactions to log.

In her boredom she boiled the kettle almost half hourly, made Royston a dozen cups of tea a day. He asked for coffee. She made him tea. 'I'm sorry, Royston – I forgot.' Royston did not scold her. She was young and still learning, a buxom blonde Caucasian with a healthy pair of legs. Besides, he had matters of far greater import to consider.

The way Royston saw it, when Roxanne walked out on him (crept out more like, while his attention was distracted) he temporarily lost his mind. First of all he harnessed the instinctive cunning of the deranged to track down her new abode. Trailed her home from work to obtain the address. Called on Roxanne's mother; ostensibly to express his sorrow at the unfortunate parting; in truth to rifle the telephone pad as soon as Mrs Bliss looked the other way.

Armed with such illicit information, and spiked by a greatly increased intake of alcohol, he embarked on a wholly irrational campaign aimed at ultimate repossession. There were nights when he set out with kidnap on his mind. This particular stage of madness came to an abrupt end when Roxanne's admittedly horny but unquestionably psychopathic flatmate took an unprovoked swipe at his manhood with a cruel serrated edge. At this juncture he thought; 'She's just not worth it!'

Thereafter, resigned that she was gone, he sank further into the mire of alcohol and marijuana, and granted unfettered license to Pussysniffer I. In the course of such activity he ran across several of his old buddies from the street corner days. One evening, in an all night drinking den, he sat in confab with Gladstone, Chamberlain, Churchill and Wes. Gladstone was spinning some yarn about a warehouse stocked with furs, and seemed to be requesting a form of participation.

The plan was to rob the warehouse and steal the furs, and the way Gladstone figured it the requisite number of participants was five. Three to shift the merchandise, one to drive the van, another to keep watch. Wes was the driver. They wanted Royston as lookout.

'All you do is stand there. You get an equal split. Ten, fifteen grand.'

Wounded in love, wronged by society, desperate for money, Royston said yes. The warehouse proved to be an industrial unit just south of the river. Gladstone had an inside contact who had set everything up.

Wes stayed in the van, the back doors gaping. Gladstone, Chamberlain and Churchill entered by an unsecured window. And Royston stood outside with a flashlight in his hand. If anything unforeseen happened he was supposed to give a signal. Flash. Flash.

Flash. If he daren't risk the light the alternative was to whistle.

Whistle? That was a laugh, he thought, not laughing. I can't whistle. I didn't tell them that. I can't swim either. Swim? What a ridiculous thing to think of. Oh man, it's so scary out here. I hope the other guys don't hear my knees knocking. But I swear I never seen it so dark. Where are all the stars tonight? What happened to the moon? Feels like the night is swallowing me up.

Stood outside the warehouse he recalled another dark night, back in 1981. Only this earlier occasion was illuminated by the sinister eyes of bobbing torches and the crackling toupees of buildings ablaze. His own involvement came about in much the same manner. This time in the youth club. Gladstone, Chamberlain, Churchill and Wes. 'Be on the street tonight. Gonna happen. Don't miss it.'

The press later labelled it the Brixton riot. For Royston it was more like a sleigh ride through hell. Within half an hour of the commencement of hostilities he didn't even care which side he was on – the stone-throwing Rastas and the truncheon-wielding coppers equally steeped in menace. Glass shattered above him. Molotov cocktails exploded in his ears. When he thought that no one was looking the frightened sixteen-year old crept away and hid down an alley behind a battalion of dustbins. Waited till all was still. Walked home and watched the reruns on TV.

The warehouse job passed off without mishap. The three thieves emerged with the booty and the van sped away. On the journey back to Brixton Royston regained composure.

'There wasn't nothing out there. I was ready with that flashlight, ready with that whistle. But there was nothing to report.'

In the end his cut was five grand. 'Unforeseen

overheads. Decline in the fur trade.' What could he do? What could he say? At least with the goods disposed of the chances of detection were slim. So he pocketed the cash, marked it down to experience. Avoided those boys when he saw them on the street.

Sat in his room, his wad beside him on the bed, he recalled the words he once said to Roxanne.

'I'd quite like to be a private eye.'

She laughed at him for that. A week later she left him. But it was true, goddammit! The young Royston, that hunted haunted impatient creature, devoured detective books and comics as if they were food. A private eye works alone. A private eye commands respect. And that, more than anything, was what he craved now.

And so he invested the five grand. Advance rental. Basic office equipment. Wallet full of business cards. Snazzy leaflet, professionally distributed. A new suit of clothes. All he needed now was for a client to walk through the door. It wasn't like this in the books and comics, or in films or on TV. The credits roll. In strolls the sponsor.

His frustration got the better of him. He thumped on the desk. Sharon popped her head around the door.

'Yes Royston.'

'Sorry baby. It's nothing.'

'You want a cup of tea?'

'Coffee, please.'

'OK boss.'

Nice kid. Have to pay her soon.

He sat back and lapsed once again into reflection. What he wanted most of all was for a client to walk through the door. What he wanted next to that was for Roxanne to stop by. Just to see him. Sat here. Behind that sign. 'Roy Bone – Private Eye'.

Royston still felt badly about Roxanne. He had always regarded her as his own special dish. For

91

long years a forbidden fruit; then suddenly established as the chef's speciality, dressed and garnished and laid out before him. He recalled the little girl; her coy smile, bashful curls. The young Royston misspelled her name – ROX ANN – on half the walls in town, bore his community service bravely the one time he was caught. But he was glad now that she rejected him then. She did the right thing. Took herself to college. Secured an education. Allowed the hottest lover in town to simmer at her pleasure.

Then he recalled the mature Roxanne. Proud ambitious far-seeing Roxanne. Tall slender sensuous Roxanne. The world's biggest eyes. The world's whitest teeth. An engaging companion. An enthusiastic lover. A creature able and willing to lay in the inferno.

Sharon brought him his drink. He looked at it disdainfully, as if it were unclean.

'This is tea.'

'I'm sorry Royston – I forgot.'

He slapped her behind.

'That's OK baby.'

She wiggled to the door and then stopped.

'Royston?'

'Yes baby.'

'When do I get my wages? I don't like to ask but it's been two weeks and I have to pay my mum and I need a pair of shoes and my boyfriend Kevin . . .'

'Soon baby. Very soon.'

Dexter Humpage stood in the doorway and scrutinised the silver nameplates. Here we are. Fourth Floor. 'Roy Bone – Private Eye.'

Three or four copies of this fellow's mailshot had been delivered through the letterbox at KCS. They had remained in Krunt's in-tray for a day or so, and then been deposited in the bin. Happening to notice them, Dexter had salvaged one for his own perusal. 'All cases considered. Discretion assured.' At the time he had foreseen no call for a private eye, so he too had crumpled the paper and cast it aside. But the fellow's name had stuck in his mind. And here he was now, waiting for the lift.

Today was Thursday. Wednesday Dexter had made another stab at salvation. He had worked late and then headed straight for the Pulsing Strobe, the night-club in which he had picked up Nadene. She wasn't there. He hadn't dared to hope. But he struck up conversation with a Californian tourist who said her name was Spirit. Thirty-five years old. Even tan. Brutal anorexia. Scrubweed hairdo. Faraway eyes.

She was fascinated by Dexter's occupation. In her opinion God was a computer, therefore what Dexter did was, like, spreading the Message. When he left the club she clung to his arm. When the taxi stopped in Fulham she refused to let go.

But almost from the outset he knew it wouldn't work. She didn't excite him. Was all skin and bone. Wore silly flip-flop sandals. Drank Bourbon neat. Smoked cigars. Was about as sexy as Charles Manson, and probably as dangerous.

She excused herself to go to the bathroom. When she returned she had somehow lost her clothes. Dexter gulped, and dressed her with his eyes. He wanted to explain that it just wasn't on, to address her seriously as one sensible adult to another. But she was Californian. So that was out of the question. Besides, she would never understand. She had al-ready matched their zodiac signs, their bio-rhythms and their birthdays in Chinese. The only thing left for them to do was fuck.

Only Dexter couldn't.

In his desperation he struck upon a crazy idea. He knew it was crazy, but he did it all the same. He feigned an epileptic fit. The trouble was that he had never actually had an epileptic fit. Or witnessed one. Or even tuned in to a reliable description. So he had

93

to work from hearsay and a drunken imagination. Beyond that his performance was based loosely on Jack Nicholson in a number of well-known film roles.

He threw back his head, gargled loudly on saliva, emitted a distinctive clucking sound from the back of his throat. Then he embarked on a rooster walk all around the living room, his head springing back and forth from his shoulders like a flushed and straining yo-yo. From time to time he veered from his course and pecked at imaginary crumbs on top of the TV set and the armchair. For some reason Spirit began to clap her hands and whoop.

Dexter lay on his back and howled like a wolf. He rolled onto his stomach and beat at the floor. He jumped up, rushed at the wall, and butted it firmly. He pretended to be a windmill, a fire engine, an alarm clock, a cow.

All to no avail. The truth was that she loved it. It turned her on. Steam began to billow from between those skinny thighs. Her tongue dangled way down below her chin.

Dexter held up a hand to halt her hungry advance.

'Spirit,' he said. 'There's something I have to tell you.'

She took his hand and kissed it.

'What's that, baby?'

'I'm HIV positive.'

'That's all right. So am I. Let's kill each other. The ultimate, huh?'

He threw her out. She clung to a lamppost.

'Scumbag,' she cried.

He threw out her clothes.

'Yeah,' he said. 'Have a crap day.'

Dexter emerged from the lift onto the fourth floor landing. For a moment he hesitated, thought of dodging back. The doors crept teasingly and then snapped to. The point of no return. Half a man's gotta do what half a man's gotta do.

He stepped through the appropriate entrance and found himself opposite Sharon. Mmm, he thought. Rather tasty. He angled his head to grab a peep at her legs. Stop it! Stop it! It'll only end in tears.

Sharon looked up from The Sun crossword – an eternal conundrum of two across and one down. Initially she thought that Dexter was an apparition, that she had been idle so long she had begun to hallucinate. However, the surreptitious glance beneath the desk confirmed that he was real. Absorbing all this she almost purred with anticipation. A chance, at last, to run through her paces.

She smiled broadly.

'Good morning sir. May I be of assistance?'

Normally, in his working guise, Dexter ate receptionists for breakfast and spat out the bangles. Now though he felt unusually ill at ease. The smooth-talking salesman playing away from home.

'Er. Yes. My name is . . .'

Hold on. Don't give too much away.

'Page. Mr Page. And I would like to see Mr Bone.'

'Do you have an appointment, sir?'

'Er. No. Is that necessary?'

'Well sir, Mr Bone has been rather busy of late. But if you'd like to take a seat I'll try and interrupt him and see if he can manage to fit you in . . .'

She wiggled to Royston's door. Dexter remained standing. Watched her fixatedly. Left. Right. Left. Right. Cheeks of her ass.

She slipped through the door and whispered to Royston.

'Excuse me, Mr Bone. There is a Mr Page outside who would like to see you. Are you particularly busy at the moment?'

Royston leapt from his seat and scorched her with his eyes.

95

'Busy? What you talk about girl? I ain't been busy in two long weeks. Bring him in quick before he gets other ideas.'

Sharon made dramatic shushing sounds, finger on lips.

'Royston! Don't make it all so obvious. Let him think that your time is precious. That way he'll respect you more and you can bump up his bill.'

Royston sat down again. You have to hand it to these white kids. When it comes to commerce they really know the score.

Joining in the game he looked at his watch.

'All right Sharon . . . Er, Miss Cobb. I think I have a few minutes in which to see Mr Page.'

Sharon smiled at him. You have to hand it to these black guys. When they fall off their high horses they're really rather cute.

She returned to Dexter.

'Mr Page . . . You're in luck. Mr Bone has a little free time between appointments. He'll see you now.'

She escorted him into Royston's office and shut the door behind him. When Dexter first saw Royston it came as quite a shock. Dr McKenzie – take two.

Royston's smile clouded over. He knew that look so well. That tidal wave of polite surprise.

'What's the matter, Mr Page? You not expect a black detective?'

Dexter struggled to regain his composure.

'Er. No. Yes. Sorry. It's just. You know. The stereotyped image. Philip Marlowe. Sam Spade. Oh. Er . . . No offence. But you know what I mean? Sherlock Holmes, Hercule Poirot . . .'

'You never seen Shaft?'

Dexter pushed an apologetic smile and wondered would that do. Thinking once more of income Royston agreed to bury the hatchet – and not where Dexter feared. He rose and offered his hand.

'No matter. I'm Roy Bone.'

Dexter clasped the hand gratefully, and forgot about his alias.

'Dexter Humpage.'

Royston leapt on this as if it were a vital clue.

'*Hum*-page? *Hum*-page?'

'Er. Yes. That's right.'

Royston shrugged.

'Coffee. Tea. Page. *Hum*-page.'

For a moment Dexter wondered who was the more insane. He on his delicate mission. Or this rambling fool before him. But he banished such speculation, applied himself to the task in hand. When your ass is in the tunnel your legs have to follow.

He and Royston both sat down.

'Now then Mr *Hum*-page. What can I do for you?'

'I want you to trace someone for me. Although I don't have much for you to go on. No photograph or anything.'

'What exactly do you have?'

'I have a name. Nadene Braxton.'

Royston picked up a pen and tried to write on the notebook. The pen wouldn't work. Affecting great nonchalance he continued his questions.

'Uh-huh. Description?'

Dexter constructed a rough verbal sketch. Royston picked up a pencil. The lead snapped.

'You know where this lady lives? Lived? Works? Hangs out?'

'She's a northern girl, living in London. I think south of the river. But I don't remember where. Clapham. Streatham. Somewhere like that. Needless to say she isn't in the phone book. And I believe that she works in a health shop, but again I don't know the name or the location. Last Saturday night she was in the Pulsing Strobe nightclub. And that's it, I'm afraid.'

'Uh-huh. Won't be easy you know.'

By means of a series of swift trials Royston had now found some ink that flowed. And already he was scheming. Because this young lady sounded very familiar.

Dexter plunged a hand into his jacket pocket.

'Oh. And I have this. It belongs to her. She left it at my flat.'

He handed over Nadene's wristwatch. For Royston that clinched it. The hand. The breadknife. The colourful timepiece. His manhood winced afresh. He pulled himself together.

'What information do you wish me to obtain?'

'Her address. And circumstances. Some sort of report on her daily routine. Does she live alone? What nights does she go out? What nights does she stay in? Does she have a boyfriend? A husband? A lover? Here is my home number. Contact me there. If I'm not around leave a message on the answerphone.'

Royston sat back and cupped his hands behind his head. He recalled the disparaging look on Dexter's face as he entered. The white kids don't have a monopoly on this enterprise lark.

'You realise, Mr *Hum*-page, that this may take some time? And involve certain expenses, as well as my standard fee? I will have to ask you for a modest retainer.'

Dexter took out his wallet. This was life or death. He wasn't counting pennies.

'How much do you require?'

Royston wasn't sure. How much had he promised Sharon? A hundred a week. Two weeks gone by.

'Shall we say . . . Two hundred pounds?'

Dexter counted out the cash.

'One more thing Mr *Hum*-page. May I ask your purpose in seeking this information?'

Dexter opened his mouth and then closed it again. He too had seen the films and read the books. 'That, Mr Bone, is my affair.'

'As you wish it.' Royston showed him out. Sharon looked up.

'Good-bye Mr Page.'

Royston turned on her.

'*Hum*-page! *Hum*-page! What are you? Deaf?'

He escorted Dexter to the lift, and then returned.

'I'm sorry baby. Didn't mean to shout.'

Sharon looked aggrieved. She cupped a hand to her ear.

'Sorry. Didn't quite catch that. I'm a little hard of hearing.'

He bent over her, pushed back her fringe, kissed her on the forehead.

'I'm sorry baby. OK?'

Her cheeks flushed scarlet. He really was cute.

'OK Royston. You're forgiven.'

'Tell you what baby. Make me a tea.'

'OK Royston.'

She made him coffee.

Dexter Humpage left the building and returned to KCS. On the street he passed Nuttall Mann. Neither one noticed the other. Both were preoccupied by thoughts of their own.

Following his dismissal by Krunt, Nuttall was quite naturally furious. What he required, he thought, was some legal advice. Needless to say he could hardly afford a costly consultation behind the lofty portals of Lincoln's Inn. So he took a trip to a gay bar and picked up a barrister named Sean.

They spent the night in Sean's bed. Sean thought Nuttall rather nervy and tense. Nuttall thought Sean gluttonous and a lot less than tender. Both of them said that everything was fine.

They lay in silence for a while, then Nuttall stroked Sean's hairy chest and made tentative enquiries about the law of unfair dismissal, filling in the details of his own grisly experience.

'I'm sorry old son, but you've no chance there. You'd only been employed three months, so unfair dismissal doesn't apply.'

Nuttall lowered his hand and began to massage Sean's testicles.

'Nuttall . . . That's lovely.'

'How about slander?'

Sean oohed and aahed and showed signs of fresh arousal. Nuttall suspended the massage pending a sensible reply.

'Well,' said the lawyer, somewhat indignantly. 'There is certainly the basis of an action for slander. Prima facie. Blatant defamation in front of everyone in the office. On the other hand, despite the inflammatory language and the derogatory terminology, the essence of what Krunt said is essentially true – as evidenced by your presence here in my bed. And if I were to be subpoenaed . . .'

Clearly anxious for an adjournment of the discussion he clambered on top of Exhibit A. Nuttall shoved him off. For his part he was beginning to question his choice of advocate.

'Sean, I'm serious about this. What if I deny being gay? Would that help to nail the bastard?'

'Not worth it, old son. His counsel would tear you apart. Marquess of Queensberry/Oscar Wilde situation. And you know what happened to poor old Oscar.'

Feeling rather demoralised, Nuttall played his last card.

'There is one other thing. One of the files that I knocked off Krunt's desk. It fell open in front of me. I couldn't help but see it. At first it looked like a load of foreign gobbledygook. But I soon realised that it was in fact a list. Names and addresses, I think. And there were peculiar symbols entered alongside. Figures too. Five thousand. Ten thousand. That sort of thing. I'm absolutely positive it had nothing to do with computers. He's into something else, I know he is. Protection. Prostitution. Drugs. Gun-running. Maybe all of those things. Don't you see – it all fits. His mysterious background. His volatile temper. The rapid turnover of staff at KCS. The way I see it KCS is little more than a front. A headquarters. A legitimate set of books. While behind the facade his activities are wholly illegal. What do you think, Sean? Is there anything I can do?'

Sean was growing tired of this unpaid labour.

'Not much, old son. You could go to the police. But there's really nothing for them to act on. No hard evidence. They wouldn't sanction a raid on such a flimsy pretext. Probably view it as malicious spite from a disgruntled ex-employee . . .'

'So there's nothing at all?'

'You could engage a private eye to snoop around this Krunt.'

Nuttall considered this. Private eyes cost money. All the same . . .

'Tell me, Sean. Do you know any private eyes?'

'Funny thing. Received a mailshot from a guy not so long ago. Unusual, isn't it? Mailshot from a private eye?'

'Do you remember the name?'

'Actually I do. I remember thinking that it sounded like a character from an ancient B movie. What was it now? Yes. Roy Bone.'

'An address?'

'Give me a break. I didn't memorise that. But I still have the leaflet lying around on my desk.'

'Will you call me tomorrow? With the address?'

Sean became wily. All that was missing was the robe and wig.

'I may do, old son. If you will do something for me this very instant . . .'

Sharon looked up. Eureka! Two in one day. She put her nail-file into her handbag and dropped the newspaper in the bin.

'Good morning sir. May I be of assistance?'

Only this one didn't look at her in quite the right way. Not in the way that, in her experience, men usually looked at her. Oh, he was friendly, and polite, and good humoured. But he didn't touch up her breasts with his eyes. He didn't even care whether or not she had legs beneath the desk. So what was wrong? Was her make-up in tatters? Or, at the age of eighteen, had the dreaded first wrinkle finally surfaced on her face?

She asked Nuttall to spell out his name. Then she and Royston enacted the same routine, and Nuttall was ushered in. He gave Royston the lowdown on Krunt. Firstly the open side, then the speculation. He added that he himself was an ex-employee, but made no mention of the sexual revelations, the office broadcast and all.

At the end of it all Royston remained confused.

'Forgive me, Mr Mann. But what exactly do you want me to do?'

'I want you to dig around. Make some enquiries. For myself I am utterly convinced that there is something there. Something big. And to break it open would benefit us both. For my part I would be happy to see justice done. And for you . . .'

He spread his hands wide to indicate limitless possibilities. In fact he was making it up as he went along.

'Reward money? Public esteem? Enhanced reputation? Clients galore?'

Royston considered this. Maybe yes. Maybe no. Still in two minds he laid down the patter about fees and expenses and a modest retainer. Nuttall flannelled some more.

'The truth is, Mr Bone, that I am currently awaiting a transfer of funds. As of the present moment I am able to deposit only a minimal sum . . .'

The detective detected a distinctive odour. That of bullshit.

'How much?'

'Fifty.'

'That ain't much.'

'How much of your time will fifty pounds buy?'

Royston gave the matter some thought.

'Couple of hours.'

Nuttall looked pleased. Royston battened the hatches.

'At the outside.'

'Then make a start. Let me know what you come up with. Maybe, by that time, I will have access to my funds.'

Royston said nothing. Nuttall laid the notes on the desk. Royston put them in his pocket. They shook hands. Nuttall left.

Royston sat down again and thought that things were looking up. The Nadene Braxton case possessed limitless potential. If the truth were as he suspected then he could locate her straightaway. Only *Hum*-page didn't know that. Therefore, in the absence of other profitable work, he could string it out for quite some time. Such a course would not, in his opinion, be dishonest. After all, what right had *Hum*-page to benefit from a purely fortuitous circumstance? Why shouldn't he sweat and suffer just like everyone else?

The Joe Krunt case was a different matter. He would have to think long and hard on that one. But at the very worst he had picked up fifty pounds for nothing. So he couldn't complain.

He called for Sharon. But she was in the ladies, arguing with the mirror. A few minutes later she re-emerged. She smiled at Royston, but much of her zip and zest had disappeared. Why had Nuttall Mann looked at her like that? When she herself could find nothing wrong? What was he? A fairy or something? Or had she suddenly gone out of fashion? Was it time to dye her hair?

'Two weeks' wages,' Royston said.

Her face brightened as he handed her Dexter's wad.

'And as an extra bonus for your loyalty and commitment . . .'

His idea was to give her Nuttall's fifty as well. Then prudence took hold and held him in check.

'A further ten.'

'Thank you, Royston.'

Her gratitude was touching. She wiggled to the door. He began to feel guilty for not giving her the fifty. She was such a nice kid. She deserved something more.

'Sharon.'

She turned towards him.

'Yes Royston.'

'How'd you like to take a ride on the Ecstasy Express?'

8

Lickie Loose was jolted into consciousness courtesy of her radio alarm. The digital display read 9:04. She had tried to set the thing for nine o'clock, but she was useless with technology. 'Featherbrain me,' she would say. 'Lucky I got big tits, eh?'

She yawned and stretched, sat up in bed. Her 'kingsize coconuts' flopped on the duvet. The radio was wailing something bland and monotonous. Lickie couldn't identify it. 'These modern records all sound the same.' That was what Lickie's mum said. And Lickie echoed the sentiment. It may even have been her own hit single. She really wasn't sure.

The music faded and in dived the DJ.

'Gweat sound there, weally gweat. Wussell Maycock with you on Wadio One. Timecheck now. Six minutes past nine. That's what it says on the big cwock here in Wondon. Means it's time for me to extend a vewy special gweeting to a vewy special person who I know tunes in woundabout this time. No names, but if you wead your newspapers you may have an inkwing of the wady concerned . . .'

Lickie switched it off in disgust. The shwivelled wittle wimp was making a habit of this. It was becoming embawwassing.

She had had enough trouble turning him out of the house last night.

'Oh weally Wickie,' he whined. 'Won't you wet me stay?'

'No Wussell – I mean Russell. I have to work tomorrow and I don't want you disturbing me when you get up at five a.m. to do the breakfast show.'

'Oh Wickie, I'll be ever so quiet.'

'No Russell. That's final.'

'I don't know. Wickie. Sometimes I think that you don't want to sweep with me.'

Just occasionally, Wussell, you hit the nail on the head. Of course I don't want to sweep with you. Who would? You have all the sexuawity of a fweshly-burst boil. All that fwenzied huffing and puffing. All those whispered words of wuv. It's wike pwucking daisies. Is he inside me? Is he not? The twuth is, Wussell, that I never wanted to sweep with you. The 'welationship' was all Albert's idea.

'Listen girl,' he said, familiar cement mixer churning in his larynx. 'You thick or what? You got a record out, right? So what's the best way, the guaranteed way of hyping it up the charts? Sleep with a bleeding DJ. Turn him over in the sack and he'll give you three plays an hour. Lightly toast him once or twice and you'll massacre the airwaves.'

Albert (for business and publicity purposes he was known by the single moniker) was Lickie's agent and manager. The press referred to him as a former East End wide boy, and hinted at illegitimate activities in the dim and distant past. Lickie thought that this was grossly unfair. For despite his sometimes forthright manner and occasionally unorthodox methods he had acted like a second father to her, and had advanced her career by leaps and bounds. When she signed to his 'stable' she was plain Maureen Chivers, flashing her wares in seedy strip joints. Nowadays she was dining with kings.

(Well, Prince Charles is a future king isn't he? Maybe I wasn't invited to his table, but I did shake his hand. At the kiddies' charity doodah. He walked along the line real brisk like, and then he hung around and spoke to me. 'Hello,' he said. 'How's tricks?' I don't think for a minute that he was only after an eyeful. A jealous tongue will put a slant on anything.)

Lickie clambered out of bed and padded naked into the next bedroom, which had been converted into a miniature gymnasium. She didn't really understand why she had ever acquired this old fashioned town house. What's the point of borrowing money to buy a mini-mansion when you can have something perfectly adequate and pay for it in cash? Especially when all you're used to is a cramped little terrace full of brothers and sisters.

But Albert had lectured her long and hard about the advantages of obtaining tax relief at higher rates, and the cast-iron potential of property investment, and so, anything for a quiet life, she had signed on all the dotted lines. And on reflection she supposed that he was right. He ought to know what he was talking about. He was her manager. He had her interests at heart. She put her faith in him.

Dismissing such idle speculation she toned herself up for her morning workout. This was yet another Albert innovation.

'It's very important to stay in condition. I know you look a knockout but you got to think of tomorrow. When you girls go you go all the way. Some of those press boys would love to stick the knife in. Especially the ones who were keen to stick the other thing in only you wouldn't let 'em. Think of it as an insurance policy. Erecting a dam against the eroding waves of nature.'

And so Lickie adhered (more or less) to a daily programme. She pumped a little iron; lay on her back and swung her legs in the air; gripped a horizontal beam and hauled herself up and down; hopped on an exercise cycle and pedalled to bloody Brighton. And then, as a finale, an Albert special. A variation on the traditional toe-touching routine.

Naturally, in view of Lickie's physical geography, the usual fingertip method was out of the question. The Albert inspired modification ran something like this. Right nipple – right knee, left nipple – left knee. Right nipple – left knee. Left nipple – right knee. And so on for twenty repeats.

When she was done with the strenuous bobbing and jerking she hopped into the shower and turned up the jets so that they hissed against her body like so many slippery snakes. Sometimes, as she lingered like this – showering, soaking, lathering, drowning – she felt it quite the most perfect time of the day, and wished it would last for hours. As if to immerse herself in purity and cleanliness were somehow to reclaim those qualities in her life, and to liberate the body she had grown up with from the false claims of men. Funny the things you think of in the shower. Eh?

She stepped from the water-palace and danced with a towel, her mind moving methodically towards the next batch of rituals, those of hair, make-up and clothing. More of Albert's homespun philosophy.

'You're in the public eye, girl. Which means that you're fair game. For our best friends the snappers. You never know when one of 'em's gonna poke his lens through the window. So don't you dare step down those stairs without your act together.'

Her hair presented no problems. She wore it long, straight and splashing, and had always found it responsive, almost toadying, to the brush strokes she applied. By contrast make-up was a chore, make-up was like homework. She dibbed and dabbed, a reluctant scholar; making spelling mistakes with lipstick, grammatical errors with mascara. For herself she wasn't convinced that it mattered all that much. The cheaper I look the more some people seem to like me. In a magazine poll I was voted the nation's favourite tart. Strawberry finished second.

Clothing, of course, varied with circumstance. Today she was making a guest appearance at a local funday, all in aid of charity. The weather was fairly good. She might have to skip about a bit. The public would expect a glimpse of her 'sizeable assets'. She considered for a moment, then slipped into brief underwear, a low-cut semi-transparent blouse, and a pair of sailing shorts. No stockings or tights. Thought about putting on a pair of pumps, but opted instead for familiar heels (she was only five foot two). Can always slip my shoes off. Squeeze the grass between my toes. Like I did when I was younger.

With everything (more or less) in place she headed downstairs. When Lickie's mum called around on Sundays to clean the house she also left seven frozen dinners and seven frozen breakfasts, together with appropriate instructions for microwaving the same. Which meant that when she was at home Lickie never went short of two cooked meals a day.

Lickie thought about her mum. Who by this time would have been in work for more than two hours. Lickie had told her to pack it in. Had offered her money. But she wouldn't hear of it. Stubborn angel. Lickie marvelled at the way her mum coped. Three children still at home. An alcoholic husband. A full-time job. Looking after Lickie's house as well as her own. Some examples are impossible to emulate. And Lickie knew that she would never match her mum.

Alone in the kitchen she nuked this morning's portion and then picked at it unenthusiastically (the rigorous physical jerks had left her stomach feeling ruptured). At the same time she scanned the tabloids and discovered that for once she wasn't in any of them. She hoped Albert wouldn't be angry. She didn't think he would be. He was still pleased as punch about 'The two faces of modern woman'.

'You looked wonderful, girl. And you remembered all those lines what I told you to say.'

Anyway, she would soon find out. Because the next scheduled event was Albert's daily phone call.

Albert liked to contact each member of his 'stable' at least once a day. As well as Lickie his 'stable' consisted of two black boxers with tearaway reputations, three Scottish footballers with tearaway haircuts, a Welsh soap opera star who thought he was Richard Burton, and an alternative comedian who thought he was funny.

At ten thirty precisely the telephone trilled. Lickie rushed to answer it. She always looked forward to Albert's morning call. Speaking to him set her right for the day.

'Hello . . . Albert?'

The cement mixer growled.

'Listen girl. How many times have I told you not to answer the phone like that? What if it's someone else? What if it's the press or TV? They'll think you can't do nothing for yourself. That you need me round there to wipe your pretty little arse.'

'Sorry Albert.'

'All right. Don't worry. But you think on. Now then. You know what you're doing today? This charity beano?'

'Yeah, I know. The Voluntary Committee are sending someone round for me at noon.'

'Ten out of ten. You make my parrot sound like a page three girl. Only joking, my love. So you go out there and knock 'em dead. They been pestering me for months to get you to do it. And it's all good publicity. Show your teeth for the snappers. Your teeth and your whatsits. Now then. What else? How about your smellies? Are you wearing the right smellies? Are you plastered in D'U?'

'Oh Albert, you know I can't stand the stuff. Why can't I just do the commercials and leave it at that? You know I prefer . . .'

'Lickie. Listen to me. You know what's in the contract. I told you, didn't I? You have to bloody wear it. All the time. Otherwise you're sponsoring the opposition. Now the minute you put this phone down you run up them stairs and smother yourself in D'U. If one of their executives passes you on the street and he don't like what he whiffs then we're both up you know where creek without a paddle between us. They'll sue for their money back. And I've already spent mine, you know what I mean?'

'Sorry Albert.'

'All right. Forgiven. Now the meeting for the TV show is Thursday week. You know about that. We also have to meet the guy who's producing the album.'

'I didn't know we had to meet him. I thought we just gave him the tapes and he made them better.'

'No, no. We work together. This album is gonna be a classic. As a matter of fact I quite fancy a go in the studio myself. I was in a skiffle band once, you know. I might even push for a co-production credit.'

'I'd like that, Albert.'

'On second thoughts I don't think this feller would buy it. Cut his income, you see.'

'I suppose.'

'All right then. What are you doing tonight? Going out with Wussell?'

'Yeah. Worse luck.'

Lickie was determined to unburden herself about Wussell. She felt sure that Albert would understand.

'Listen Albert, I've had it up to here with Wussell. I can't stand the sight of him. In his wipped denims and his Wadio One T shirt . . .'

'Patience girl. One more hit single. Album in the shops. Then we're fucking made. In the meantime you just keep him on the hook . . .'

'Yeah, but Albert. You don't have to sweep with him.'

'And nor do you, my love. Not now he's sampled the goods. Tell him you're on a celibacy kick. These people are very gullible . . .'

'Tell him I'm on a what?'

'Tell him you've got an 'eadache.'

Lickie sighed. It was no use arguing with Albert. But while he was here she had something else to ask

111

him. She summoned the courage and spat out the words.

'Any news about the film part?'

A long pause. Lickie thought the line had gone dead, then Albert spoke again.

'No luck yet.'

Her eyelashes fluttered and her heart skipped a beat.

'Will you try for Mel Gibson?'

'I am trying, darling. But his people are very obstructive, you know what I mean? Now listen. I have to go. Trying to line up a title fight. Got to speak to Mickey Duff. You have a good day, you hear? Wear your D'U and be nice to Wussell . . .'

'Bye Albert.'

Albert was gone. Lickie hurried upstairs and smothered herself in D'U.

Babs Hammer entered the room supporting a coffee tray. She placed sugar and milk within reach of the three men. Then handed a cup to each individually.

First of all to her husband, Charlie. Charlie looked ruddier than usual and excessively tense. It was obvious that he was thinking. And in such a condition he was best left alone.

The second cup she passed to Fat Legs Eddie Roman. Eddie was dressed as badly as ever – perspiring gently, pulling on a cigarette. He looked up at Babs.

'Cheers Babs. You're a princess, you know that?'

His thoughts flitted back to a steamy afternoon, late summer 1966. Eddie called around at the Hammer residence to drop off some illicit merchandise. Charlie was out at work (Eddie, of course, didn't work), but Babs was at home, along with the nipper, then only a few months old.

'Eddie, there's a light fitting come loose up in the bedroom. And Charlie's not home till six . . .'

Before he knew it Eddie was out of his Beatle boots and into the sack, turning under and over with a rampant Mrs Hammer, the new-born brat wailing in the background, left unattended for an hour at least.

'Thanks Eddie,' Babs said, when they were finished. 'Sometimes with Charlie it's difficult, you know.'

The incident had never been repeated or referred to since, but returned to Eddie vividly on occasions such as this, when Babs brushed his hand with hers, and seemed to swivel her hips especially for him.

The third cup she handed to Fast Mits Finnegan. The scar tissue beneath his eyes twitched nervously. He ran a hand over a head shorn of hair.

'Thank you my darling.'

His special recollection was of a February morning, 1967. Babs had often said that she would like to call in at the gym and watch him training, but it came as a shock when she suddenly appeared, young Johnny gurgling in his pram, no sign of Charlie anywhere at all.

Fast Mits stepped up his exertions in an effort to impress her. She seemed to revel in the atmosphere of the place. The sweat, the liniment, the dull heavy pounding. The skipping, sparring, weights and workouts. There were six boys going through their paces that morning. A light-heavyweight (Fast Mits Himself), two middles, a welter, a feather and a fly. Steam rising, muscles tensing, Babs accommodated them all – biggest first.

The greatest prolonged thrill of her life, she later said to Fast Mits (as he walked her home, pushing the pram). And though not one of those six boys achieved overmuch in the ring, each had a golden memory worth at least two Lonsdale Belts.

Babs left the room, closing the door behind her.

'She's all right my missus,' observed Charlie to the others.

'A good 'un,' said Eddie.

'The best,' said Fast Mits.

Each passed a moment in silence – in memory, as it were, of Babs.

'All right,' said Charlie, returning to the original business. 'I think we've covered everything. All that remains is the matter of disguise.'

Eddie looked away. Fast Mits groaned.

'We have to be thorough,' said Charlie, defiantly. 'We can't leave anything to chance. She may have big tits but they don't cover her eyes.'

He lifted a cardboard box which had been lying beside his chair. At that moment the door burst open and in bounded Robin the Rottweiler.

'Hello,' said Charlie. 'Here comes the fourth member of the gang.'

The way Charlie saw it the job was a cinch. Not that that stopped him worrying. You have to keep worrying. Otherwise you lose your edge.

The plan had been concocted by himself and Albie Alibi. Or rather 'Albert' – as Albie now wished to be known. In the old days Albie was never a tremendously active villain. Not one to blow a safe or cosh a copper. But he was always in the union. A man to tip you the wink. To act as intermediary. To fence a little merchandise. And, as his nickname suggested, in times of emergency to vouch for your good conduct.

For a modest consideration Albie would say you were with him. At the dogs. At the pictures. In the boozer. Round his house. The only thing he wouldn't say was that you were sharing his bed. Which in those days, in the East End, was very understandable.

Fifteen years passed and Charlie didn't see Albie. Albie seemed to have taken himself out of circulation.

And then one night they ran across each other in a crowded public house. At first Albie didn't notice Charlie and almost melted away. Charlie pursued him, shook his hand, slapped his back. They shared a few choice memories, and later retired to Albie's pad. Albie had spent some time in the States and picked up new ideas. He referred to himself as 'Albert'. And said that he was moving into management.

From then on Charlie monitored Albie's progress. His rise was little short of meteoric. First the boxers, then the footballers, then the branch into showbiz. Cuts of purse money, transfer fees, advertising contracts. Albie dressed better, drank better, entertained more lavishly.

But greed breeds greed, yes indeed. And Albie was not yet averse to a little under-the-counter dealing. He and Charlie hit on the kidnap scheme one evening over whisky. It seemed so easy, so foolproof and all. A gang of trustworthy boys kidnap one of Albie's artistes. Working behind the scenes Albie manipulates the unsuspecting victim so that he or she is delivered into their clutches. The kidnappers then negotiate directly with the artiste's manager. Who takes the tricky decision not to call in the law. Uses his influence and powers of persuasion to extract a ransom from selected payers. Delivers it personally into the hands of the criminals. Secures release of star. Everybody happy.

The only real teaser concerned the identity of the lucky victim. The boxers were ruled out. They were hot boys – Fast Mits Finnegan would barely last a round. The footballers were similarly scratched from the field. The form they were in, their clubs would probably be happy to dredge headless corpses from the Thames and cash in the insurance. The soap opera star was a strong possibility. The alternative comedian a non-starter (no one would pay). But by far the pick of the bunch was lovely/luscious/lascivious Lickie Loose.

One: she was by far the easiest to overpower and hold.

Two: she had placed all her business affairs in the capable hands of Albie, and seemed to trust him implicitly.

'Take for instance this new house of hers,' Albie said to Charlie. 'Bleeding white elephant really. Rambling monstrosity. But this estate agent geezer says to me that he'll cut me in halves if I can shift it for him. So I has a word with The Alps – that's what I call her – and next thing there you are. Thank you very much.'

Three: Albie reckoned he would have no trouble in extracting a moderate ransom demand (say quarter of a million) from either D'U Cosmetics, or Lickie's record company, or maybe a glossy magazine. She was so popular, he said, that if need be he could probably raise it by public subscription.

Four: following her release the story would run and run. Serialised in the press with accompanying pin-ups. Wecited over the wadio by woyal Wussell Maycock. Kickbacks for Albie. Here, there and everywhere.

And so it was arranged. A bogus charity funday, fully documented in Albie's files. Lickie at home awaiting unknown chauffeurs. Several hours to play with before anyone would even realise she was gone.

The way Charlie saw it the job would finance his retirement.

Suitably smothered in D'U, Lickie sat watching a video of her latest appearance on Top Of The Pops. Albert said that it was good for her to analyse her own performance. That she would learn things. Avoid mistakes in the future.

With this in mind she tried hard to find a critical

perspective. But to be honest there wasn't much to observe. Just a lot of bouncing around and out-of-sync miming. What to note in the mental jotter?

Wear a bra.

Control your mouth.

She rewound the video and reflected that she didn't know very much about this function she was due to attend today. Except that it was some sort of local funday held somewhere out in Essex. Various celebrities attending. Proceeds to charity. Probably have to take part in silly games. Sign a lot of autographs. Albert had asked her to take along an item of clothing to be raffled off. She had suggested a pair of jeans. But he had said no. Make it knickers. And he knew best.

At noon precisely the doorbell chimed. Lickie checked herself in the mirror, then hurried out into the hall. She unhitched the safety chain and opened the front door wide. Found herself confronted by two decidedly odd looking characters.

The first was squat and wore a wide pinstriped suit that flopped all around him. A bushy black moustache sprouted from his nostrils and overhung his upper lip – wiggling and drooping like a cluster of upturned centipedes. Two further moustaches doubled as eyebrows. While his forehead was gripped by the rim of a trilby.

The second man was taller and wore a jumper and jeans. A long grey scarf was wrapped around the lower part of his face, so that he resembled a bandit in a TV Western. The skin around his nose and eyes was stretched and stained like that of an old man, yet his hair sprouted upwards in the raw fluorescent spikes of a pantomime punk. Both men wore false noses – big red bee stings that seemed to glisten in the daylight.

'Good afternoon Miss Loose,' said Eddie Roman, mumbling through his moustache. 'My colleague and

I represent the Voluntary Funday Committee, and we are here to escort you to the main event.'

Lickie was unable to stifle a giggle.

'Oh, I see. In the spirit of things already. Is that it? Eh?'

'Yes miss. One likes to dress the part.'

Lickie pinched Eddie's shoulder.

'I love the funny suit.'

Eddie's moustache came in handy – to mask his solemn frown. Lickie turn to Fast Mits Finnegan.

'And the make-up around the eyes. Must have taken you hours.'

More like years, Fast Mits thought. And cop a load of them boobs.

Lickie invited the two men to wait inside while she dashed upstairs to slip on her jacket. She re-emerged holding a plastic bag, which she handed to Eddie.

'Here's the knickers,' she said.

Eddie looked dumbfounded. No one had told him about the knickers.

'You know. The knickers. For the raffle.'

'Oh. Right.'

He passed the bag to Fast Mits.

'The knickers,' he said.

On the way to the car Fast Mits slouched behind, opened the bag and took a peep inside. There they lay. Neatly folded. Royal blue. It was not much known to his friends but Fast Mits Finnegan had always been fascinated by women's underwear. He tended to remember his conquests by the garments they wore next to their skin. For instance the slinky white panties he ripped off Babs Hammer that day in the gym. And his overriding temptation now was to cast off his false nose, dunk his bewigged head deep into the plastic, and sniff long and hard for a lingering scent.

They reached the Ford Fiesta which was parked by the kerb. Eddie opened the driver's door and asked Lickie to sit alongside him. Fast Mits climbed in the back and sat on the plastic bag.

'Suppose you're more accustomed to riding in limousines miss,' said Eddie, deferentially. 'But the funday is a charity event. No unnecessary overheads. I'm sure you understand.'

As the car pulled away he slipped off his red nose. All very well driving an inconspicuous motor. But what if everyone in town is gawping at your beezer?

The Fiesta wound slowly through the outskirts of London. Lickie sat back and listened to the car stereo. With Wussell's show over it was safe to switch on the wadio. When she glimpsed the other two she thought that both were behaving strangely. The short one in the clown's suit seemed to be angling his face away from her as if he didn't want her to see him without his false nose. While the tall punky one in the back was again holding the plastic bag and staring at it intently.

Before too long the city slipped away and Lickie recognised the boundaries of Epping Forest looming large. Eddie turned off the main road and drove slowly along a narrower track, the woodlands thickening on either side.

'Hello,' he said. 'Feels like the motor is cutting out.'

Lickie looked at him rather anxiously. He paddled his feet up and down – not even touching the pedals – and then, so far as she could see, he whipped the key out of the ignition and swung the wheel left, allowing the car to judder to a halt, half on the road, half off it.

'Well,' said Eddie. 'That is a blow. The damn thing just died on me.'

Lickie switched off the stereo.

'Hadn't you better do something?' she said. 'Look at the engine? Call the AA?'

Just then a Mercedes rolled into view from the

opposite direction. It crept slowly across the road and halted in front of the Fiesta.

'Ah,' said Eddie. 'A friendly fellow motorist has stopped to offer assistance.'

Charlie Hammer stepped out of the Mercedes. Lickie's suspicions boiled over.

'Well,' she said. 'If he's nothing but a friendly fellow motorist – how come he's wearing a red nose too?'

Eddie almost smiled. She was a bright kid, sure enough. The irony was that Charlie wasn't wearing a nose. It was just his normal bulbous beetroot-shaded beak.

Eddie nodded to Fast Mits, who sprang into action. He dropped the plastic bag and took from his pocket a handkerchief soaked in chloroform. He then draped his arms around Lickie's shoulders and clasped the soggy anaesthetic firmly to her face.

The fumes made Lickie groggy. Conjured a wavy image of her old school dentist – a tiny bald chappie with a broad pervert's leer. He kept her coming back for fillings and extractions, and each time she awoke her breasts were somehow sore.

A sudden resilience pulsed through her veins and she bit the hand that gagged her. Fast Mits dropped the handkerchief and yelped aloud. Lickie forced open the car door and made a daring run for it, trying to keep a straight line between the tarmac and the trees.

This, she thought, is where all that bloody exercise should stand me in good stead. But her high heels were crippling and she had to kick them off. Her feet then fell victim to all the twiggy bits in the grass. And her breasts boomed against her like a pair of hostile cannons. And her vision was left askew as a result of the chloroform. The forest and the road swept to and fro across her eyeline. Dizziness. Giddiness. Mum! Albert! Help!

The three kidnappers gave chase. But Charlie and Eddie soon fell by the wayside – in Charlie's case quite literally. Eddie helped him up. They wheezed in unison. Pinned their hopes on Fast Mits.

Fast Mits jogged steadily and felt surprisingly good. It was a long time since he had done this sort of thing. Even in the old days he never took his road-work seriously. Many a frosty dawn he smuggled a packet of fags into the pocket of his shorts and stopped off behind a bush for a smoke half way. And then there was the lonely farmer's wife who let it be known that he never need go short of an early morning brew. Sometimes they went three rounds, other times six or eight. Every now and then the full championship distance.

Returning to the present his chest began to pound and his legs to weaken. But the girl was weakening too, zigzagging crazily from one side to the other. Fast Mits was doddering now, breathing like a wounded ox. But one last effort and . . .

He threw himself at her and they clattered to the ground. His wig fell off. She struggled and kicked. He grasped her in a bear hug. Their legs entwined. The erection was inevitable. His hands moved to her breasts.

Charlie and Eddie arrived on the scene.

'All right champ. No need to feel her up.'

Lickie now had lost all sense of bearing. Eddie had brought the chloroform but it was surplus to requirements. When he was sufficiently recovered from his exertions Fast Mits slung her across his shoulder and carried her back to the cars. A passing motorist slowed down in astonishment.

'Riding accident,' panted Eddie, still rather breathless.

'I'm not surprised,' said the motorist. 'If she goes riding dressed like that.'

As soon as the coast was clear Charlie opened the

121

boot of the Mercedes and Fast Mits dropped her inside. The three villains then sat in the Fiesta to assess the state of play.

'Everything's fine,' Charlie said.

He mopped his brow and added:

'No sweat.'

Eddie remained in the Fiesta and drove back to London. Charlie and Fast Mits transferred to the Mercedes and drove to the M25. Lickie would be semiconscious, or at least would awaken soon. The idea was to give her a sense of motion and distance. The M25 merely circles in a wide arc around London. Charlie and Fast Mits settled themselves for two laps at least.

Some hours later the Mercedes left the motorway and headed back into Essex. Albie had managed to rent a cottage that stood conveniently alone within the outer reaches of the forest When making his telephone enquiry he employed a carefully mimicked Welsh accent. 'Ah yes,' the owner said. 'You're a Pakistani gentleman.' So he switched the name of the proposed tenant from Owen Owen to Patel Patel.

Charlie parked the Mercedes in the driveway of the cottage.

'Disguises,' he said.

Fast Mits scowled, and reluctantly applied scarf, nose and (somewhat soiled) wig. Charlie himself donned a thick balaclava and a heavy pair of shades. Fast Mits then stood guard as Charlie opened the boot. Lickie emerged dazed and bewildered, but able to find her feet.

'Where are we?' she asked.

'No one will find you here,' Charlie said. 'Out in the wilds of Cornwall . . .'

He stopped himself, as if regretting the revelation.

'It doesn't look like Cornwall to me,' said Lickie. 'Looks more like Epping Forest.'

'What do you know, you dumb bitch?' interjected Fast Mits.

They took her inside. Charlie walked into a standard lamp, then stumbled over the sofa. Admitting defeat, he took off the shades. For her part, as she crossed the threshold, Lickie thought she heard a dog bark.

The downstairs area comprised a hallway, living room and kitchen. Upstairs were two bedrooms and a bathroom. One of the bedrooms was to be Lickie's prison. Albie, or rather Patel Patel, had earlier telephoned a tradesman and instructed him to install bars on the window and a lock on the door. 'The child sleepwalks,' he had said, by way of explanation.

Lickie sat on the bed. Charlie stood over her. Fast Mits hovered behind.

'Right,' said Charlie to Lickie. 'Let me give you the lowdown. Behave yourself and this will all be over in a couple of days. All you have to do is stay in here. My friend will be downstairs and he will look after you. If you want him knock loudly. He'll bring you food and drink and let you go to the loo. But don't try any funny business. My friend is very genial most of the time but if you upset him he can just as soon turn nasty . . .'

Fast Mits emitted his best menacing snarl, but found it muffled by the wraparound scarf. Charlie continued.

'And even if you do manage to get past my friend – well, you still won't get far. Take a look out here . . .'

He led her to the barred window. In the back garden Robin the Rottweiler was prowling around. As if conscious of their attention he raised himself on the rockery and stared up at the window. Ooh, Lickie thought (she couldn't help it) – hasn't he got a big plonker?

'As you will see,' Charlie said, 'the dog is firmly

tethered. But the leash is sufficiently long to allow him to reach every window and door. And if anyone he doesn't recognise steps out of this cottage alone . . .'

His voice tapered off, as if the prospect were so grisly as to defy contemplation. Out in the garden, loyal Robin fired off a volley of barks. Good boy, thought Charlie. You tell her.

He and Fast Mits left the bedroom, securing the door.

'All right,' said Charlie, as they descended the stairs. 'I'll head back to London and make contact with Albie. I'll be back with Eddie early in the morning. You shouldn't have no trouble. Easy night ahead. Only don't forget to wear your clobber each time you go in there.'

He went outside, petted Robin briefly, then started the Mercedes and left. Fast Mits shook off his disguise, took a beer from the fridge, sat down on the sofa. Above him he could hear Lickie padding restlessly to and fro. From the window he could see Robin, now slumbering on the lawn.

Fast Mits finished his beer and opened the plastic bag, which he had earlier rescued from the back seat of the Fiesta. He raised the knickers high and looked at them awhile, then placed his fingers inside the elastic and stretched it wide. He checked quickly left and right, then pulled the knickers down over his head and collapsed into sweet reverie.

Charlie Hammer returned home shortly after six. Babs seemed a little suspicious of his story that Robin had been detained at the vets.

'Didn't seem nothing wrong with him to me,' she said. 'He only went to have his nails clipped. And that was this morning.'

'Ingrowing nails,' said Charlie. 'Very painful for a dog.'

Leaving his wife in the kitchen he picked up the telephone and dialled Albie's number.

'Everything all right?' Albie asked.

'The bee's knees. Regular as clockwork. Smooth as silk.'

No need, Charlie thought, to mention the near botching of the anaesthetic or the pursuit in the woods.

'So,' he said. 'What's the timetable now? How soon will somebody miss her?'

'Well,' said Albie. 'Wussell Maycock is due to pick her up tonight. He's bound to think it odd when she isn't at home. Hopefully if he contacts anyone he'll contact me. That's what he usually does when he wants to track her down. Meanwhile I'll call the chairman of D'U Cosmetics. I'm sure he'll cough. Just think of the spin-offs. The public will flock to buy the product that rescued Lickie Loose. At least that's what I'll tell him. We'll see what he says and take it from there. I'll call you later.'

Charlie said good-bye and put down the phone. Babs yelled to say that dinner was served.

'I hope Robin's all right,' she said.

'He's fine,' said Charlie. 'Be back in a day or two.'

9

Royston Bone leaned back in his chair and put his feet up on the desk. By his right hand lay a box of six cigars. By his left a personally engraved lighter. Both of them presents from Sharon Cobb.

At that moment young Sharon entered the office. She did so backwards, pulling behind her a service trolley, which she parked inside the door. She smiled at Royston, then lifted his feet and placed them on the floor. She took from the trolley a large white tablecloth and laid it out on the desk. A napkin she tucked inside Royston's shirt. She then placed before him a plate of freshly cut salmon sandwiches, an uncorked bottle of wine and a tall stemmed glass. These were followed by a large puffy sponge cake, an item she looked on with particular delight.

'I baked it myself,'

'Thank you baby.'

'You're welcome.'

She curtsied gracefully and left him to it.

Back in reception she lapsed into a dream state, gazed absently at the notepad in front of her, on which she had scribbled the same legend maybe one hundred times.

'Sharon luvs Royston'.

Sharon was eighteen years old. For her life had not been easy or hard. The truth was that she had never even thought about it all that much.

Her parents were not rich but they earned enough to pay the bills. When she was very young they bought her state-of-the-art dolls as advertised on TV. When she was a little older her mum taught her how to apply lipstick and eye liner, and her dad warned her about all the low-down tricks that young men would try, and advised her how to rebuff them with a single sharp word, or, if that failed, with a kick in the bollocks.

Sure enough the young men played out their roles, and for the first time in her life Sharon disobeyed her dad. You have to be amenable. If you want to remain popular. Many of her girlfriends walked out the school gates and into the maternity clinic, but Sharon was wise to that one. She learned about the pill in a Social Awareness seminar, and thereafter swallowed it religiously. After all, she reasoned, you don't want to be stuck with a young one too early in life. You want to wait until you're at least twenty-one.

She left school and took a post as a receptionist in a local garage. Initially she was on a government training scheme, but when the scheme ran out the boss agreed to keep her on. Maybe the boys in the workshop drew up a petition, for they all seemed to like her. Bill. Ben. Chas. Dave. The sex, of course, was a great disappointment. But after about the fifth time you don't expect anything more. You lie back and fake it. It doesn't last long.

She went out with Kevin for over a year. Only finished with him the day before yesterday. Kevin was the workshop foreman's son. Still at college. He was very clever. So he said. But when he was out with his mates he just fell into the crowd. Football chants. Drunken curries. Another two minute wonder. Just like his dad.

She took the job with Royston because the money was so much better. A hundred pounds a week compared to seventy-five. At first she was a little uncertain about working for a black man. But she overcame that. You have to integrate, she told herself. You don't have much choice. They're everywhere now.

For two long weeks it seemed she had made a horrible mistake. Interminable days with nothing to do. Flimsy excuses in place of a pay packet. And then, out of the blue, it all fell into place. A couple of clients walked in off the street. Two weeks' wages plus a bonus safely in her purse. And those magical words, which still echoed in her ears.

'How'd you like to take a ride on the Ecstasy Express?'

That night Royston took her out for a drink, and later back to his place. Along the way he marked her card about the Ecstasy Express. It was a long dark steam train which hurtled through the night. Its driver the most skilful to ever mount a footplate. At its head a gleaming lantern with a magnetic glow.

He said that in its time the Express had called at many stations. But wherever it went the people cheered and applauded. Laid garlands beside the track. Often erected plaques in memory of the event. Begged and pleaded for the Express to return. Which sometimes it did, but more often than not it sped on and away towards pastures new.

By the time he finished the tale Sharon was sitting on his bed. The wine and the words making her giddy. His fingers stroked her cheekbones and massaged her shoulders. His tongue entered her mouth and almost wrenched out her tonsils. Then he drew back and adopted a mysterious tone.

'Listen baby ... Think I hear something coming ... Sounds like a train ...'

He cupped a hand to his ear. Wrinkled his brow to indicate intense concentration.

'Yes ... Definitely a train ... And you know something, baby? Sounds like the Express ...'

Her eyes grew wide like those of a schoolgirl. She was so excited she wanted to jump up and down.

'Listen baby. You hear it?'

He turned his back on her. The noises began softly and then grew louder.

'Choo-choo-choo-choo ... Woo-woo ... Woo-woo ...'

She barely even noticed that he was stepping out

of his pants. Still with his back turned he made a station announcement.

'The Ecstasy Express is approaching fast. All passengers must be ready at the edge of the platform . . .'

Sharon didn't remember taking off her clothes. She must have done it in a trance. But she did remember the way Royston slowly turned around.

'Isn't it a fine train?' he said. 'Don't you just love it?'

She could hardly wait to demonstrate her devotion. She leapt towards the lantern and scrambled aboard.

Royston finished his sandwiches and drained the last of the wine. The sponge cake, he thought, would wait until later. Through the slightly opened door he could hear Sharon singing. One more satisfied customer. Maybe he should amend that sign just a little.

'Roy Bone – Stud'.

But for all the pleasure he dispenses a man still needs cash. Royston was thinking of phoning Dexter *Hum*-page and requesting a further advance. First though he would have to verify the whereabouts of Nadene. Which meant calling Roxanne. Only he didn't want to do that while she was in work. He had a feeling the switchboard there had been primed to frustrate him. He would call her this evening. At home.

So what to do now? How to pass a few hours?

He considered for a moment, then stood up and called aloud.

'Sharon honey . . . I hear a train . . .'

Roxanne washed and Nadene dried. When they were finished they sat together on the sofa. Roxanne had a couple of weeks to go, working out her notice at her old job. But her commitment had already switched to Cordelia.

They had held a second meeting, to sketch the

129

outline of Roxanne's responsibilities. Once again Cordelia was so awfully nice. So much so that Roxanne dismissed her own lingering doubts and vowed to walk through fire for this woman.

In fact Cordelia required significantly less than that. She wanted Roxanne to conduct a series of interviews. The subjects would, of course, be women – from varying walks of life. Roxanne would examine their backgrounds and extract their opinions. Later she and Cordelia would study the typescripts and assess the roles these women played in society today.

Roxanne viewed it as an exciting project and was anxious to begin. Almost immediately she hit on the idea of staging a dummy interview with Nadene.

'It will help me enormously. Help me map out the ground.'

'Sounds fun,' said Nadene.

And so they fixed a time. Ate dinner together. Sat down. Roxanne uncapped her pen and set the tape recorder whirring. Nadene looked a little concerned.

'I thought that this was just a trial run.'

'It is, it is. But I have to simulate actual conditions.'

In truth Roxanne was scheming. For if this went well she was sure she could use it. Where else would she find a more fascinating subject? Nadene the unfathomable. Nadene the dilemma. Enough material for an entire volume. Of course she would never use the tapes without Nadene's permission. But she saw no reason why her friend should withhold that. If anything she might welcome a full and frank analysis. It might prove therapeutic – unravel some mysteries, even for her. Or am I getting carried away?

Roxanne had laid advance plans to structure the investigation professionally. She had listed in a notepad a series of brief self-prompters, leaving sufficient space after each one to jot down critical comments and observations. The idea was to run through

Nadene's life chronologically, hopefully homing in on crucial phases and junctures.

For the most part she found Nadene agreeably compliant, ever ready to trot out an appropriate anecdote. The first remark on Roxanne's list read 'Earliest memory?' On this one Nadene was quite specific.

'I was one or two. We had a coal fire then. My mother warned me not to touch the fireguard. Well it looked harmless enough to me. So I crawled up to it and touched it. Snatched my hand away quick. Looked up at my mother. She was smiling triumphantly. I was determined to defeat her. So I coiled my fingers around the wire mesh, gripped it tightly to the palm of my hand. The pain made my head sing, but I refused to let go. My mother held me with one arm and tried to extricate my fingers. In the end I passed out. If you don't believe me take a look . . .'

She opened her right hand. Roxanne leaned forward to inspect it. A thin red scar snaked across the palm. Roxanne shuddered. Her pen hovered above the notepad but she didn't write anything. She would return to that one later. With the aid of the tape.

The next prompter read 'Early home life'. In response to this Nadene began to recite poetry. Something about Daddy being a bloody bastard and brother lying dead in the bath. Roxanne looked confused, and left another blank.

'Infant and primary school,' she said. 'Any particularly vivid memories?'

'Being caned by the headmistress. Me and Keith Wakefield. He said that all girls were sissies. I set out to prove him wrong. It was a hell of a scrap while it lasted. You would have enjoyed it. I snagged him with a straight right. His nose pumped blood. Then he caught me with a left hook which dislodged one of my teeth. This made me really angry. I kicked his right shin so that he hopped about in pain. Then I kicked his left shin which meant he had nothing left

131

to hop on. I dragged him up off the floor and held him over a desk. You know those school desks with lids that open upwards? I opened the lid and put his head inside. Then I brought the lid down on top of him. It made a wonderful sound. Bong! It was like Big Ben. I'd struck nine o'clock before the teacher broke us up.'

Roxanne scribbled hastily: 'Early victim of sexism. V. aggressive response.' She turned the page and read aloud the next heading.

'Fears and insecurities.'

Nadene shuffled her legs, lost a little colour, seemed to regress to those earlier years.

'You remember the Ripper? The Yorkshire Ripper? Well he was at large when I was eight, nine, ten. He was running up a cricket score, murdering women. And it was all happening in our own backyard. As you walked home from school the boys would chant: 'The Ripper's gonna get ya! The Ripper's gonna get ya!' And my dad would say: 'Don't wander off – you might run into the Ripper.' I studied all the press reports. God, it was horrific. Outside the house I was jumping at shadows. Every man I saw was a potential suspect. One of the neighbours figured high on my list. And then I arrived at an alternative theory. The Ripper was my dad. Why not? He was violent. He hated women. And on the evening of the next murder he was out of the house. He went out every night, mind. Down the pub, you know. But for me that clinched it. I psyched myself up to go to the police. Then I backed off. What if they didn't believe me? And my dad somehow found out? Eventually of course they nabbed Peter Sutcliffe. Even then for a while I thought they'd got the wrong man.'

Roxanne wrote: 'Ever present threat of violence/ violation.' She then skirted quickly around the topic of senior school. She knew from other conversations that Nadene possessed an entire catalogue of X-certificate stories concerning sex and violence, drink and drugs, revolt and insurrection. Roxanne had always thought that half of them were made up. Now she wasn't so sure. Either way she believed that if repeated now they would only complicate the issue. Whatever the issue was.

'What's next then?' Nadene asked.

'Early work experience.'

'I was a supermarket checkout girl for a couple of months. But I wasn't cut out for it. I'd get hopelessly mixed up. Charge all the wrong people for all the wrong things. One bloke looked at me disgustedly, turned to his wife and said: "She's got more tits than brains." I looked at his wife, turned to him and said: "I've got more tits than your wife." The bloke kicked up a fuss and one of the assistant managers came over. The bloke started whining: "This girl said she's got more tits than my wife." The assistant manager looked from one side to the other. "By God, she's right," he said. In the end the assistant manager and I were both sacked for impertinence. We went down the pub to drown our sorrows. He said that for himself he didn't mind losing his job. But he was really concerned for his wife and children. Three pints later he asked me to go to bed with him.'

'You didn't, I presume?'

'As a matter of fact I did. He was useless. Like all the rest.'

Roxanne did her best not to appear outraged. Fortunately black girls don't blush.

'Any other work experiences before you moved to London?'

'Yes. I was a barmaid. In the Bled Pig. It was a horrible job. Gargoyles grinning across the bar. "Pint of Smiths and a blow-job, love." They were very witty.'

Roxanne discarded her notepad and began to ad lib.

133

'What did your parents feel about you moving to London?'

'I only mentioned it once. My mum said: "You'll end up on drugs." My dad, the Ripper, said: "They'll find you down an alley with your throat slit." After that I just saved my money and packed my bags and didn't tell them anything.'

'And did you find London very different to Bradford?'

'Not really, no. The people use bigger words and go to plays now and then. But they're basically the same. The main thing for me is that I don't have anyone breathing down my neck. No family, no school teachers, no kids that I grew up with. It's like I've found my own space. Even if I'm not too sure what to do with it.'

Roxanne knew that there was one more subject she really ought to broach. She did so with utmost caution.

'Nadene. Would you like to talk about your attitudes towards sex?'

Nadene was bold. Perhaps a little rash.

'I may as well do. That's as close as I ever get.'

And so they opened negotiations. Roxanne probed warily. Nadene reiterated her previously stated views – on the unproven legend of the cataclysmic cock – but an uncharacteristic hesitancy seemed to shadow each sentence. A current of tension sparked from one girl to the other. Unspoken words hovered between them.

'Turn dyke. Or join a convent.'

'Turn dyke. And let me be there.'

Needless to say Roxanne wrote nothing. Then Nadene lowered her eyes and her face seemed to soften. She was perhaps on the brink of something like confession. Roxanne half-sensed this. Then the telephone rang and scattered her senses. She switched off the tape recorder and hurried out into the hall.

134

'Hello,' she said, picking up the phone.

'Roxanne? Hi baby. It's me. Royston.'

Roxanne struggled for something useful to say.

'Oh. Hi.'

'How you doing baby? It's been quite some time.'

'Yes. It has. I'm fine. Fine.'

'Well look baby, I was wondering if we could meet . . .'

Roxanne recovered her composure.

'Royston, I don't know about that . . .'

'Hey, no panic. No heavy scene. Just as friends. Little chat, you know. We've known each other since we were kids. No sense in drifting apart completely. I ain't gonna try nothing you wouldn't approve of. I'm pretty settled in my own life right now. But I'd sure like to keep in touch . . .'

Roxanne thought once more of her brilliant audacious plan. Of pairing Nadene and Royston. Well here was an opportunity, if she wanted to take it.

'Look baby. We could just meet at lunchtime . . .'

Roxanne wished he would keep quiet while she debated with herself. Nadene will never be cured by verbal therapy. Branding herself on the fireguard. Fighting with boys. Hunting the Ripper. Nadene is a one-off. Way beyond the scope of Cordelia's project.

Royston continued.

'You still work in town? You know that wine bar . . .?'

Roxanne grasped the nettle.

'All right. Tomorrow at one.'

Royston and Roxanne arrived in the wine bar at roughly the same time. Royston bought the drinks and they found themselves a table.

'Well baby,' he said. 'You sure look good.'

Eyes. Teeth.

'Thank you very much.'

She looked him in the eye.

135

'You look good yourself.'

He brushed back his hair.

'You're speaking the truth.'

They both smiled. Some things don't change. Royston then asked about what Roxanne was up to. She told him about the forthcoming assignment for Cordelia. He said that he was pleased. He then laid a business card face down on the table. Roxanne turned it over.

'Roy Bone – Private Eye'.

'Oh Royston,' she said. 'Are you really?'

'Sure thing. The man on the beat. Mixing with the heat. Working on a couple of cases right now . . .'

'Really? What cases?'

Royston tapped his nose.

'Sorry baby. Confidential. You know?'

Roxanne insisted on buying the next drinks herself.

'You still living in Clapham?' Royston asked her.

'That's right.'

'With that girl . . . What's her name . . .? Nadene . . .?'

Roxanne was a little puzzled. She didn't think that Royston knew Nadene's name. She supposed it must have slipped out some time.

'Yes,' she said. 'With Nadene.'

Royston dipped a hand into his jacket pocket. He took out Nadene's wristwatch and placed it on the table.

'This belong to her?'

Roxanne was genuinely surprised.

'Why . . . Yes. Where did you get it?'

'Second-hand shop in Brixton. Saw it on the shelf. Thought it looked familiar. The breadknife . . . You remember?'

Roxanne giggled.

'Yes. I remember.'

136

'What did she do?' Royston asked. 'Pawn it or something?'

The look in his eye said he already knew the answer. Roxanne gave it anyway.

'No. no. She left it behind. Er . . . In someone's flat.'

'Oh yeah? Whose flat was that?'

'I don't know. Dexter someone . . .'

'Dexter *Hum*-page?'

'Why yes. I believe so.'

'Think I know that guy,' said Royston cryptically. He pushed the watch at Roxanne. 'Anyhow, you give her that. Tell her no hard feelings.'

'Thank you.'

The jukebox in Roxanne's head played 'Now Or Never'.

'Royston,' she said. 'There's something I'd like to ask you. And funnily enough it concerns Nadene.'

What to do? What to do? How on earth to dress it up?

In the end she plumped for that rare option, the truth. She told him everything. All about Nadene and her unsuccessful quest. Then she informed him of what she thought he could do.

At first he rocked back and laughed, as if afraid to take her seriously. A closer study of her face revealed that this was no jest. He hovered awhile and then lunged forward, his dark eyes on stun.

'And will the lady in question pay for this service?'

Roxanne was quite disgusted.

'Royston! I thought that you were coming up in the world. Not sinking to the level of a common whore.'

He rocked back again, seemingly deep in contemplation. Then he began to laugh. A loud, pleasant, engaging sound. Roxanne knew that she was in.

'OK,' he said, his chest swelling out. 'I'm your knight in shining armour. Just arrange the time and place.'

Roxanne smiled and promised to do that. Then she

finished her drink and said she had to go. Royston hung around for a further half hour. By the time he alighted on the fourth floor he was feeling a little tipsy. He brushed past Sharon's desk.

'Any calls?' he asked briskly.

'No Royston. But I bought you this.'

He stopped and turned around. She handed him a brown paper package. He opened it carefully. Inside he found a folded white shirt of fashionable cut. Immaculately pinned. Wrapped in clear plastic.

'Baby, you shouldn't have. You're spending all your wages.'

'I thought you'd like it.'

'I do baby, I do.'

He pushed back her fringe and kissed her forehead. She smiled sweetly.

'Coffee Royston?'

'Please baby. Yes.'

He retired to his office, leaned back, put his feet up. The man on the beat. Mixing with the heat. Private eye. Stud. Man for all seasons.

Flushed with such confidence he dialled one of the telephone numbers left by Nuttall Mann.

'Good afternoon. KCS. Fran speaking.'

'Give me Krunt.'

'Who's calling, please?'

'It doesn't matter who. Just say that it's important.'

A long pause. Sharon brought the coffee and placed it on the desk. Royston watched her as she wiggled from the room. Then a voice snapped in his ear.

'Krunt.'

At first he thought it was an insult and set himself to respond. Then he remembered who he was and what he had set in motion.

'Hello Krunt. My name is Bone. Roy Bone. I'm a private investigator. And I have reason to believe

138

that you are engaged in certain activities of which —
shall we say? — the authorities are not aware.'

Krunt spoke angrily.

'What? You crazy? Who are you? Get off the line.'

'Oh no. You don't shake me so easily. You see,
Krunt, I have seen the file. The one you keep on your
desk. The list of names and addresses. The strange
symbols. You know the file I mean?'

Krunt slowed down.

'What exactly do you want?'

Royston stopped to consider and almost backed
off. But the wine was still with him. As was Sharon's
adoration and Roxanne's request. The man on the
beat. Mixing with the heat.

'I want to arrange a meeting. You and I. That
seems the best way to resolve this situation
amicably.'

Krunt was decisive.

'OK. Come round here. To KCS. Tonight. When
everyone else is gone. Say nine o'clock. Let yourself
in at the back. Come up the stairs to the second floor.
See you later, Mr Bone.'

Royston opened his mouth. But Krunt was gone.

The phone call had a rapidly sobering effect on
Royston. At three o'clock he told Sharon to take the
rest of the afternoon off.

'Will I see you tonight?' she asked hopefully.

'No baby. I have to work tonight. See you in the
morning.'

'OK Royston.'

She kissed him on the cheek and left. Royston took
the long-bladed knife from the top right hand drawer
of his desk and placed it in the inside pocket of his
overcoat. He then locked up the office and took the
tube back to Brixton.

Immediately he emerged from the underground he
set out to track down Gladstone, Chamberlain,

139

Churchill and Wes. He found them in the betting shop.

'Hey listen,' he said. 'You boys wanna help me out tonight? I could use a little muscle.'

Gladstone pressed for details. Royston didn't say much. Just that he had to meet a dangerous customer and felt in need of back-up. When Gladstone smiled it was the smile of a rattlesnake.

'How much exactly is this proposition worth?'

'Well it ain't worth nothing just yet. I ain't got no money. I just thought, you know, that we were friends and I helped you out on the warehouse job . . .'

Four faces leapt at one.

'Ssshhh . . .'

'Oh yeah. Sorry. Well I guess you know what I'm saying . . .'

Four backs turned. Four hands filled in betting slips. One lonely detective headed back home.

Up in his room Royston considered abandoning the case. Calling and cancelling. Bluffing it out that it was all a mistake. Needn't even do that. Could just not turn up. Yeah, but he had given his name over the phone. This guy Krunt could easily track him down. So maybe it was best to confront him face to face. Look him in the eye. And apologise profusely for wasting his time.

Shortly after eight Royston took the tube back into town. Then walked slowly towards KCS. There was only one car parked in the courtyard round the back. And the loading bay was open, just as Krunt had indicated.

Royston stepped inside. It was horribly dark. He crept around on tiptoe. Until he stumbled over the bottom step of the stairs and the echo filled the building. He lay there in a heap, almost paralysed by fear. The night outside the warehouse. The Brixton riot. All those sensations alive once more.

But nothing happened. No one came. Royston stood

up. Dusted his clothes. Began to climb steadily. The soles of his shoes slapping against the hollow wooden steps. His heart hyperactive. His right hand poised just inside his coat.

He reached the second floor. Felt his way through reception. The sales office too was swamped by darkness. Desk shapes basked like crocodiles hiding in the gloom. Royston squinted for a light switch. Wished to God he'd brought a flashlight.

And then the lights snapped on, leaping at Royston like ferocious tigers. He whipped out the blade and hopped from foot to foot, looking all around him, forming a circle of one.

A man emerged from a side office doorway. Not a young man. A face like granite.

'Mr Bone, I presume?'

The voice was recognisable. Royston opened his mouth to speak. Was then aware of a very loud cracking sound and an overwhelming feeling that it somehow involved his skull.

When he came to it seemed like hours had passed. In fact it was only a couple of minutes. There was a dull painful throbbing in the back of his head. And not one of his limbs responded to his commands.

This was because two large men in dark suits were carrying him between them. They were descending the stairs. The man called Joe Krunt walking ahead. Each jolt, twist and turn caused Royston to wince.

They reached the ground floor, where Royston had come in. They then descended further, down into the basement. One more time Krunt switched on the lights.

To Royston's uncertain eye the basement of KCS resembled a medieval torture chamber. A grand inquisitor's chair behind a grand inquisitor's desk. A long wooden bench equipped with a rusty metal vice. A brazier lined with ashes, thankfully unlit.

At a signal from Krunt the two men set Royston

141

down. His legs buckled and he crumpled to the floor. The men hauled him up again, wrenching at his arms. By an intense effort of will he managed to remain standing.

Krunt stood in front of him. They were of roughly equal height. But Krunt seemed to tower.

'Mr Bone. On the telephone you said that you had seen one of my files. I believe that was a lie. Am I right or wrong?'

Royston hesitated. Krunt slapped him hard. Right hand. Only face.

'Mr Bone. I am not a man to be kept waiting.'

'A lie,' Royston croaked.

'Good,' said Krunt. 'Following our telephone conversation I had you checked out and, to my surprise, discovered that you really are a private investigator. I therefore assume that this foolhardy mission was instigated by a third party. Am I right?'

He raised his slapping hand. Royston nodded frantically.

'Yes, yes.'

'Good. We are making significant progress. All that remains is for you to give me the name of your client.'

Royston shook his head.

'Can't do that.'

He prepared to be slapped – swung his own head from left to right in anticipation. Instead Krunt took from his pocket Royston's long-bladed knife. He moved the weapon up and down in front of Royston's eyes – a menacingly hypnotic motion.

'Such a fearsome item to carry on your person . . .'

Royston envisaged stitches and the loss of his good looks. Then, to his great surprise, Krunt threw away the knife so that it clattered against the wall.

'Myself,' he said, 'I prefer to use something a little cleaner . . .'

This time he produced a solid black handgun. It

142

snuggled against his palm like a doting puppy. Royston's eyes darted madly in search of an escape route. The two henchmen flanked him to the left and right.

In a slow deliberate movement Krunt raised the gun and pressed the barrel against Royston's left temple.

'The name . . .?'

Royston wanted to tell him but was rigid with fear. The words wouldn't come. The bastard words wouldn't come.

Krunt took a step back and fired the gun. The flight path of the bullet singed Royston's hair, the closest trim he had ever had. The terrifying explosion echoed in his ears.

'You see,' said Krunt. 'I could easily blow your head off. Or maybe even worse . . .'

He lowered the gun and pressed it into Royston's groin. The Ecstasy Express in imminent danger of derailment.

'Give me the name.'

Royston made one last effort.

'Nuttall Mann,' he said.

10

The chairman of D'U Cosmetics was a bastard and a half. That was the opinion of Albie Alibi.

'I am most distressed by the plight of Miss Loose,' Sir Laurence T'Oliver said, on the telephone from his home. 'But there is no way that I alone can sanction the payment of a ransom demand. And certainly not a sum of a quarter of a million pounds. The best I can do is to convene an emergency board meeting early in the morning.'

Albie hammed up the agony, with no little style.

'But Larry,' he sobbed. 'My little girl is *out there*. Her *life* is on the line.'

Sir Laurence turned away from the receiver and sniffed with disdain. He wished this horrid cockney oik would refrain from such demeaning familiarity. Larry, indeed! The cheek of it.

He decided that this late-night conversation had just about run its course. He vaguely recalled the big-titted bimbo engaged by his marketing department in a desperate attempt to boost flagging sales, and naturally he was concerned that she was now at the mercy of ruthless cut-throat brigands. On the other hand that did not mean that he was about to lose either his commercial judgement or a good night's sleep.

'Albert,' he said. 'You always have the option of alerting the police.'

Albie insisted that he dare not take that chance. The well-being of his poor baby was far far too precious. He had to abide by the kidnappers' instructions.

'Well then, all I can do is to call you noon tomorrow.'

Babs Hammer was still in bed. Charlie called to her from the foot of the stairs.

'Right love. I'm off.'

Babs emitted a shrill squawk, and a moment later appeared on the landing in her dressing gown.

'Where are you going? You didn't say nothing. Who was you on the phone to last night?'

Charlie frowned. He'd thought she was asleep.

'That was Albie. Bit of business come up.'

'Where are you going now?'

'Same thing. Bit of business. All right?'

He fixed her with a look that said: 'Button it, my love.' Babs pushed her luck an inch or so further.

'What about Robin? When is he coming home? Will it be today?

Charlie wriggled his fingers – a strangler's twitch. By a great effort of will he remained outwardly calm.

'He'll be home in a day or two. Tell you what I'll do. I'll call around at the vets and see how he is.'

And with that he was gone. Babs slipped off her dressing gown and went back to bed. Charlie's peculiar behaviour was getting on her nerves. She wondered whether or not she should seduce the milkman.

Charlie picked up Eddie Roman. Side by side in the Mercedes they reviewed the state of play.

'What have you done with the Fiesta?'

'It's safe. In a lockup in Battersea. But Charlie . . .'

'What?'

'I still don't see why we couldn't have used your Johnny's place?'

'No way. My Johnny's a good boy, but this is one little caper he knows nothing about. You don't understand, Eddie. This Lickie Loose. She's like a goddess to him. You must have seen her pictures all over the garage.'

'Yeah, but Charlie. If it come to a showdown between his favourite wet dream and his one and only father . . .'

'I don't know, Eddie. I just don't know.'

Eddie absorbed this, then asked how Albie was doing. Charlie told him about the chairman of D'U Cosmetics being a bastard and a half. A look of concern creased Eddie's criminal features. Eddie was all too familiar with the knock on the door and the click of the handcuffs. They haunted his dreams, plagued his sanity.

'Bloody hell,' he said. 'It sounds a bit iffy.'

Charlie took a confident tone – a bold attempt to stifle Eddie's doubts and his own.

'Don't worry,' he said. 'Board meeting this morning. Albie's getting a phone call at noon. Then he'll call us.'

Eddie calmed himself.

'So no one knows that she's missing, like?'

'Only . . .'

Charlie switched on the radio.

'Wussell Maycock with you, wocking on the bwek-fast show . . .'

And switched it off again.

'Only the DJ. He contacted Albie last night. Asked where she was. Albie sold him some story. You know Albie. Prime bullshit artist.'

'Yeah.'

The Mercedes approached the driveway to the cottage. Charlie and Eddie were startled by the sight of a black-clad figure on a push-bike. The figure was heading towards them, but weaving uncontrollably from one side of the path to the other.

Charlie hit the brake. The cyclist swung left, wobbled precariously, then disappeared over the handlebars down into a ditch. By the time he emerged Charlie had the window down ready to abuse him.

'What the . . .'

Charlie spotted the dog collar just in time. For

146

though he was no saint, Charlie was still not inclined to swear too vociferously at a man of the cloth. Just on the off chance. You know.

'Vicar,' he said. 'I'm most dreadfully sorry. I didn't see you at all.'

The flustered vicar gave the impression that the tumble in the ditch was the least of his concerns. He glared back towards the cottage.

'I, sir,' he said, 'have just survived a confrontation with a thoroughly frightful beast.'

Charlie and Eddie looked at one another. Neither was quite sure whether he was referring to Robin the Rottweiler or to Fast Mits Finnegan.

As if to aid them in their dilemma the vicar turned around and lifted his coat. A patch had been torn from the seat of his pants.

Charlie and Eddie still seemed unsure, though the odds had now swung slightly towards Robin.

'You must accept my apologies,' Charlie said, hedging his bets. 'We left him to guard the cottage while we were away.'

'I've a good mind to go straight to the police.'

Charlie dipped in his inside pocket and produced a twenty.

'Don't do that,' he said. 'Here, take this. For the parish funds. Keep it for yourself if you like. But no police. Eh?'

The vicar took the twenty, rescued his bicycle, and pedalled away. Charlie parked the Mercedes by the side of the cottage. He and Eddie got out. Robin ran to greet them, tongue hanging out. He then made a retching sound, and coughed up a soggy piece of thread. Charlie bent down to pat him.

'Naughty old Robin. Booked his passage to hell. You and the Hound of the Baskervilles. Down there together.'

Eddie gave the coded knock (two-four-six-eight-who-do-we-appreciate?), and Fast Mits let them in. Charlie looked at him sternly.

'What's going on here?' he demanded. 'Holy bleeding war?'

Fast Mits offered a stumbling explanation.

'Yeah well,' he said. 'I hears a knock on the door. I has a peep and he looks harmless enough so I opens up. He starts wittering about this collection for the church roof. I'm just in the process of telling him what to do . . .'

Charlie's eyes bulged, like those of a toad. Fast Mits corrected himself.

'. . . In so many words like, when I hears a scampering of feet and the next thing I know old Robin is swinging like a pendulum from the parson's arse. Never seen nothing like it. I had to laugh.'

'Hilarious,' said Charlie. 'Cost me twenty quid. Comes out of your share. All right?'

At that moment he noticed the navy blue knickers lying on the carpet. His expression alone asked the obvious question. Eddie filled him in on the origin of the undergarments. Fast Mits chose to leave it at that.

The three sat down to smokes and cuppas. Charlie and Eddie passed on the news from Albie. Charlie then asked how Lickie was bearing up.

'She's fine,' said Fast Mits. 'No trouble really. Eats her food. Drinks her drink. Goes for a whatsit.'

A saucy gleam appeared in the ex-champ's eye.

'But I'll tell you what. She's sure fine looking. She's something else. Those bloody great . . .'

Charlie shushed him.

'I know what they're like.'

The gleam hardened, became a rapist's leer.

'You know what?' said Fast Mits. 'I can't help thinking . . .'

'Thinking what?'

'Well. You know. What an opportunity, like. You, me and Eddie. We're no spring chickens. We may never get another chance like this.'

'Fast Mits. What exactly are you suggesting?'

'That we. You know. One at a time.'

Charlie surrendered his cool – indulged in a series of theatrical gestures.

'Are you punch drunk or what? Let me tell you something. What we have here is a painless operation. Which is the best kind. We kidnap the girl. The company pays the ransom. We release the girl. We all go home happy. So let's leave it at that. No complications. All right?'

Fast Mits sighed. His erection crumpled.

'OK,' he said. 'It was just a thought. Being here alone. I get to thinking.'

'Well don't,' said Charlie. 'It's fucking dangerous.'

Sir Laurence T'Oliver took his place at the head of the boardroom table. He laid out his notes, and quietly surveyed the faces to his left and right. Serious men in early middle age – Henderson, Magtooth, Motley and all. At the far end of the table sat the only woman on the board – Clementine Boog-Watson from personnel.

Sir Laurence called the meeting to order. An expectant hush fell upon the room. For in the hour between nine and ten speculation had raged.

What was it all about? This sudden summons. Take-over? Damaging court action? Liquidation? Redundancies? No one felt safe.

Slowly and deliberately, the chairman divulged the true reason for the gathering. Miss Lickie Loose, a 'fashion model' engaged by the company for a high-profile advertising campaign, had been kidnapped by parties unknown, and a ransom demand of a quarter of a million pounds conveyed to D'U via Miss Loose's manager. As yet both police and public were unaware of this circumstance.

As the story unfolded so a visible wave of relief swept over the other board members. Someone else's butt. Not ours. Thank God for that.

Sensing this communal relaxation, Sir Laurence snapped them to attention.

'The question is simple,' he said. 'Should we pay?'

His eyes flashed left and right. Henderson looked at Magtooth. Magtooth looked at Motley. No one looked at Sir Laurence.

'Suppose,' the chairman continued, 'that we do pay, and as a result of such payment Miss Loose is released unharmed. It is obvious to me . . .'

Anticipatory murmurs of 'Yes' and 'That's right'.

'. . .That such an eventuality would greatly benefit D'U Cosmetics. Undreamed of publicity and widespread goodwill.'

'Hear, hear.'

Sir Laurence halted. His fellow directors all examined their fingernails. Relief was not long coming.

'Suppose, however, that we sign the cheque and Miss Loose is not released. An opposite scenario. Commercial acumen laid open to ridicule and contempt.'

'True, true.'

Sir Laurence homed in on one of his underlings.

'Tell me, Rupert. As marketing director, how would you weigh the alternatives?'

Rupert Henderson scowled inwardly, while those around him breathed again. Why me? Rupert thought. Why bloody me?

In the event he composed himself and waffled splendidly, repeating what Sir Laurence had said, adding a little embroidery, reaching no conclusions whatsoever. To everyone's surprise Clementine Boog-Watson raised a hand and asked to speak.

'May I just say, from a woman's point of view, that Miss Loose must be suffering considerable distress.'

The boys all nodded, respecting her product knowledge. Uneasy silence settled once more. Then Rab

Motley, the finance director, made a decisive inter-
vention.

'Gentlemen,' he said. 'And you, Clem, of course. I
see it this way. It isn't really a case of marketing
strategy. It's a simple case of funding. To meet this
demand would be sheer folly. It has been a difficult
year for D'U, and our position at the bank is perilous
enough. If quarter of a million were to simply disappear ... Where would that leave our cash flow? Our
profit forecast? Our very liquidity?'

Sir Laurence nodded grimly. Half an hour ago, in
private, he had primed Rab Motley, handed him the
script. Now he took the helm with renewed determination.

'It goes without saying that Rab is correct. The
cold financial brain. Steadying the wilder, though
thoroughly laudable impulses that some of us may
have felt. We *cannot* pay. Are we all agreed on
that?'

'You bet, Larry!'

'Never in a million years!'

'However,' Sir Laurence added. 'This sorry affair
will not end with a decision by D'U Cosmetics. The
ransom demand will almost certainly be directed
elsewhere. Someone else may pay. Someone richer,
more foolhardy. And in time the story will emerge.
And mischievous minds will put a slant on anything.
We exist in a competitive environment. We have
many rivals, many enemies. Do you see the headlines? This company branded as uncaring, parsi-
monious ...'

'Good point.'

'Indeed.'

Sir Laurence scanned his audience. He had them in
the palm of his hand.

'Clearly,' he said. 'The best solution for all concerned would be the speedy release of Miss Loose
with no cash changing hands. However, the girl's

manager insists that we do not involve the police. Does anyone have an alternative suggestion?'

Rab Motley again.

'Could we not engage some form of private investigator?'

Sir Laurence pressed the intercom and summoned Miss Dalyrimple.

Miss Dalyrimple was forty-eight years old and had been employed as Sir Laurence's secretary for twenty-three years, following him from golden handshake to golden hello. She arrived at the office at eight a.m. to lay out his agenda for the day, and left at six thirty after personally emptying his ashtray. In her free time she compiled cross-referenced scrapbooks of newspaper clippings and trade circulars. On the first of August she started saving for Sir Laurence's Christmas present. She earned eight thousand pounds per annum.

Miss Dalyrimple shuffled into the boardroom, hopelessly in awe of the exalted proceedings. Sir Laurence addressed her matter-of-factly.

'Private investigators? I believe we had something through not so long ago . . .'

'Why yes, Sir Laurence, I believe we did . . .'

She scurried away, to return a moment later with a large ring-binder file opened at Roy Bone's mailshot.

'Is this what you're thinking of, Sir Laurence?'

'Indeed it is, Miss Dalyrimple. Thank you so much.'

Miss Dalyrimple departed. Sir Laurence tapped out the number. He remembered laughing when the leaflet landed on his desk. He hoped the fellow would not disappoint him now.

Sharon Cobb answered the telephone.

'Good morning. Roy Bone Detective Agency.'

'Good morning. May I speak to Mr Bone, please?'

The poor girl sounded distracted.

'I'm sorry, Mr Bone isn't here at the moment. To tell

you the truth he hasn't been in for a couple of days and I'm awfully worried. I hope he isn't hurt or in any sort of trouble. What do you think? Do you think he's all right?'

Sir Laurence hung up. It had gone much better than he had dared to hope. Now, at last, he was about to get his way.

'Gentlemen,' he said. 'And you, Clem. We can ill afford to waste time with private investigators. I feel it is our duty to contact the police.'

Half an hour later Dirk Magtooth was in a public phone booth. Hell, he thought, if you glimpse a chance you snatch it. Sir Laurence himself would approve of that. And if the company's bank balance was rather poorly, then Dirk Magtooth's was on its deathbed.

Sir Laurence had called the cops from the board-room, and was now crossing London in a chauffeur-driven Bentley, heading for Scotland Yard. 'You may rest assured,' he had said, 'that I will insist upon a thoroughly discreet operation. There is no way that this will leak to the press."

Magtooth, however, knew differently. He remembered the unscrupulous reporter who had come sniffing around at the time of Sir Laurence's latest divorce. On that occasion Magtooth, like the others, had maintained a dignified silence. Now he was desperate for cash.

He dropped his coin into the slot and was connected with the switchboard of a daily tabloid.

'May I speak to Porky Waring, please?'

'One moment sir.'

Dirk Magtooth lowered his hat and raised his collar, disguising himself to such an extent that to the passing observer he was a man without a face. The telephone receiver simply disappeared into a gap in his clothing.

'Hello. Porky Waring.'

'Hi. Dirk Magtooth. D'U Cosmetics. I've got a hot scoop but I want twenty grand.'

In the end Dirk Magtooth settled for ten. He gave it to his bank, and his bank gave him breathing space. Meanwhile Porky Waring put his by-line to the sensation of the year. Kidnap story pages one to three. Photographs of the victim pages four to eleven.

The fact that such maximum exposure might endanger the life of 'Loose, twenty-one' never once crossed Porky Waring's mind, nor that of his editor, Dinsdale Snape MBE. For the 'intrepid' Waring and the 'courageous' Snape formed a lethal combination. In recent years they had, for example, printed a detailed route map indicating the 'secret' hideaway of a notorious supergrass; persuaded a foolhardy photographer to straddle a precarious ravine in order to snap a princess taking a lesson from a ski instructor; driven a prominent churchman and charity worker to attempted suicide over the 'exclusive revelation' of a thirty-year old Peeping Tom charge. So a 'onetime stripper' was small beer to them.

Once the story broke Scotland Yard had little option but to co-operate. Chief Inspector Tommy 'Cuffs' Todd held a press conference, which was screened on national TV. The telephone number of a confidential information line was displayed for all to see. And within hours the police had more to go on. Several witnesses reported that Miss Loose was seen entering a white Fiesta, the other occupants of which were two men wearing false noses. One of these witnesses managed to recall the first three letters of the registration.

There was also a call from a man who claimed to have witnessed the aftermath of a 'purported riding accident' on the outskirts of Epping Forest. Fortu-

154

nately for some this loyal citizen had a tendency to confuse a Mercedes with a BMW, and was most insistent that he had seen the BMW in question heading directly for the M25.

'J-J-Jesus Albie,' stammered Charlie into the telephone receiver. 'We're f-f . . .'

'Steady on,' said Albie, dragging on his forty-first cigarette of the day (it was nine thirty a.m.). 'What we got to do is stay calm. Now listen. Tell Fast Mits to stay put. No reason at all for the Filth to stumble on the cottage. Don't let The Alps know that this has happened at all. Let her think she's on her own.'

He dashed his cigarette; then cradled the receiver between chin and shoulder as he lit a replacement.

'Tell Eddie to dump the Fiesta. In the crusher. In the quicksand. In the bloody ocean. I want it gone. Meanwhile you get around here sharpish. I got to see the Filth again at noon. I want to speak to you first.'

Albie sat in his office with three representatives of the Filth. Once again they pored over the fictitious paperwork regarding the fictitious funday. Once again they went over the details of the supposed telephone call from the kidnappers.

'I told you,' said Albie. 'It went something like this. Foreign sort of accent. "We got ze girl. We want quarter of a million. No tricks. And . . ."'

Albie glared at the officers.

'"No police!"'

Later they took him to the Yard to make a further statement. Tommy 'Cuffs' Todd looked embattled, harassed. He had been up all night. He was running on caffeine.

Tommy and Albie were old acquaintances. They went back as far as 1964, when young PC Todd booked fledgling operator Albie for peddling counterfeit tickets to the FA Cup Final.

'Look Constable,' said Albie, then. 'I got real ones too. I can get best grandstand for you and your girl. Practically in the royal box.'

'I don't trust you, Albie,' said Todd, now.

'The name,' said Albie, 'is Albert.'

Meanwhile Charlie Hammer strolled around the West End looking for telephones that worked. Each time he found one he shut himself inside the booth and dialled the incident room. Once connected he adopted one of a rota of accents and offered highly misleading information.

Throughout each call he stared at his wristwatch, and once twenty seconds had elapsed he disconnected the line. That way they would never trace him. Following Albie's instructions he put subtle stress on the flight to Cornwall. Every third call comprised a sighting from that neck of the woods. The in between calls were a mixed bag, largely ad libbed. Scotland. Wales. Yorkshire. West Germany.

The accents he used were rather good, though he said it himself. So absorbed was he in his little piece of method acting that he barely noticed the occasional reversions to his more natural dialect.

'Ooh arr, it be 'er orl roight. You know what I mean?'

Johnny Hammer bit a chunk out of his own left hand and spat the mingled flesh and blood thock! into a waste bin. He was in the office of Johnny's Unbeatable Bargains. On the desk before him lay the mingled news-sheets of seven or eight national dailies. The Lickie Loose story – initial splash. The Porky Waring exclusive, and the blatant plagiarism of his rival hacks.

Johnny had read all the words and looked at all the pictures. He looked up now at the pictures on the wall. The same girl. The same face. For once it was

the face that he looked at. Not the mountain range or
the forest or the valley or the plateau. Just the face.
Young. Beautiful. Immensely tragic.

Johnny hunched in his stolen jacket, crumpled a
stolen logbook, and wondered what the world was
coming to. When a girl like Lickie Loose couldn't
walk the streets in safety. What a sad, sick society.
Johnny hung his head. He wanted no more of it. He
wanted out. Then he kicked back his chair and
snarled at the walls. He wanted a vigilante group. He
wanted revenge.

Glancing at his stolen wristwatch he noticed that
it was just after noon. He flung open the door and
bellowed at one of his lads. Young Phil came trotting.

'Go and get me an evening paper. First edition.
Should be out.'

'I'm just draining the Montego, boss, and . . .'

'Sod the bleedin' Montego! Get the bleedin' paper!'

Recognising murderous intent, Phil scampered off.
Johnny wandered outside and stamped around the
pound. A rich-looking punter was eyeing up a Jag.
The Jag's price sticker allowed for a fifty per cent
margin. Johnny walked past, didn't notice a thing.

Ten minutes later Phil returned with the first edition
of the evening paper. The Loose case, of course, made
the headlines again; ahead of the cabinet reshuffle
and events in Eastern Europe. Johnny scanned the
report. He skimmed over the familiar stuff, then
halted as he reached the fresh evidence. A white
Fiesta. The first three letters of the registration . . .

Babs Hammer answered the telephone.

'Hello.'

'Hello Mum.'

'Johnny! How are you, my love?'

'Look Mum. Is Dad there?'

'No. He isn't. He's behaving ever so strangely.'

'Yeah?'

'Yeah. And Robin's still at the vets.'

'The vets?'

'Yeah. I don't understand it.'

'Well look Mum . . .'

'Just a minute. There's the door. I'll see if it's your Dad . . .'

Johnny waited. Young Phil poked his head around the door. Johnny waved him away. Phil hesitated. Johnny motioned with his fist. Then he heard his father.

'All right, son? How's tricks?'

'Dad. You know this Lickie Loose business?'

'Yeah. Shocking.'

They exchanged a few details, regurgitated from the press. Then Johnny came to the point.

'Listen Dad. You seen the Standard? This white Fiesta . . .'

'Er, no . . . But now you mention it I did hear something on the radio . . .'

'Well look Dad. That's the motor what I fixed for Fat Legs Eddie and Fast Mits Finnegan.'

Charlie thought he'd play it cool.

'No. You're mistaken. Eddie and Fast Mits? Kidnap? Not their game at all.'

'Dad. The registration. I changed the plates myself.'

'Well maybe they sold the car. Quick profit sort of thing.'

'I don't think so. Eddie said they wanted something inconspicuous like. They had something planned.'

'Well look son. There ain't nothing you can do.'

'Dad. I got a lot of time for Eddie and Fast Mits. And I can stomach most things. But when they mess with Lickie Loose . . .'

Charlie forgot about playing it cool – injected some good old fashioned menace.

'Look son. You're from the East End. They're from the East End. There's a code of honour to observe . . .'

Johnny did not bend.

158

'I'm sorry Dad . . .'

Charlie experienced a terrifying vision of exercise yards and morning slop outs. He made a last desperate play.

'Johnny. I know Eddie and Fast Mits much better than you do. I'll look into it. I'll find out. I swear I will. You just sit tight. I'll let you know. You got my word.'

Parental authority saved the day. Or at least the afternoon.

In her temporary bedroom, with its locked door and barred window, Lickie Loose was oblivious of headlines and commotion. All she saw was the forest and the lawn and the fierce dog with the large penis. Then when it was dark she saw nothing at all. She wondered what was happening in the world outside. Was the world aware of her ordeal? And if so, how was the world taking it? Was it making a fuss? Pestering the family? How was Lickie's mum bearing up under pressure?

One thing which helped keep her sane was the thought of Albert. Good old Albert. He would know – she was sure of that. He would be handling the situation, negotiating with these people. Representing her interests. As always. Good old Albert.

How long had she been here now? Two days? Three? Four? It was so dull. So monotonous. She did not feel frightened. For the gang had not threatened her in any way. She just felt bored. Sitting here with nothing but her own thoughts for company. She exercised. She dozed. She exercised. She dozed.

She heard raised voices from below, as if the three of them were arguing and shouting at each other. A door slammed. Something fragile smashed against a wall. For the first time Lickie felt a little scared. She tried to make out what was being said. Some dispute about who was leaving and who was staying and who was in the shit and who was being fucking stupid. There was then a period of hush, followed by the opening of the front door, two sets of footsteps outside, the revving of the Mercedes, its departure down the drive.

Lickie lay down on the bed, decided she had been foolish to feel so complacent. Of course she was in danger. She was in the hands of criminals. And by the sound of it all was not well between them. Perhaps their plans were backfiring. The police closing in. What would happen then? Would they set her free unharmed? Or silence her for good?

A steely resolve formed in her mind, a determination to extricate herself from her prickly predicament. And now was an ideal time to make a play. For if events had followed their usual pattern she was once again alone with the tall spiky-haired one. The one who brought her meals and escorted her along the landing. And of the three he was the most obviously vulnerable. She had seen the way he looked at her across the breakfast tray. She had heard his ragged breathing outside the bathroom door.

Lickie gathered courage, summoned feminine wiles.

Meanwhile Fast Mits had his head in the knickers once again.

11

Nuttall Mann found employment at the Gay Peacock nightclub. It was the first time he had worked behind a bar. But he soon picked up the job. The customers too. Found himself floundering in a familiar whirl-pool. All you need is love. All you get is sex.

One afternoon Nuttall picked up the telephone and dialled Roy Bone's number. He did not have the cash to sponsor a full investigation of Krunt, but he thought he might as well know where his fifty quid had gone. In the event all he heard was the girl receptionist twittering in his ear. Maybe Bone had absconded. Maybe Bone was dead.

The young barrister Sean stayed out of the Gay Peacock. He was avoiding Nuttall. Legal aid work he could do without. But others came into the club specifically to check out the handsome new barman. The manager was pleased with his latest recruit. Granted him a modest rise. There were tips too. Silver coins stacked in a half pint glass, along with scribbled phone numbers and complimentary con-doms. The rent got paid. Just.

And then one night there was an unexpected caller at the club. At first Nuttall didn't even recognise him. They were clamouring at the bar. He took orders from lips, barely noticed faces. Dripped whisky from the optic, sprayed soda from the siphon. Took the grubby five pound note. Fumbled in the till for change. It was then that their eyes met.

'Nuttall Mann! I don't believe it!'

'Sparky! My God!'

Steven Sparks remained strikingly attractive, though lines on his face suggested worry of late. Nuttall gaped at him. It all came flooding back. His initiation in the school gymnasium. Across the vault-ing horse. On the trampoline. Half way up the wall ladders.

The PE instructor had entered the club alone. Stood beside the dance floor he enjoyed an orgy of eye contact, but politely rebuffed each offer that came his way. At eleven o'clock Nuttall had a fifteen minute break. He and Sparky took a table in a shady lovers' nook.

'Well,' said Nuttall. 'How's life at Rumpiggots?'

It was a less than genuine enquiry. More of a tentative ice breaker. For something about Sparky said that Rumpiggots was consigned to history. And in the shady nook, over whisky and soda, the man himself confirmed that this was so.

Following Nuttall's abrupt departure from home, Rowley and Alice set about apportioning blame. They blamed the punks. They blamed the immigrants. They blamed the jobless. But above all else they blamed the school.

Pacing his study, brow knitted in a frown, Hopkins the headmaster expressed the opinion that it was all an unfortunate misunderstanding. He spoke of male homosexuality as if it were an activity akin to picking one's nose.

'Oh no,' he said. 'I'm sure that none of that sort of thing goes on around here.'

But Rowley and Alice were not to be bought so cheaply. During his rise to eminence in local political circles Rowley had gained much valuable experience in the kicking up of stinks, and that afternoon in the headmaster's study he threatened to direct every low blow and cheap trick in the book at the lofty but somewhat limp-wristed spires of good old Rumpiggots. Rowley wanted a scapegoat. Rowley wanted blood. Mindful of the school's reputation, mindful of his own pension, Hopkins agreed to an internal investigation.

The angry parents temporarily placated, and, more importantly, removed from the premises, Hopkins, sixty-three, summoned his deputy, Haddock, who was fifty-four.

'Fishy,' said Hopkins. 'You're a younger chap than I. And closer to the staff. Poke around a little . . .'

Fishy raised his eyebrows.

'. . . See what you can find.'

Fishy Haddock assured the head that his quest would be diligent. The truth was that he already knew the truth. He had read the signals. Not to mention the legend 'Sparky – well dodgy' plastered about the school. For Fishy Haddock was no stranger to the joyful spurts of secret sodomy.

At public school there was a boy named Pagitter . . .

As a young master there was a chap called Worrall . . .

Even in recent months he had come close to drooling over the rippling torso and firm buttocks of the gym teacher, Sparks. Every so often, in the marital bed, he would flip Catherine over and slip her one up the rear, just for the sake of twisted nostalgia.

A week after accepting his assignment Fishy Haddock returned to Hopkins with a dossier on Sparks. The headmaster thanked him, and said that from here on in he would deal with the matter himself.

As soon as Sparky entered the study he knew the game was up. The old boy's beak cast a shadow like a gallows. There was not a hint of mercy in his steely hooded eyes.

After much unofficial plea bargaining Rowley and Alice agreed not to prosecute. The clinching factor was a payment of five thousand pounds. Hopkins took the money from the headmaster's reserve fund. Told the bursar that it was an *ex gratia* payment to a former member of staff who had fallen on hard times. When the bursar looked at him disbelievingly he gave her a hundred and told her to keep quiet.

Sparky formally resigned, acknowledging the fact that he would never work in Education again. In the months that followed he was forced to sell both home and car in order to meet mounting debts. Sat in the shady nook with Nuttall he concluded his story. The train to London. The drifter's escape.

At that point the manager of the Gay Peacock burst in on the cosy twosome. Nuttall had overstayed his break. There was chaos at the bar. Sparky wrote down an address, and left the nightclub. Nuttall scurried like a madman to rescue his reputation.

At three in the morning he clocked off, his position intact. A black cab nosed hopefully from a bay of shallow lamplight. Nuttall climbed into the back, and gave the driver Sparky's address.

Dexter Humpage was like a bear with a sore head. He couldn't open the paracetamols.

He prised, unscrewed, pulled and forced. The little white bottle grinned up at him, its threaded maidenhead firmly intact. Dexter glowed like a shepherd's delight. Rivers of sweat dripped from his jowls. His impotence danced madly; thumbed its nose, blew raspberries.

He dropped his head into his hands and began to sob aloud. Who would have thought it? Dexter Humpage. Star salesman. Fifty grand a year man. Wailing like a baby. At his desk. In the office. His legion of young charges just a door knock away. His credibility clinging by its weak worn fingertips.

The phone rang. Dexter sat up, dried his eyes. Fran Lipp connected him to a potential sale – an ambitious young publisher whom he had treated to lunch earlier in the week. On that occasion, over wine and cigars, Dexter had promised to run up some favourable costings, to see what he could do. In truth he had run up nothing but the white flag of surrender.

And now the man was on the line expecting a systems specification. Dexter searched for automatic pilot. He waffled hopelessly, tripped over his own jargon. The publisher listened for five minutes and then hung up. Another commission out the window. Dexter didn't care.

It seemed that everything was hitting him all at once. For several days now Krunt had been in the foulest of tempers. Looking older, meaner; sounding harsh and foreign. He had sacked three people, and bawled everyone out, Dexter included. The storm seemed to date back to the public humiliation inflicted on Nuttall Mann. Or maybe just after that. But it was difficult to trace any possible connection.

Dexter knew that in many ways the time would never be more opportune for him to make his break and set up on his own. Plunder the client list. Present his forecasts to the bank. Sign his distribution deal. Trust to market forces. Yet he knew equally well that in his present condition of diluted humanity such pioneering activity was out of the question.

He had just about given up on the detective, Roy Bone. Two hundred pounds. But it wasn't the money. He could only conclude that the man was a con-artist. Each time Dexter phoned he ended up giving therapy to the distressed receptionist. Looked like Bone had ripped her off too. The bl . . . The bastard.

Dexter wandered to the window, opened it, breathed resuscitation. He looked down to the street. No Roy Bone meant no Nadene Braxton. The whole thing was psychological now. He was utterly convinced that only she could solve his problem. His Problem. His PROBLEM. She was out there somewhere with the remedy in her pants. Oh, there were others who were willing to try. But that only made matters worse . . .

Fran Lipp put the mirror in her handbag and covered the WP. Krunt's letters would wait. She had more important work to do.

The way Fran saw it, she had pussyfooted around for far too long already. Her reputation was at stake.

Not to say her future. She had more or less informed the rest of the office that she and Dexter Humpage were hitting it off. Fortunately he had not seen fit to issue any denials. But Fran felt the time had come to flaunt a little proof. Preferably an engagement ring. At the very least an arm-in-arm parade for all to witness.

Fran was sure that Dexter wanted her. She could see it in his eyes. The way they settled like butterflies on her breasts and knees. So what was it, she wondered, that was holding him back? Fidelity to some secret girlfriend? A sense of office decorum? No good reason, she was positive of that.

What Dexter needed was a taste of the goods. She would hold his nose and force them down his throat. Feed them to him intravenously if all else failed. Fran knew that she was good. Various captains of industry would attest to that. So once Dexter had dipped his bread in the honeypot he would never again be content to spread mere marmalade.

And now was the time to lay the picnic before him. Krunt in a meeting. Most of the young salesmen out on the road. The other girls busy behind chattering machines.

Fran rose from her desk and strode with purpose. Dexter Humpage. Come on down.

Dexter Humpage initialled the quote and placed it in the typing tray. He was battling hard. To salvage something from the wreckage of the working day.

The door opened, then closed again. Dexter looked up. Fran was bearing down on him. Her face set in a mask of determination.

She hoiked her skirt above her knees and leapt at the desk with a side scissors kick. Her bum bounced once on the surface and then dropped squarely onto Dexter's lap. Her thighs fell one either side and knotted themselves around him, crushed his hips so

166

completely he almost sent out for replacements. Her breasts bounced his heart. Her hands clawed his back. Her mouth attacked his face and damn near swallowed it whole.

And Dexter sat there. He rocked and then he sat there. Lashed to his seat by this rampant sex bomb. She was steaming. She was dripping. And Dexter felt ... Nothing. Nothing, that is, except absolute panic, unadulterated fear.

Fran swung herself sideways and they crashed to the floor. She kicked the chair out of her way and set upon her victim. With rough decisive fingers she snapped his tie in two and ripped the buttons from his shirt. Then she crooked her neck and nuzzled at his groin. She took his zip in her teeth and wrenched it its full length. Her tongue passed through his boxer shorts like a knife through butter. But something was missing. She couldn't find it anywhere.

And then she did (it had made itself small). Her tip kissed his and stung him into action. He leapt from her, left her chewing air. He staggered to his feet. She staggered to hers. He raised a hand to placate her. She advanced on him regardless. He dodged behind the hatstand and held it between them. She moved right. He blocked her with the hatstand. She moved left. He blocked her again. And then she ploughed through the middle, fought briefly with an overcoat, cast the stand aside.

Dexter took refuge behind the filing cabinet. She flushed him out. He backed towards the window. She closed off all his options.

All except one. For the window was still open. The ledge outside maybe eight inches wide. Dexter backed out slowly and edged himself along. Fran hung out of the window and grabbed at his legs. Her fingers brushed his trousers. Lucky he wasn't wearing flares.

Dexter shuffled along until he could shuffle no further. Then observed with horror as Fran too began to clamber through the window. At that moment, alerted by the commotion, a couple of young salesmen burst into the office. Fran steadied herself, tailored her strategy to the mood of the moment. Fran was nothing if not resourceful.

'No, Mr Humpage,' she cried. 'Don't do it. Please don't jump. I implore you.'

For the first time Dexter looked down. OK, he said to himself. It could be a lot worse. It's only two floors. Hardly a tower block.

His second notion was a trifle more disconcerting. Yes, he thought, but if you fall you will surely die. Splatter on the concrete so they have to scrape you off with knives. Your body like jelly and your brains like mush.

A stiff breeze numbed his body where his shirt and tie were torn. His fingers clung precariously to the window frame behind him. Another glance down revealed a group of passers-by who had gathered to witness the spectacle. Dexter's right foot slipped slightly. A piece of tiling broke and plummeted. The mob sighed like a football crowd when a chance goes begging.

Dexter was aware of several people in the office behind him. Their heads took turns to peek from the window. And then he noticed something else. At first he didn't believe it. But it was certainly true. For there she was. Down below. On the edge of the crowd. Honey flavoured bob. Smooth contours. Leather jacket. Tight jeans. Nadene Braxton. Baby, it's you.

Something stirred inside him. Something which had not stirred for quite some time. And of course his fly was gaping from Fran's oral assault. And perched out on the ledge he could scarcely cross his legs. His boxers first bulged and then allowed the beast fresh air. Did the crowd really gasp, or was it his imagination?

The sight of Krunt at the window killed off Dexter's erection. Down below Nadene Braxton glanced at her watch and hurried up the street. Krunt barked at Dexter in no uncertain terms.

'You vill come inside this instant and halt this fucking nonsense!'

Carefully, inch by inch, Dexter did just that.

Joe Krunt assigned his two most trusted henchmen, X and Y, to track down Nuttall Mann. Their instructions were specific. Flush him out. Bring him here.

To achieve this objective X and Y journeyed to the heart of the London gay scene. The bars. The clubs. The amusement arcades. The public lavatories. With them they carried a blown-up print of a passport photograph. Krunt insisted that each KCS employee furnish him with a passport photograph. Krunt was a man of foresight and guile.

For a couple of days the quest proved fruitless. No one recognised the handsome young man in the black and white snapshot. Then X and Y happened upon some acquaintances of Nuttall's from his early days in London. They tramped around old haunts, traced a previous address.

In many instances the gay community were somewhat reluctant to offer their assistance. Accustomed to harassment, their natural instinct was to defend their own. However, as X and Y discovered to their delight, traditional methods of persuasion tend to carry all before them.

'I'm sorry,' said the young barrister, Sean. 'I don't know the name or the face.'

'That's not what we were told,' said X.

Sean adopted his courtroom tone of righteous indignation.

'I assure you . . .'

169

Y's forehead swung like a mallet, bashed Sean firmly between the eyes. They were in the gentlemen's lavatory of a public house. Sean landed on his back. His arm dangled in the gutter. He saw birds and bees and stars and stripes.

X leaned over and hauled him to his feet.

'OK,' said Sean. 'I'll tell you what you want to know.'

And so the trail led to the Gay Peacock. X and Y clocked the barman, noted his shifts. In collaboration with Krunt they selected a suitable occasion to make the snatch.

On the appropriate evening X and Y entered the club together. Bought drinks. Took a table. One or two patrons eyed them suspiciously. And it was true that they looked a little out of place. Two middle-aged men, thick set, dressed in black. Sitting quietly, rigidly, amongst the bright young dancers and amorous canoodlers. Sensing this, X made a grasp at authenticity. Y's hand lay on the table. X placed his own upon it, caressed it gently with his fingers. Y snatched his hand away. Shot a filthy look.

Behind the bar Nuttall Mann was feeling good. At least he was feeling better than he had felt for some time.

Sparky had a flat in Finchley. Nuttall was moving in there. That would halve his rent.

Sparky had a job in a North London sports shop. The proprietor was of retirement age. Sparky had put together a scheme by which to buy him out. All he needed was backing from the bank. If he got it he would go ahead, and bring in Nuttall as a junior partner.

The sex was good too. The companionship. (Whisper it gently) the love.

Nuttall had told Sparky all about KCS – the means of his dismissal, the abortive attempt to enlist Roy

Bone. Sparky said that it was just one of those things. That Krunt was a vicious reactionary, anxious to conceal some dark proclivity of his own. That the file on the desk was no doubt something quite routine. That Roy Bone was obviously a fly-by-night and best left alone.

In other words Sparky felt that Nuttall should forget the past and try to start anew. As he collected glasses and approving glances Nuttall thought that Sparky probably was right.

Satisfied that all was well, X and Y left the club early. X parked the car just down the road. In the early hours there was plenty of space. Then he and Y sauntered on the pavement. To kill the time they smoked cigarettes.

The last punters filed drunkenly into the night. A few minutes later Nuttall Mann emerged. He was with the manager. X and Y looked at one another, expressing concern. This might upset their plans.

But the two did no more than exchange a few words on the steps of the club and then head off in opposite directions. X and Y trailed Nuttall. He did not turn around, seemed absorbed in his thoughts. X spurted ahead of him.

'Excuse me,' said X. 'Are you Nuttall Mann?'

Nuttall looked up. His first thought was of the police. The bastards never leave you alone.

'Yes,' he said. 'But wh . . .'

Y slugged him from behind. X caught the limp body and carried it to the car. They drove around to KCS.

When Nuttall Mann recovered consciousness he was down in the basement. He rose groggily to his feet. Put out his hands to steady himself. He was flanked by X and Y. He felt decidedly ill.

171

Like Royston Bone before him, Nuttall Mann saw himself inside a medieval torture chamber. A grand inquisitor's chair behind a grand inquisitor's desk. Krunt was in the chair. Nuttall slumped against the desk.

Just when he thought that things could not get any worse he realised that they could. For he was suddenly aware of a fierce heat behind him, as if a giant open furnace were lapping at his back. Sticky perspiration glued his shirt and trousers. He moved his head around slowly. A long wooden bench equipped with a rusty metal vice. Orange flames leaping high from the confines of a brazier. An ominous glow of coals. Sturdy poker at the ready.

Krunt strode around the desk and commenced the interrogation routine.

'You saw the file on my desk?'

'No.'

Slap.

'You saw the file on my desk?'

'Yes.'

'You hired Roy Bone?'

'No.'

Slap.

'Yes.'

Nuttall mopped his brow. Wiped smoke from his eyes.

'Tell me. Why did you hire that numbskull to pry into my affairs?'

Nuttall realised that it was futile to lie.

'I was upset at the way you fired me. I thought the file might contain some incriminating evidence. I engaged the private eye to investigate for me.'

'And you see where it led you?'

Nuttall tried to be conciliatory. He knew it was pathetic. But the words came all the same.

'Yes. I see that. Look. If you let me go I swear that I'll never ...'

172

Krunt smirked. The gargoyle recipient of a very dirty joke.

'Oh yes, fag-boy. I will let you go. But first I must leave my mark.'

He signalled to X and Y, who took Nuttall between them and hauled him over to the wooden bench. Once there they proceeded to strip off all his clothes. Finally they held him, face pressed against the surface, splinters in his scrotum, backside jutting, legs dangling.

Nuttall could no longer see Krunt. But he heard the distinctive accent. Almost talking to itself.

'Yes, I must certainly leave my mark.'

Nuttall wrenched one shoulder free so that he could look behind him. Krunt was holding the poker in the fire, heating up the point. It was shaped like a spearhead. It glinted like an evil eye.

X and Y secured him again, took away his vision. Face down, Nuttall was sickeningly aware of rough hands on his buttocks. X seized the right cheek. Y the left. They paused a moment and then wrenched them apart as far as they would go. Everything in the room seemed to rush inside the crack. The heat. The smoke. Above all the fear.

Nuttall braced himself for the poker. He prayed it would be soon. And over in an instant. Surely it would be. He would faint. He would die. He might as well die. For he would be horribly disfigured. Hideously crippled. He would never walk again. He would never sit down.

The penetration, when it came, was nothing like an iron spearhead. More like a half-hard member, smothered in Vaseline. Though he could not see it, Nuttall somehow knew that it was blue-veined and skinny, aged, ridiculous.

It probed around nervously, like a choirboy in hell. Barely entered the passage, although the gate was gaping. And then it came. A squirt and a dribble,

which ran down Nuttall's leg. X and Y released him.
He rose as best he could. Turned around to see Krunt
putting himself together.

Nuttall recalled what Krunt said in the office, on
that fateful day.

'I have eyes in my head. I see things maybe others
do not see.'

And he recalled what Sparky said in the gym, all
that time ago.

'There are certain telltale signs. It takes one to
know one.'

For a moment Nuttall felt almost triumphant.

'So,' he said to Krunt. 'Who's a fag-boy too?'

The taunt incensed Krunt, sparked him to action.
He raised the poker high and screamed in Nuttall's
ear.

'I am not a fairy! Not a fag-boy!'

Krunt calmed himself; held the business end of the
poker perilously close to Nuttall's face. This time he
whispered.

'I am a homosexual. That's all.'

He stepped back, motioned to X and Y. They threw
Nuttall his clothes. Nuttall dressed quickly. Krunt
still had the poker in his hand.

'Needless to say you will forget that all this happened. No more private eyes. And no police.'

Nuttall nodded. Krunt considered for a moment. A
certain venom returned to his eye.

'One more thing,' said Krunt.

'What's that?'

'My mark.'

Krunt jabbed with his forearm. The gleaming end
of the poker grazed Nuttall's jaw. Nuttall passed out.

12

Johnny Hammer sat in his father's favourite armchair. Charlie was out again. Robin still not home.

Babs came into the room carrying a tray. A coffee for herself. A four-pack for Johnny. She sat down opposite her son. Johnny ripped off the first can, cracked it open, poured half the contents down his throat.

'So,' he said. 'Dad's been acting strange?'

'Yeah,' said Babs. 'I'll say.'

Johnny finished the first can and tore open the second.

'And Eddie and Fast Mits have been round here?'

'Yeah. Last week it was. Secret conference. Doors closed.'

Johnny rose from the armchair and paced about the room. He drained the second can and dropped it in the bin. Babs uncorked the third can for him.

'It's Robin I'm worried about,' she said. 'He's been gone for ages. Well. Ever since that day. I don't believe he's at the vets at all. I think there's something up.'

Johnny picked up the third can, draped his free arm around his mother's shoulders.

'Don't worry, Mum.'

'Well. I miss him.'

Blimey, Johnny thought. What is it between her and that dog? But whatever it was he did not dwell on it, for all the time a notion was forming in his mind.

He emptied the third can and strode into the kitchen. (He needed space to think.) Ravenously hungry, he opened the fridge. A dozen bottles of milk, snowy and perfect. Johnny reached beyond them and picked up a loaf. He shredded the wrapper, grasped half the slices, fed himself greedily. Yes. Yes. It was coming together.

He dropped the remainder of the loaf, left the fridge door swinging. Back in the living room he employed the fourth can to wash down the bread. He belched loudly, then spoke to his mother.

'Mum. I think I've got it.'

Babs looked up at him, eyes open wide.

'What is it, son?'

Johnny wished he had a fifth can. Deprived of vital sustenance, he spoke as clearly as he could.

'It's like this. They're all in it together. Dad, Eddie and Fast Mits. Eddie and Fast Mits lift the car. Kidnap Lickie. Drive her out to some isolated spot. Chain her up. Lock her in. With Robin standing guard.'

Babs grasped her son by the arm.

'Johnny. I think you're right.'

She fell silent for a moment, then said:

'Poor Robin.'

Johnny pulled away from her and walked around the room. He did his best to think aloud.

'Now-then. The-papers-said-there-was-a-ransom-demand . . .'

Babs let out a shriek.

'Yes! Yes! Your father was on the phone with Albie. Albie is the girl's manager . . .'

Johnny thumped the wall.

'That's it! That's it!'

Babs rushed for the first aid kit and bandaged Johnny's fist. He sat down in the armchair. His mother brought him another four-pack. Using his good hand he went to work on it.

'Tell me, son. What are you going to do?'

'I don't know, Mum. That girl. She means everything to me . . .'

'Yes, but Johnny. He is your father. You must think back over all the years . . .'

Johnny did just that. He loved his Mum and Dad. Yes, but there was a downside too. Charlie was always a stickler for discipline, a firm advocate of corporal punishment in the home. Johnny recalled the flat of his father's hand. The bone of his father's knuckles. The point of his father's knee. The toe of his father's boot.

Johnny leapt from the armchair, leaving three cans unopened. He dashed for the front door. His mother pursued him, and tugged at his sleeve.

'Johnny. Not the Filth. Don't turn him in. Your own father.'

Johnny stroked his mother's hair, and kissed her on the cheek.

'Mum,' he said. 'You have to let me do this my way.'

With that he was gone. Babs turned to the mirror on the wall. A worried frown stared back at her.

'Oh dear! Oh gawd! Oh my!'

A moment later he was back. Pressing the doorbell. Stepping inside.

'Johnny. What is it?'

'I need a piss. Badly.'

Lickie Loose heard footsteps on the stairs. She braced herself. This was it. This had to be it.

She had already laid the groundwork. Yesterday. When the tall spiky-haired one came up with a tea tray. On that occasion Lickie reclined on the bed and crossed her legs teasingly.

'My,' she said. 'I'll bet that you're a handsome fellow. Underneath that silly disguise. So why don't you prove it? Take off your scarf. Your nose. Your wig.'

The kidnapper blushed. (She thought they called him 'Vammits', but she wasn't really sure.) He mumbled like a schoolboy.

'Can't do that, Miss.'

Lickie winked at him.

'I like you,' she said. 'I don't like the others, but I

do like you. It seems such a shame. Us being here alone. And living on separate floors.'

The plate and cup rattled on the tray. Vammits set it down. Lickie leaned forward and stroked the back of his hand.

'Before this thing is over. Maybe you and I . . .'

Vammits snatched himself away, left the room, bolted the door. Lickie heard him enter the adjoining bedroom. She heard the springs vibrating. So she knew she had him hooked.

Later that evening the other two called again. More loud disputes. The Mercedes left around ten. Vammits spent half the night pacing up and down.

And now he was pushing open the door. He entered. Tried hard to frown but managed only a soapy grin. He set down the breakfast tray. Lickie jumped up from the bed and embraced him lightly.

'Oh,' she said softly, feigning surprise. 'I'm so glad to see you. I've been here so long. I feel so scared and lonely. Hold me. Please.'

Guided only by instinct, Vammits clasped her to his chest. She clung to him a while, then wriggled herself free. She sat back on the bed, and patted the mattress beside her.

'Come on,' she said. 'Sit down here.'

Vammits looked at her. His eyes confirmed what his body knew already. She was not wearing a bra.

Her 'prime attractions' heaved visibly, weighting her blouse. While her thighs climbed raunchily from her skimpy sailing shorts. Her tongue as loose as an unlatched window – she sent it out sneaking like a thief in the night.

'Well,' she said saucily. 'Who's a shy boy, then?'

Vammits hitched his trousers and shuffled towards her. He sat down on the bed. Lickie let out a giggle and leapt at his neck. She tore the scarf free and dropped it on the carpet.

'Hey,' said Vammits. 'You shouldn't . . .'

She darted again and grabbed the false nose. The elastic snapped. She tossed the nose aside.

'My oh my. You are a handsome devil . . .'

He rubbed his face where the elastic had stung him.

'Yes but . . .'

Her next move snatched the wig. She flung it out through the door and onto the landing. Then she lay back and laughed. Vammits moved angrily. He hovered above her, then froze; halted by the force field of her 'twin booster pack'.

Lickie reached up and tickled his chin.

'What's your name?' she said.

'They call me Fast Mits,' said Fast Mits. Then he bit his tongue.

She took one of his hands in hers.

'Fast Mits?' she said. 'Were you . . . A fighter?'

'Southern area light-heavyweight cham . . .'

'Why! You're famous . . .'

Lickie grabbed his neck and pulled him down on top of her. His hands shot to her breasts. His fingers dug painfully, but Lickie endured it. She chewed at his ear and wrapped her legs around him.

'Oh Fast Mits, Fast Mits . . .' she moaned.

He unbuckled his own pants and tugged at Lickie's shorts. She raised her knees to block him.

'Fast Mits,' she said, seriously now. 'Do you have a rubber?'

Fast Mits stopped what he was doing. He looked about dazedly.

'Uh . . . No.'

Lickie addressed him matter-of-factly, like a friend.

'Well look. I can't afford to take a chance. You understand, don't you? My career and everything . . .'

'Yes. Er . . .'

'But I can do this for you . . .'

She pulled down his trousers and yanked at his underpants. His penis came out bobbing and weav-

179

ing. She ran her tongue along it and then took it in her mouth. She sucked it to her right cheek, then switched it to the left. It was like brushing her teeth with a rancid sweaty toothbrush.

Fast Mits gurgled. Lickie feared that he might shoot. So she spat him out, then took him more gently. Her lips kissed the head. Her tongue circled around it. Then she bit on it as hard as she could.

Fast Mits screamed loud enough to bring a cemetery to life. Out in the garden Robin began to howl.

Calm and purposeful, Lickie grabbed the ex-fighter's testicles and crushed them together. The sound he made now was closer to a death rattle. Lickie squeezed. And squeezed. And squeezed. And squeezed.

Fast Mits lost consciousness. Lickie skipped out of the room and locked the door behind her. Half way down the stairs she realised that she didn't have her shoes. But she hardly had time to go back and claim them.

She slipped into the kitchen, thinking that she would escape the back way. Then she froze with horror. For there was Robin. A canine face, raised at the window. Panting and spitting.

Lickie searched for logic, a way to appease him. She looked around for dog food. Surely there must be some. A tin of meat. A box of biscuits.

She clattered through the cupboards but drew a mighty blank. She stopped to consider. Maybe there was something else. Some toy that would amuse him. She carried her search into the living room. And there on the floor lay the navy blue knickers. It was a long shot. But . . .

Lickie picked up the knickers. They were soiled and damp. She turned up her nose, held them at arm's length. Used her free hand to unlock the kitchen door. Tossed the knickers out into the yard.

Robin sniffed at them inquisitively. Took them in his mouth. Managed to wrap them around his nose.

As Lickie tiptoed outside she was beset by a sense of impending doom. Robin looked up, eyed her suspiciously. She almost threw in the towel. Retreated there and then.

A curious thing happened. Robin turned away from her. Lay down with the knickers. He seemed quite contented. Lickie made haste.

She scampered through the forest, wincing at twigs and fir cones underneath her feet. Her plan was clear and simple. She would keep going in a straight line until she came to a main road. Then she would attempt to flag down a passing motorist. Someone was bound to recognise her. After all, she didn't have a bra on.

Tommy 'Cuffs' Todd combed his moustache and picked up the telephone.

'Good morning Commissioner,' he said. 'I'm sorry to disturb you at this early hour.'

'That's all right, Todd. What is it? The Lickie Loose case? Have you cracked it?'

'Why yes sir, I believe we have. It's much as I thought. Seemed clear to me once I knew that Albie Alibi was the girl's manager. A bad sort, Albie. I know him of old. So I put a man on Albie. And he led us to Charlie Hammer. We've wanted to nick Charlie for many a long day. It's my belief that he's been involved with . . .'

'Yes, yes. Get on with it, man.'

'Yes sir. Sorry sir. Well sir. Our enquiries regarding the Fiesta led us to suspect Eddie Roman and Fast Mits Finnegan. Two old cohorts of Charlie's. So it looks like the old East End gang. In above their heads, I should say.'

'If you know all this, Todd, why haven't you moved?'

'Would have done, sir. But for a bit of bad luck.

Yesterday we had a tail on Charlie Hammer, hoping he would lead us straight to the girl. Unfortunately the police vehicle concerned stalled at traffic lights and we lost him. However, Charlie is now back at home and we have the place staked out. It's only a question of time, sir. Until he makes a move.'

'Excellent. Stick to it.'

'Only one thing I'm not so sure about, sir. And that's whether we have enough evidence to connect the other three to Albie. But once we get them down in the cells I'm sure we'll make them squeal. The average criminal is yellow at heart, and . . .'

'Yes. Quite.'

'Well thank you sir. I won't take up any more of your time.'

Todd put down the phone.

'Fool,' said the Commissioner.

Charlie Hammer lay in bed. He knew he should have got up at the crack of dawn. But he was knackered and shagged out. It had been a stressful few weeks. The intricate planning. The precise execution. The intrusive publicity. The nerve racking wait.

The 'no' from D'U Cosmetics. That was the biggest blow. Albie was now in secret negotiation with Dinsdale Snape, the tabloid editor. Albie reckoned Snape would cough. Charlie prayed it would be soon. His poor old ticker couldn't take much more of this.

Get up, get up, his senses told him. Yeah, but the quilt is so snug, the pillow so soft.

Babs Hammer lay by Charlie's side. She was quite happy to stay in bed a while yet. At least until 'Milko' had called on his rounds. Just in case he expected a repeat of yesterday's order. Surely he would realise. With the Mercedes in the drive. But he was such a randy so and so. He was really such a giggle.

The telephone trilled. The Hammers had an extension in the bedroom. It was on Charlie's side. He groped with a sleepy hand and missed it by a foot. By contrast Babs made a purposeful dive and almost scooped it up first time. She had endured too many of these mysterious morning calls. She wanted a piece of the action.

Charlie felt his wife upon him. At first, half awake, he thought that they were making love. Then he realised that they were fighting for the phone.

He pushed Babs away, and sat up in bed. She punched him in the back, and tried to reach around him. After a brief struggle he secured her in a headlock. He used his free hand to lift the receiver.

'Hello,' he panted.

It was Albie. Albie sounded distressed.

'Listen Charlie. They're onto us. Just heard it from my contact in the Filth. I been ringing the cottage but there's no reply. I don't know what's happened to Fast Mits.'

Under the quilt Babs made a grab for Charlie's testicles. Fully awake now, he blocked her with a thigh and squeezed her neck tighter.

'What do you want me to do?' he said to Albie.

'Get down there. If The Alps is still there you'd better bind and gag her. Try to find Fast Mits. Remove any incriminating evidence. Then get the hell out. And don't contact me again until I let you know it's safe. You can do it, Charlie. I'm banking on you, son.'

Albie hung up.

'Cheers,' said Charlie.

'Urrr . . .' said Babs.

Johnny Hammer sat behind the wheel of a Jag. The Jag was parked just down the road from Johnny's parents' home. It had been there all night. For Johnny was taking the law into his own hands. The next time Charlie made a move Johnny was going after him.

On the back seat lay a ruck of empty cans. Just beneath the driver's door a frothy puddle of urine. Johnny dashed a cigarette into a brimming ashtray, and blinked his eyes to stay awake.

A little further down the road sat Baines and Rogerson. They were plainclothes policemen. In an unmarked police car.

They had radio contact with Chief Inspector Todd.

Charlie Hammer emerged from his front door. Babs Hammer appeared at the bedroom window and flung an alarm clock at him. It struck him on the head and bounced off onto the lawn. Charlie rubbed his head and unlocked the garage door.

He backed the Mercedes down the drive and sped off up the road. Jolted to consciousness, Johnny sped off after him. Baines sped off after Johnny. Rogerson talked to the radio.

Charlie Hammer braked the Mercedes outside Eddie Roman's lodgings. Johnny Hammer braked the Jag. Baines braked the unmarked police car.

Charlie was far from happy with the turn of events.

'Listen Charlie. They're onto us.'

Well great. Just terrific. Bang goes the comfortable retirement. Simple case now of precious freedom versus a stretch in the Scrubs.

'Don't contact me again until I let you know it's safe.'

Oh, right. I get it. Albie wriggles out. Albie looks after number one. Albie does what Albie's done throughout history. Albie takes a wide berth and thereby safeguards his liberty.

So why doesn't Charlie do the same? Because Charlie can't. Because Charlie's fucking dog is tied up outside the cottage. Because Fast Mits Finnegan is out there alone and the last time Charlie put money on Fast Mits Finnegan the then southern area light-heavyweight champion was knocked out cold inside two minutes at Bethnal Green. Because if the situation is retrievable then Charlie don't trust no one but himself to do the old retrieving. Because if Charlie simply stayed at home worrying he would probably have a bleeding heart attack.

On the other hand if Charlie's going down then he's taking someone with him. Hence the phone call to Eddie Roman (Charlie sitting on Babs, pinning her shoulders with his knees) before leaving home. Rehash of Albie's message to Charlie. Hence Eddie now, stumbling down the driveway, looking like death.

Eddie got into the car. The Mercedes roared away from the kerb. So did the Jag. So did the unmarked police car.

Charlie and Eddie soon realised that they were being followed.

'It's the Filth,' said Eddie.

Charlie squinted into the mirror.

'No it's not,' he said. 'It's my Johnny.'

Johnny was too intent on following the Mercedes to be aware of the unmarked police car. Meanwhile Baines and Rogerson were somewhat perturbed by Johnny's presence.

'Who's the joker in the Jag?' said Baines.

'Get past him,' said Rogerson.

Johnny swung the Jag from side to side, success-fully blocking the idiots behind him. He rolled down the window and shook his fist.

'Wankers!' he screamed.

Charlie began to drive as they drive in the films. In his younger days he had driven that way himself. Only he was a bit out of practice, so he missed the pedestrians and market stalls by the narrowest of margins, and when he drove on the wrong side of the road the other drivers only just had time to get out of his way.

Johnny clung more or less to his father's bumper. Baines and Rogerson were not so lucky. The Jag in front of them clipped the edge of a market stall. They swerved to avoid the cauliflowers and skidded on the eggs. The unmarked police car spun a hundred and eighty degrees. Its rear end hit a wall. A canopy collapsed on top of it. A box of tomatoes hit the windscreen and exploded into juice.

Rogerson talked to the radio.

'I'm sorry, Chief Inspector. We've lost them again.'

The Mercedes sped out of London. The Jag still loomed in the rear-view mirror.

'Don't drive to the cottage,' said Eddie. 'Not with Johnny behind us.'

'What d'you think I am?' said Charlie. 'Stupid or what!'

He swung left. The Mercedes bounced along a cobblestoned driveway. In the passenger seat Eddie Roman jerked up and down. Up ahead a farmyard loomed.

Behind them Johnny attacked the driveway much too fast. He felt he was being riddled by machine gun fire. He wished he hadn't drunk quite so many cans.

A man with a pitchfork tried to halt the Mercedes. Charlie pressed the horn and drove straight at him. He dived over a low wall and landed in a pigsty.

Charlie drove around the farmhouse, scattering hens and worrying sheep. He noticed an open barn, slowed down, drove inside. The interior of the barn was high and wide. Sunlight crept in through the door and then surrendered to a deep black well. Charlie edged the Mercedes forward, into the well. He briefly flashed the headlights. Before him stood a huge mound of hay, stacked from floor to ceiling. It loomed above the car like a terrifying scarecrow.

The Mercedes nosed into the hay. Nosed and nosed until only the boot protruded.

'Bloody hell,' said Eddie.

'Shut up,' said Charlie.

Out in the yard the hens and sheep had just about regained their composure. Then Johnny drove around the farmhouse. This time the poor creatures didn't even bother to flap and scamper. They just surrendered to their fate.

The Jag paused briefly outside the open barn. Johnny peered inside. Saw nothing but blackness. Hit the pedal once again.

A few minutes later Charlie reversed out of the hay and into the farmyard. The Mercedes bumped over scattered animal corpses. The farmer and his three sons (average height six foot six) came running from the farmhouse. They lined up in front of the Mercedes, wielding mighty cudgels. The man with the pitchfork raised his head above the pigsty wall and cried out a warning. Charlie was already accelerating at the gang of four.

Three escaped with glancing blows, minor cuts and bruises. One, the eldest son, managed to throw himself onto the bonnet of the car and perched there on his knees. He lunged forward, big red face pressed against the windscreen.

Charlie hit the water jets. One of them zapped the farm boy's eye. Then Charlie hit the wipers. The first blade clipped the farm boy's nose. He rocked back, wobbled precariously. Charlie swung the wheel sharply, left and right. The farm boy fell off.

Charlie parked the Mercedes a little way from the cottage, left it part camouflaged under branches and foliage. He and Eddie took time to slip into their disguises. They then approached with stealth.

The exterior scene was serenity exemplified. Robin lay chewing at some old rag. Nothing else moved.

Charlie bent down to pet Robin.

'Bloody hell. He's got the knickers.'

'Here look,' said Eddie. 'The kitchen door's open.'

Charlie and Eddie went inside. The ground floor was deserted. So was the upstairs, except for the locked bedroom. Charlie rapped on the door. They heard a moaning from within. If the two possibilities were Lickie and Fast Mits then it was definitely Fast Mits.

Charlie stepped back and kicked at the door. He then hopped up and down the landing, nursing an injured foot. Eddie saw that there was only one thing for it. He hunched his head into his shoulders and charged at the door. His skull met the wood and the wood cracked first.

Charlie and Eddie entered the bedroom. Fast Mits lay writhing on the bed, clutching at his wounded genitals.

'She's done a runner,' said Charlie.

'Must be out in the forest,' said Eddie.

Leaving Fast Mits to his misery they ran back downstairs. Out in the garden Charlie unleashed Robin. By this time Robin had just about shredded the knickers,

'Go on boy,' said Charlie. 'Find yourself the real thing.'

Robin bounded off into the forest. Charlie and Eddie lumbered after him.

Johnny Hammer drove around the boundaries of Epping Forest. He was sure they had her tucked away somewhere here. That Cornish stuff in the newspapers was nothing but bullshit. East End villains never stray far from the Mile End Road.

As he drove, Johnny cursed his own rotten luck.

He had lost the Mercedes somewhere in the farm-yard.

At the end of the cobblestone driveway he had stopped to consider. Sprayed the windscreen to clear it of chicken blood. Looked left and right. Gambled left. Driven round in circles.

A little further on he had pulled up in a lay-by. Not to check directions. But to puke at the roadside. On the back seat the empty cans grinned.

Now he had the radio on to aid his concentration. Since Lickie's kidnapping became public knowledge Wussell Maycock had been off the air. 'Too distw-essed' to go through with his show. Well thank heaven for small mercies, Johnny thought to himself.

A chart hit faded and up piped the replacement DJ. Would like to play a special message. Recorded by someone familiar to the listeners.

Yes, it was him. Wussell. Pwactically bweeding fwom the speakers.

'Hewo wisteners. Wussell Maycock speaking. Nor-mawy I addwess you in a fwivowous vein. Today my tone could not be more sewious. Because, as you pwobabwy know, a wady vewy dear to me is at this moment in the hands of wuthwess cwiminals. I speak, of course, of Wickie Woose, who was abducted wast week. I am on the air now to make a pwea for information. Someone somewhere must know some-thing. Mustn't they . . .?'

Johnny couldn't handle it. This wimp. Who couldn't even speak properly. Whining over the airwaves, broadcasting to the nation. Why, a real man would be out in the field, carrying the fight. Just as Johnny was.

He raged with indignation. Meanwhile the appeal continued.

'. . . Pwease contact your neawest powice sta-tion . . .'

Johnny couldn't handle it. The Jag. He hit a sharp

bend. Swung the wheel far too late. Careered off the road.

The car ripped through a fence and rammed into a tree. It came to a halt; engine coughing, wheels spinning. Johnny was thrown forward. His head hit the windscreen.

The dream began as a vortex of light.

Then it steadied.

Orange triangles on a purple backcloth.

Johnny himself. A grown man. In the foetal position. In the black shell of the womb. A can of lager in his hand. A cigarette in his mouth.

Johnny's mother, Babs. Dancing like Salome, casting off her veils.

Robin the Rottweiler. Tongue hanging out.

Charlie, Eddie and Fast Mits. In black suits, white shirts and spotted bow ties. Dancing on stage. Big band playing. Silver canes twirling.

The forecourt of Johnny's Unbeatable Bargains. Empty.

Lickie Loose. Naked. Oozing in a sumptuous sunken bath. Raising a foam smothered leg. Splashing the water. Beckoning. Calling someone to join her.

Who? Who?

Johnny himself. In his loudest shirt and his best jeans and trainers. Walking down the street. Turns into a driveway. Big posh house. Rings the front doorbell. Butler shows him in. Walks through the hallway. Into the reception room. Sees the sunken bath. Lickie's head above the water. Approaches. Beaming.

Is halted in his tracks. The bath is full of Wussell Maycocks. Miniature Wussell Maycocks. Hundreds of them. Grinning like leprechauns. Half submerged in the water. Forming a protective chain around Lickie.

Lickie raises herself slightly. She has a Wussell

190

Maycock on each breast. She dips a hand into the water and gropes around between her legs. Pulls out another Wussell Maycock. With a smile on its face.

A sudden flurry of chicken feathers and sheep's hooves.

Vortex of light.

Johnny came to and got out of the car. Hardly knowing what he was doing he blundered into the forest.

Almost immediately he saw Lickie Loose, naked, running towards him. He thought he was still dreaming. In an effort to find out he punched himself in the nose. The blood spattered on his shirt. He knew he was awake.

Lickie's flight from the cottage had been a troublesome one. The treacherous undergrowth cut her feet and scratched her legs. Whichever way she headed the forest seemed to grow denser. And then, to cap it all, she turned to see the Rottweiler bearing down upon her.

He bounded over a rise, leapt a couple of bushes. Lickie knew she had to do something, otherwise he would be at her throat. She remembered the knickers back at the cottage. How he liked to chew and sniff them.

His eyes met hers, not thirty yards apart. She whipped off her blouse and dropped it in the bracken. Robin kept on coming, then skidded to a halt. He lay down on the blouse, began to tear it into strips.

Lickie made off again, put distance between herself and the confounded hound. Only to hear, five minutes later, the familiar breathing and the scampering of doggy feet. Acting quickly, she stepped out of her shorts and hung them on a branch.

Robin jumped at them, just failed to reach. He psyched himself up, gave an almighty leap, took them in his mouth. At first he swung like a pendulum;

then he, shorts and branch all crashed to the ground. For a moment he was silent and still. Lickie hoped that he was dead. Then he raised himself, nose and mouth in operation.

The pursuit was repeated. Lickie opening a gap. Robin closing her down. All she had left was her last pair of knickers. She took them off and showed them to the dog. Then, thwarting his approach, she thrust them down into the hollow of a tree. The last she saw of Robin he was up on his hind legs (all three of them), ferreting anxiously in search of the knickers.

And now, it seemed, rescue was at hand. Albeit from an unlikely quarter. A rough young man with a cut forehead and a bloody nose. Ah well. Beggars can't be choosers. Any port in a storm. All that shit.

'Help,' cried Lickie, faintly.

The young man merely gawped. She told her lungs to do better.

'HELP!' she bellowed, loudly.

Johnny had no problems with identification. He knew her naked form like the palm of his hand. In fact she made an amazing likeness. To her tabloid image.

He stood with arms outstretched. Dizzy with exertion, Lickie ran to him. He embraced her. Felt her nipples, stiff with cold. Her groin against his.

A moment later they were on the grass. Her breast in his hand. Her neck in his mouth.

He threw his leg over.

Lickie summoned her last energies and forcibly ejected him.

'What are you?' she cried. 'Some sort of fucking rapist?'

Johnny rose to his knees. He was disgusted with himself. A knight in shining armour overcome by a dirty mind.

'I'm sorry,' he said. 'I'm truly sorry. I'm here to help you. Please believe me.'

Lickie considered. Behind her, somewhere, stalked the fearsome beast. Under the circumstances she decided to bestow the benefit of the doubt.

Johnny took off his bloodstained shirt and wrapped it around her. She wore it reluctantly. It made her skin crawl. He then took her hand and led her back to the Jag.

It was then that they met with a surprise. For next to the Jag stood Charlie and Eddie, both out of breath.

'Johnny,' said Charlie.

'Dad. Eddie. What are you doing in that ridiculous pantomime clobber?'

Charlie and Eddie took off their disguises. The confrontation grew claws.

'I'm warning you, Dad,' said Johnny. 'Don't you stand in my way.'

'And I'm warning you, son. You just hand her back to me.'

They glared at each other. Lickie felt horribly weak. She longed for her mum. She longed for Albert. She wouldn't have said no to Wussell bwuddy Maycock.

At that moment Robin emerged enthusiastically from a cluster of trees. After a long hard struggle he had managed to extricate the knickers from the hollow. But, boy oh boy, had they been worth it!

He came to a halt between Charlie and Johnny.

'Here boy,' said Charlie.

Robin cocked an ear.

'Here boy,' said Johnny.

Robin cocked another. His eyes darted from father to son. He looked mightily confused.

Charlie bent down and rubbed his fingers together.

"Come on, old son. Who looks after you? Takes you walkies? Fills your food dish every night?'

Robin appeared sympathetic to this call. Moving

193

hastily, Johnny leaned forward and slapped a hand against his thigh.

'Yeah, but who takes you rabbiting? And slips you extras under the table?'

Robin couldn't handle it. He freaked out. Turned and fled. Off into the forest. Howling as he went.

It was left to the men to do battle for the girl.

'This is your last chance,' said Charlie. 'Hand her over now.'

Johnny braced himself for combat.

'You'll have to take her from me.'

Charlie nudged Eddie, and propelled him forward. Bloody hell, thought Eddie. Why me?

All the same he did as he was bid. He and Johnny squared up to each other. With Charlie and Lickie as anxious spectators.

Johnny was much bigger than Eddie, and many years younger. But fighting is nine parts psychology, and in this respect Eddie felt he had the edge. For Eddie was a hoodlum when Johnny was just a kid, and Johnny knew that. Johnny would have it in his mind that he could never beat Eddie. This gave Eddie confidence.

Johnny threw one punch and Eddie lost his confidence. He hit the deck sharply. Blimey, he thought. The death of psychology.

Johnny stood over Eddie, as if expecting more. But Eddie had a sore head and felt very old indeed. He closed his eyes and feigned unconsciousness, happy where he was.

Where Eddie believed in psychology, Charlie trusted to surprise. He rushed at Johnny and tried to kick him in the nuts. But Johnny half turned and took the blow on the hip. In the same movement he grabbed his old man round the neck and they crashed to the floor. And there they lay, grunting and groaning, wrestling, gouging.

Lickie picked a careful path around them and

headed for the road. As if on cue she heard sirens and a screeching of brakes. Car doors opened. Uniforms emerged.

Lickie broke into a trot. Tommy 'Cuffs' Todd ogled her for a moment, then passed her to the custody of an accompanying policewoman. Meanwhile he and his men sauntered across to disturb the battling Hammers.

'You submit?' snarled Charlie.

'Never!' cried Johnny.

13

Royston Bone was a troubled man. He couldn't settle to anything at all.

The day after his ordeal at the hands of Krunt he simply stayed in bed. The alarm beeped at eight, as was its custom. Royston leapt up with a war cry, like a trooper from a trench. He grabbed the clock in both hands and smashed it against the wall. He then went back to bed; put his head under the pillow, and didn't move for twenty-six hours.

During that time he flitted constantly between the edgy paranoia of wakefulness and the endless nightmare of sleep. A thousand times he relived the deathly sensations of the dungeon. The whistling bullet that parted his hair. The loaded barrel that threatened to part his genitals. He would wake up and scream. He would wake up and shudder. When a car backfired outside the window he almost shat the bed.

Once or twice his conjectures turned to the unfortunate Nuttall Mann. Unfortunate? Why, it was that lousy faggot (you can tell, man) who began the whole thing. Wandering in off the street, uninvited, with his wild assertions and his ridiculous demands. He it was who sentenced Royston to that fearful hour of hell.

But the fact remained (he couldn't deny it) that by wilting under pressure Royston had repaid the compliment many times over.

'Give me the name.'

'Nuttall Mann.'

So now, most likely, the private eye's second-only client would himself be down there, suffering some unspeakable torture. A direct consequence of Royston grassing on him.

Royston racked his brains to find some justification, some moral right to cling to.

Hell man, he brought it on himself!

You stir up a hornet's nest you're bound to get your ass stung!

He tried also to play down the extent of the retribution forthcoming. They won't actually kill him. Surely not. That would be murder. Snap a bone (distressing connotations!). Twist a limb. Maybe less than that.

There was of course the possibility of involving the police. Royston could wander round there, spill the whole story. But what was there to go on? Nothing concrete on which to convict. Krunt would play the perfect host, invite the investigating officer in, furnish him with a drink. You must see, officer, that this is a ridiculous concoction. A fancy trumped up between a nigger and a queer.

Besides, following the warehouse job, Royston had no intention of walking into any police station whatsoever. (He also had a sneaking suspicion that before establishing a detective agency you really ought to obtain some sort of licence.)

It all brought back to him the injustice of life. With particular reference to his own sorry lot. He seriously wondered whether or not he had ever enjoyed a single even break. He reckoned that he probably had not.

On the second day he rose. He was desperately hungry and he needed a pee. Having settled those requirements he washed and dressed and sat down in front of the TV. Simple escapism. Maybe that was the cure.

Several hours passed most tolerably. Game show. Chat show. News and weather. And then in the afternoon they bowled him a googly. Old detective film. Black and white. Classic of the genre.

Of course he had the option of switching it off. But that wasn't his style. He felt he had to see it through. That it constituted a crucial test of nerve.

Once upon a time he would have lapped up the

plot. Now he viewed it with a stony cynicism. Always so easy for the 'tec on the screen. Nice straightforward case. Extortion. Triple killing. He handles it his own way. Rounds up the bad guys. Grabs the girl. DOESN'T RAT ON ANYBODY!

In real life it just isn't like that.

On the third day he went out drinking. With Gladstone, Chamberlain and Wes. He remembered only too well how on the night of his undoing these disloyal cheapskates had failed to support him. With a little muscle in tow the boot might very well have found itself on a different foot entirely. Bastards, he thought. Bastards. Bastards. Bastards.

Gladstone offered an olive branch of sorts.

'Hey, Royston. Sorry we couldn't help you the other evening. Otherwise engaged, you know what I mean? How'd it go? You make out all right? Yeah?'

Two-faced bastards. Two-faced bastards. Two-faced bastards.

On the other hand Royston was determined to make no public show of weakness.

'Yeah. Fine. All right.'

'You sure about that.'

'Yeah. Sure I'm sure. Why d'you ask?'

'Your hand, man. Shaking like a leaf.'

Royston looked down and saw that it was so. He steadied the hand and his knee gave a tweak. He stood up straight and suffered a twinge in his neck. Spontaneous breakdancing. Nothing he could do.

A little later Churchill strolled in.

'Yo! Royston! Wicked haircut. Shaved on top. Who did that for you? Give me his name.'

Back at home, in something of a stupor, Royston thought of Sharon Cobb. A nice girl. A loyal girl. A reasonable fuck.

He really should have called her. She might be worried sick. Perhaps she had tried to contact him. While lying in bed he had let the telephone ring.

Maybe she had called again while he was out with the boys.

He would go to the office tomorrow. Maybe. A part of him wished that he could get out altogether. Visit his grandparents in Jamaica. That would be lovely. Sunshine and sea. Rum on the beach. Yeah, but it was out of the question. They still require cash in exchange for airline tickets. If only I could come up with, say, a quick twenty grand . . .

Pondering this he drifted into sleep.

Was awakened by the telephone. Thought of Sharon. Picked it up. It was Roxanne. She wanted to finalise his appointment with Nadene. He remembered his appointment with Nadene. Went along with what Roxanne said. Made a note of time and place. Said good-bye. Went back to sleep.

But the next time he woke up he was a different man. He felt wanted. His services required. By this troubled little girl. Nadene Braxton.

He heard a definite call. For a public demonstration of his most subtle art. He may be a rotten detective, but he was still the hottest baddest lover in town. Ask Roxanne. Ask Sharon. In forty-eight hours you can ask Nadene too.

He stood before the full length mirror in the bedroom (a present from Roxanne – she knew him too well). Yes, he thought. I look good. Cool dude. Handsome man.

But perhaps a little scruffy in a sweatshirt and jeans. He changed into a suit and checked the glass again. Better. Better. Smart. Intelligent. Man about town.

But lacking, perhaps, a certain edge. He pulled on his overcoat and hat, dragged down the brim. Yeah. Mean. Streetwise. Tangle at your peril. (How soon a man forgets.)

For his next trick he performed a routine he had perfected as a boy. First he took off all his clothes.

Then he stood before the mirror once again. Next he took the role of a brutal sergeant-major.

"Ten-shun!'

Pussysniffer I responded to the call.

Roxanne Bliss had fixed things up with Royston. She had arranged for him to meet Nadene on the evening when Roxanne herself was dining with Cordelia (convenient all round). There was only one i to dot, one t to cross. Roxanne hadn't yet got around to informing Nadene.

Several times the words had slipped towards the tip of her tongue, but somehow the occasion had never seemed appropriate. Nadene was always either washing her hair or drying her hair, taking a shower, reading in her room. As well as this she had been rather prickly of late. Their famous arguments were raging at a rate of two or three per night.

All of which brought Roxanne around to doubting herself. Was it really advisable? This virtuoso pairing of supply and demand? Roxanne tried to think of what Cordelia would do (she admired Cordelia so). Without doubt Cordelia would be strong. Stick to her convictions. Roxanne resolved to bite the bullet. Soon.

And now, with only twenty-four hours remaining, she had the bullet between her teeth. Nadene was calmer tonight. Sitting on the sofa. Relating an incident she had witnessed during her lunch break from work. A would-be suicide perched on a window ledge. Frantic colleagues poking their heads out and trying to talk him down.

'And it was weird, you know. Because I thought I recognised him. He looked like a guy I met a couple of weeks ago. I'm not sure whether I told you about him at the time.'

Roxanne wasn't really interested in this.

'You thought you knew him?'

'Yeah. But then something happened which meant it couldn't be him . . .'

'And what happened? Did he jump?'

'I don't know. It was almost the end of my lunch hour and so I had to dash off.'

'What? You mean you just left him there?'

'Why not? It was out of my hands. I mean there was nothing on the TV or in the Standard. He must have gone back inside. The wimp.'

Roxanne declined to pass further comment. She was determined not to become embroiled in contentious side issues. For now was an ideal time to advise Nadene of the arrangements made on her behalf.

She gave herself a shove in the back.

'Nadene. Do you remember Royston Bone?'

Nadene considered.

'Royston Bone, Royston Bone . . . Yes. Of course. Your ex-creep. Your persistent ex-creep. He kept coming around here and calling on the phone. I threatened to castrate him with the breadknife. Pretty effective, as I recall. He didn't come round no more.'

Roxanne sighed. It wasn't going to be easy.

'You shouldn't be too harsh on him. He does have his good points . . .'

She spoke at length about Royston's good points. Then she spoke briefly about his very best point. Nadene looked highly sceptical. Roxanne saw that there was no alternative. Like a timid deep sea diver, she just had to take the plunge.

'Well look. It's like this. I've arranged for you to meet him. Tomorrow night. I think that maybe he can do you a favour . . .'

Nadene said nothing. She didn't have to. Her face was a lexicon of horror and distaste.

Roxanne floundered.

'Think of all you told me. You said that you were searching for the cataclysmic cock. Well Royston has it, I assure you. I'm only trying to help. For God's sake Nadene . . .'

Nadene jumped from the sofa and unleashed her scolding tongue.

'Roxanne, I thank you for your dutiful efforts but I do not need you or anyone else to "fix me up". I've had more men than you've had green salads. One night in the Bled Pig I bet Carole Walker that I could pull any man in the room just by raising an eyebrow. She picked out this tough old sailor. An hour later we were at it in the park, underneath the band-stand . . .'

'What was he like?'

'Old and knotted and pickled in rum. But that's beside the point. I'll search for salvation in my own sweet way. By trial and error. And error and error. I do not need help. No. No. A thousand times no.'

'Nadene. Be reasonable. You could at least . . .'

'No. No. No. No. No. No. No. No. No.'

'So you've made up your mind?'

Nadene leapt at Roxanne. They fought briefly, then Roxanne escaped to the bathroom and locked herself inside.

The following afternoon at the health shop Nadene received a summons to go and see the manageress. She knew what it was about. An incident that took place earlier in the day.

Nadene and one of the younger assistants were in the shop alone. A man shambled in, a rough looking vagabond. He staggered to the counter and raised a big hairy fist.

'Give me all the money. You fucking bitch.'

The young assistant was panic stricken. Nadene remained cool. She dipped in her handbag and produced a can of hairspray. She let the vagabond have it. Left eye. Right eye. He left in a hurry in search of a white stick.

Nadene herself spoke to no one of this. But she observed the young assistant whispering to the manageress. And now a direction to visit the old girl. A verbal commendation, no doubt. Perhaps a cash bonus. That would be nice.

Nadene knocked on the door and entered the office. She was surprised that the old bird did not invite her to sit down. However, the reason for the meeting was indeed the morning incident. The manageress asked Nadene to describe in her own words everything that had happened.

When Nadene was done the manageress peered up at her through a pair of pince-nez.

'A can of hairspray, you say?'

Nadene smiled proudly.

'Yes ma'am.'

'Which particular brand of hairspray?'

Nadene's mood changed. For young assistant read damned informant. And with the evidence in her handbag she knew that it was futile to lie.

She named the brand. The manageress spoke on behalf of the ozone layer. For a good half hour. When at last she drew a conclusion it was predictable enough.

'And so, Nadene, while I appreciate your vigorous defence of the cash takings, I have to say that in my opinion you are totally unsuited to this type of work. I've been concerned for some time about your eating habits and your choice of clothing. But this really is the final straw. To think of that foul aerosol peddling its pollution . . .'

Nadene looked down at the pince-nez. She was tempted to whip out the spray and zap the cross-eyed bat. But she settled for a cheque to the end of the month.

On the way out she cornered the young assistant.

'I'm sorry, Ms Braxton. I was only thinking of the planet . . .'

'One piece of advice, kid. Don't ever think of anyone but yourself.'

After leaving the shop Nadene wolfed a hamburger and swallowed a Coke. Stopped by a public lavatory and stuck her hair on end. Then returned tiredly to Clapham.

As she entered the flat Roxanne was by the phone.

'What are you doing?'

'I'm calling Royston. To cancel tonight.'

Nadene put her hand over the receiver.

'Don't call him. I'll be there. What time did you say? Eight thirty?'

Roxanne was dumbfounded. Nadene walked towards her bedroom. She opened the door and then turned back.

'And he'd better be good! He'd better be the best!'

Royston Bone longed for a little more confidence. Which was not like him at all. Not in his dealings with the tastier sex.

By rights he should be full of it. After all, here he was, stood in a bar, awaiting a lady, a very sexy lady, who was coming to him in the hope of ultimate satisfaction. It wasn't a case of making her day. More a case of saving her life. And only he could do it. He had been selected. Surely every stallion's dream.

He puffed his chest and ordered another gin and tonic. The way the best professionals work. Personal recommendation. Word of mouth.

Yeah, but this would be the first time since. . . . You know what! And there was no telling how such a disturbing experience, nay brush with death, might affect his level of performance. The vision of the gun barrel was not an easy one to lose. He was haunted by what might have been if Krunt had pulled that trigger.

He had fully intended to call in at the office.

Yesterday or today. Do a little sparring with young Sharon Cobb. Work himself into a lather. Knock himself into shape. But somehow he had not quite found the motivation to leave his training camp in the hills. Not until now.

Was it wise, he wondered, to work off your ring rust in a championship contest?

He shrugged his shoulders, ordered another G & T.

Nadene walked slowly from the tube. She could see the lights of the meeting place, up ahead, over the road. Maybe Bone wouldn't show. Oh, he would show. After all, he was a man. A fully deluded member of the beaver patrol.

She wondered why she felt so nervous this time around. When she knew the hype so well. The pitifully proud pronouncements of the male sexual ego. The harder they say they come. The harder they fall. One and all.

Could this one be different? Roxanne had more or less staked her credibility upon it. Was it possible? And was it, underneath, what Nadene was afraid of? Did she really want to have her world turned upside down? Her cast-iron certainties smashed like china?

Yes. She did.

But who was this Royston Bone? What made him so special?

Royston spotted Nadene as soon as she walked in. And she looked good, he had to confess. Hair spiked. Pout seductive. Unbuttoned to cleavage. Skirt round her ass. Stockings sheer. Heels high.

But as she picked her way through the merry throng he couldn't help recalling the last occasion on which they met. In the kitchen. The flat in Clapham. The arc of the breadknife. The narrowness of his escape.

Images of torture clogged Royston's mind. Krunt's

handgun. Nadene's breadknife. Spontaneous breakdancing. Jitterbug and jive.

As soon as she walked in Nadene spotted Royston. There he was. At the bar. Gin and tonic in his hand.

And he looked pretty hunky, she didn't mind admitting. Tall and powerful, with a hint of arrogance. Strong body. Firm buttocks. She wished that he'd turn round.

When he did she was distracted by a glint in his eye. Was it fear? And could his hand be shaking?

The time had come for greetings.

'Hi Gorgeous.'

'Hi Nadene. What can I get you?'

'Same as yourself.'

'Right.'

Drinks served, they found themselves a table. Royston searched inside himself for a suitable opening gambit. Nadene bailed him out.

'So,' she said. 'You're pretty well hung?'

Over the next hour and a half they drank like thirsty fish. More a case of plying themselves than of plying each other. As far as expenses were concerned Nadene insisted on going Dutch. Which was fine by Royston. He was saving up for his flight to Jamaica.

But in terms of conversation he found it heavy going. He didn't know how to take her. This slick spiky sex addict. He didn't know what she expected. Whether she wanted him to talk dirty or sweet.

For the most part she was happy to relieve him of responsibility. Nadene talked a lot. And she talked about men. A host of male misfits came clattering from her closet. She laid them on the table and skewered their pale corpses.

Royston took it all in. A hundred dudes from Yorkshire who couldn't light a candle. A hundred dudes in London who couldn't crank a motor. More than once he wanted to break in and say: 'Yeah, but you're talking about white dudes here . . .'

At ten o'clock Royston felt he had to move. Alone in the gents he decided that the time was ripe for decisive action. The drink had done enough to blunt the breadknife and unload the gun. But was still some way short of eroding his own lethal weapon. He had one tough lady on his hands tonight. 'I hear a train . . .' would cut no ice with her.

Back at their shared table he addressed Nadene politely.

'Nadene, honey. Do me a favour?'

'Uh . . . Sure.'

'Stand up.'

'What?'

'Stand up.'

'You mean . . .?'

'That's right. Just there. By the table.'

Nadene rose unsteadily and then stood mockingly to attention. Royston moved quickly, darting like an alley cat. He swept her off her feet and hoisted her across his shoulder, so that he had hold of her legs and she was beating at his back. In this manner he marched her out of the bar.

On the street they warranted one or two disapproving glances. No one said anything. A police car rolled by. In the tube station Royston stopped at the ticket window.

'Two singles to Brixton, please.'

The clerk looked up at the grinning black man and the backs of Nadene's thighs. He then dispensed the tickets and gave Royston his change.

On the escalator Nadene had a go at screaming. No one paid her any attention. They had to wait ten minutes on the Victoria Line platform. The others down there gave them room to breathe. Growing a little weary, Royston shifted his burden from one shoulder to the other. To pass the idle time he lit a cigarette.

The train was sparsely populated at this mid-evening hour. Royston took a seat and spread Nadene across his knee. There were three other people in the carriage. A middle aged couple and a young man in a tracksuit.

Nadene appealed for their assistance.

'Help, help . . . This wild brute . . . You must . . .'

No one moved. Royston's grin spread ear to ear. He spoke like a cowboy in an old fashioned Western.

'You know,' he said. 'I do so admire a woman with spirit . . .'

Nadene started up again. Royston raised his hand and began to spank her bottom. A series of good solid thwacks echoed through the carriage. The young athlete laughed loudly.

'Give it to her, man.'

The middle aged couple smiled to each other.

'They must be so in love.'

The train made stops along the way. Passengers got on, got off. Nadene let out an occasional cry. When she did so Royston spanked her. Upside down, with the blood inside her head, Nadene tried to balance out contrasting sensations. A gross sense of public humiliation. And a sharp internal buzz which was far from unpleasant.

When the train docked at Brixton Royston transferred Nadene to his shoulder once again. He carried her up the escalator. Gave their tickets to the man. Then turned out into the street.

Somewhere along the way they passed Chamberlain and Churchill, who were just emerging from a public house. These two broke into spontaneous applause.

'Yo! Royston, baby! Right on.'

'Yowzer! Yowzer! Yowzer!'

Dangling down Royston's back, Nadene brandished

the V. A little further down the road she lost her stilettos. Royston kicked them into the gutter and continued on his way.

They soon reached their destination − the house that Royston shared. He unlocked the door and took her inside. On the stairs they passed one of the other tenants.

'Hi Royston.'

'Hi Paul. This is Nadene.'

'Hi Nadene.'

Paul disappeared into the hallway. Royston took Nadene into his own room and flung her down onto the bed.

'Right lady,' he said, unbuckling his pants. 'Now you get yours.'

Roxanne and Cordelia were having dinner at the house in South Ken. And Cordelia had really done her guest proud. White tablecloth. Flickering candle. Silverware. Crockery. Four courses, home cooked. Chilled wine. Very nice.

The hostess herself looked immaculate in the setting she had created. Her hair was like gold in the glow of the candle. Her skin like snow against a loose fitting gown. In terms of dress Roxanne had goofed again. Remembering Cordelia's dungarees at the interview, she had turned up in jeans and a short denim jacket. But it didn't seem to matter. Their understanding, she was sure, stretched beyond such things.

Over dinner they discussed the research project. Roxanne's ideas were all well received. Cordelia told her to press ahead and do things her way. They would then work together to mould the final product.

Roxanne chose not to mention her dummy interview with Nadene. It would only confuse the issue. But later, as they perched on the sofa with coffees, she did raise the subject of her flatmate and friend. And Cordelia seemed interested, so Roxanne went on. Before long she had told the complete Nadene story – only stopping short of tonight's arrangement with Royston.

'It seems to me,' said Cordelia, 'that your friend wears a suit of armour to protect a tender skin. Employs blunt rhetoric to disguise a deeper longing. You say she writes poetry? That's where you'll find the key. I'll make you a wager – that the truth is in the poetry. That was what I did, when I was in my teens. I harboured feelings to which I never could own. I poured them out in poetry. Trite, dreadful stuff. The secrets of my soul.'

Roxanne sat transfixed. Yes, she thought. The poetry.

Cordelia reached across and touched Roxanne's hand.

'Roxanne? Are you all right?'

'Yes. Yes. I'm fine.'

The taxi dropped Roxanne outside the flat in Clapham. She let herself in and switched on the lights. Conducted a thorough search to ensure that Nadene was not home.

Then, with a mingled sense of anticipation and guilt, she settled herself in Nadene's room and opened the top drawer of the dresser.

She took out the poetry and read it line by line. The progression could not be clearer. From demon kings to handsome princes. Nadene wasn't merely mellowing, she was settling down.

Roxanne thought of Cordelia. So perceptive. So wise. Then she scrabbled about the remainder of the room, searching for further evidence of Nadene's state of mind.

The last place she looked was under the bed. From there she produced the plastic bag, and emptied out the comic books. True life romances. Each and every one.

Roxanne experienced one of the worst moments of her life. My God, she thought. What have I done? Dispatched my friend to cold clinical sex. When all she cries out for is warm and heartfelt love.

'I love you,' said Nadene, and hugged Royston's neck. 'I love you. I love you. I love you. I love you.'

'Hey baby,' he said, gently petting her. 'That's cool. You know?'

She dipped beneath the duvet, took his testicles in her mouth, tickled them with her tongue. Royston's moan was deep and prolonged, enough to curdle blood. His balls were sore. They needed convalescence. They didn't need this.

Nadene re-emerged and lay on top of Royston. Used her teeth to nip the hairs from his chest. The degree of pain was less, and therefore almost pleasant. He looked down at her head, the spikes all plastered now. He took her by the neck and forced her to look up at him.

'Tell me,' he said. 'Don't you ever sleep?'

'Not tonight I don't. I'm floating on air. Oh Royston, you're the best. I only wish I'd known you when I was thirteen. You're a saint. A living, breathing saint.'

Flattered, flushed with sudden energy, Royston reached down. Pussysniffer I was in dry dock, but fingers never wilt. He called for two volunteers and drove them into Nadene. She gurgled with pleasure.

The fingers groped and oozed, their mission to fulfil. That lucky thirteenth orgasm. Lurking in there somewhere. Find it. Snatch it. Bring it home.

Up on the pillow Nadene was bobbing and jerking.

'You're a saint. You're a saint. You're a sa-eeee . . .!!!'

*

Ten minutes later Nadene slipped out of bed and put on Royston's dressing gown.

'Royston. Do you have a telephone?'

Roxanne was beside herself with worry. How was Spiky Riding Hood? Out there in the woods. With Big Bad Royston.

The telephone rang. Roxanne rushed to answer it.

'Roxanne? It's Nadene.'

'Nadene! Are you all right . . .?'

'I just called to thank you. You're a genius. You saved my life.'

'So it went all right?'

'*All right*? Are you kidding? You mean you didn't catch the tremors?'

'But I was so scared . . .'

'Roxanne, I love you. But I have to go now. Got to get back there. You know what I mean?'

Roxanne began to speak again, but was silenced by a buzzing in her ear. She put down the receiver. Collected her thoughts.

So Nadene is happy after all. Now only one thing remains.

'Feelings to which I never could own.'

Although it was two in the morning she picked up the telephone and dialled Cordelia's number.

14

Dexter -age (he hadn't Humped in a long time) played back the tape from his answerphone at the flat.

Click. Whirr. Anguished word from his mother.

'Hello Dexy. Is anything wrong? We haven't heard from you since Easter. Why can't we be together as a family any more?'

What's your problem? You're on my Christmas card list.

Click. Whirr. Brisk message from one of his biggest customers.

'A thousand apologies for disturbing you at home. But I need to speak to you like pronto. Would you call me back on . . .'

Not this side of a High Court summons.

Click. Whirr. A voice instantly recognisable. A tone both studied and relaxed. As if its owner were reading out lines in between drags on a joint. One hand holding the script, the other arm wrapped around a very sexy woman.

'Good evening, Mr *Hum*-page. Roy Bone speaking. With regard to the Nadene Braxton case. Extensive enquiries have led me to the definite conclusion that Miss, sorry Ms Braxton has left the country and is not coming back. No way. In the circumstances I think the best thing would be to forget all about her. I will keep the two hundred pounds to cover my time and expenses. There is really no point in you contacting me again. If you do I will have to charge you more. Thank you. Goodnight.'

The tape ran silently to the end of its spool. Dexter paid it no heed. He was gutted with grief. He sat beneath the window and wrapped his head in the curtain. He was not ashamed to cry. In less than a minute his face was like a lake. He mopped his tears, to make room for others. The curtain snapped from its rail and covered him completely. He didn't move. He didn't want to move. He was happy as a curtain troll. That was his lot now.

Then he jumped up and cast the curtain aside. Passing headlights washed the window. Dexter was not aware of them. He saw by his own light. A pure penetrative light which began in his brain and spread across the universe.

Roy Bone was lying. Quite shamefacedly. He had taken the money and done nothing in return. He was a con-man. Fraudster. Cheat. Never trust a ... Never trust anyone. That was Dexter's motto now.

He calmed himself. Repaired the curtain. Tried to formulate a plan. To be acting alone made him feel stronger. He picked his nose, poured a whisky, scratched his crotch, lit a cigarette.

The next day at KCS Dexter rode the bluff train. Which was what he had done since it all became too much. He shuffled papers. Erected a facade of faked industry and commitment. Bought people off. Played them one against the other. Promised the Earth and delivered only Mars Bars.

He was borrowing time at ten over base. Travelling on a shuttle between the frying pan and the fire. Anyone could have told him that he was doing himself no good. But he was far too distracted to take advice or consider consequences.

The worst day of all was the day he went walkabout out on the window ledge. Not the sort of stunt you can cheerfully mark down to latent eccentricity.

At first he was lucky. Because shock set in. He had barely uttered a word of explanation when all of a sudden he began gibbering and shaking and rolling on the carpet. Which came in very handy. In terms of gaining some temporary respite, a little time to concoct.

No one thought of sending for a doctor or an

ambulance. It was a busy time of day, and they all had other calls to make, appointments to keep. So they shut him in his office and took turns to pop in just to see how he was. It was like a freak show. And the subject of much speculation.

'They say Dexter's flipped.'

'Too fucking right. Out on the window ledge.'

'Jesus.'

'Too true.'

'The signs were all there.'

What Dexter needed to know was about Fran Lipp. The song she had sung. Piece by piece (hamming it up) he coaxed the information from his various visitors. It seemed she had taken a neutral course. Claimed to have wandered in and found him already out there. Which was reasonable enough. It got her off the hook and allowed him some scope.

Had he existed in a more sympathetic working environment – say, in a library or a slaughterhouse – he would have played along with the suicide angle. Claimed manic depression. Weighty personal strife. Lapped up heartfelt condolence and a month's convalescence on at least full pay.

But when the object is sell they don't treat you that way. They want your contacts. They want your leads. The instant you start to crack everyone grabs a chisel. Before you know it they're sweeping up the splinters.

And so he plumped for sleepwalking. Not entirely satisfactory, but given the circumstances and the time pressure the best he could come up with. He said that, overburdened by work, he inadvertently nodded off at his desk. Experienced a strange and vivid dream in which he seemed to be flying. Awoke to find himself out on the runway.

They didn't believe him. He didn't blame them. Fran Lipp avoided his eye. The young lads struggled to keep straight faces, then crept away to snigger.

While Krunt simply glared at him with eyes like flaming sulphur. Sweltering in the inferno, Dexter thought the game was up. In the end, he supposed, it was the old fear of losing the client list which just about saved his bacon.

And so he rode the bluff train. On the day after Roy Bone's answerphone message he rode it until late in the afternoon. Periodically he would call Bone's office number. In so doing he revealed an imaginative talent for mimicry, employing a varied range of voices. The unfortunate young receptionist was hopelessly deluded (she didn't suspect at all). As if on cue, she would trot out her fears and suspicions regarding her AWOL employer.

On the other hand you never can tell. Maybe Bone is sitting by her side. Holding something over her. Forcing her to lie.

In the end there was only one thing to do. Dexter had to go around there and find out for himself.

Sharon Cobb was beside herself with woe. For almost a week she had lived with a host of chilling suspicions. Accident. Injury. Kidnap. Murder. But not until now had she suspected the worst.

It was almost as if fate had today marked, circled in red on the calendar of What Must Be. As on all the other days since Royston's disappearance she had called his home number regularly on the hour. No reply. She had also called every police station and hospital in London. Nothing. As if her burdens were not enough, that strange man Dexter Humpage had made a series of incoming calls, each time adopting a different accent, all of them ridiculous and pathetically transparent. Severely tempted to pelt him with home truths, she had somehow kept cool and played along with his game.

And then it happened. At four o'clock she called Royston's number. It rang out four or five times. And then it stopped. Someone picked it up. Sharon tingled with excitement. The blood pumped in her veins.

'Royston? Is that you?'

'Hello. Who is this?'

The voice sounded funny. The speaker had a speech impediment, or was perhaps a northener. But the crucial distinction was one of gender.

'Hello? Are you there?'

Suddenly everything fell into place. It was as plain as daylight.

Royston had another woman.

Dexter Humpage breezed through the doorway, not bothering this time to consult the silver nameplates. He didn't wait for the lift to the fourth floor. He bolted up the stairs like a man possessed. About three quarters of the way up he collapsed, suffering from what he took to be a mild heart attack. But five minutes rest and a series of improvised breathing exercises restored him to his feet, and he resumed his blundering progress. He burst into Roy Bone's reception.

Sharon Cobb sat weeping and wailing, head in hands (at least it looked that way, hidden as she was beneath a scattered blonde cascade). Dexter brushed past her and into Bone's office. The horse had bolted. The cupboard was bare. Dexter pulled out each of the desk drawers. They were all empty except for the bottom left hand side. This contained an old betting slip, a packet of condoms (opened) and a few flakes of marijuana. The filing cabinet told the same story. Angry and frustrated, Dexter turned the cabinet over and jumped up and down on it, caving in the sides.

Back in reception Sharon was still sobbing; oblivious to noise, commotion, intrusion. Dexter hunted all around her. No joy. Physical exertion caused him to pause. His attention switched to the girl. It was obvious that she was not protecting Bone. All the same he would have to pump her for information.

He addressed her politely. Met with no response. Raised his voice. Nothing but boohoo. So he snatched at her wrists and gripped them firmly. Brought himself close to her tearstained face. Her eyes were vacant, lost in private sorrow. Her lips parted slightly but no sounds came. What she needed was kindness and compassion; a shoulder pad to cry on.

But Dexter didn't have the time. So he slapped her and shook her and propelled her round the room. She gurgled and moaned – nothing cohesive. Finally she fell over, a disorientated bundle of hair and high street separates and tights tights tights.

Dexter hauled her up. Her face was blue with smudged mascara. Stray eyelashes stuck to her skin. She made an effort to speak.

'I . . . I . . .'

Dexter crumbled. He wasn't a hard man. Not any more. He didn't have it in him to punish this poor creature. And so he nursed her back to health, or something quite like it. Wiped her face. Brewed the coffee. Listened in confusion to her tangled tale of woe.

One thing was clear. She didn't know where Bone was. Dexter awaited his moment, then made his own enquiry.

'I need some information regarding the Nadene Braxton case. Nadene Braxton. Do you know the name?'

She spoke slowly, mechanically.

'Nadene Braxton. Yes. Ha, ha. You asked Royston to find her. But he knew her all the time. He said it was a cinch. Too good to be true. He had two hundred pounds and he could milk you for more.'

Dexter's brow creased with fury. Why, that no good . . .

218

He thought once again of the pitiful waif in his arms. He patted her back, raised the cup to her lips. Then he pressed her for a few more facts.

'This Nadene Braxton. Do you know where she lives? Where I might find her?'

Again the words came slowly. Dexter clung to each one.

'Royston spoke of her. Ha, ha. We were lying in bed. Oh, it was so perfect. Royston and I. Side by side . . .'

This was not good. He wasn't concerned with her sex life. Only his own. He tried to redirect her.

'Yes, yes . . . But this Nadene Braxton. What did Royston say?'

Sharon struggled to remember. What did Royston say? For some reason she thought of her Aunt Elma, who was a spiritualist, or so she claimed. She used to pack them in, in the back room of the Victoria Arms. Invite questions from the floor, float off into a trance, adopt the supposed vocal inflections of dear departed friends and relatives. Gruff grouchy grandpas. Shrill spinster sisters. Sharon herself had always thought it was a racket. And yet you never know. There might be something in it. Some dormant hereditary gift. If not for communion with the dead, then for memory and impersonation.

Dexter started with surprise as the frail blonde suddenly addressed him in the hard macho tones of a second generation Jamaican immigrant. In this way Royston/Sharon advised him of a street name in Clapham. He pressed for a house number. It was not forthcoming. Royston/Sharon was already launched into his/her pillow talk routine.

'Hey, baby. Did you enjoy that? Wasn't that the best? Did you like to ride the train? Isn't it a slick train? Isn't it well oiled? Well see here. Listen to me. The Express is sleeping now. Recharging itself. But it won't sleep forever. Why don't you go down and reward it with a kiss? That way you may get to ride the train again . . .'

Dexter backed off, not a little afraid of this peculiar phenomenon. He had read the books. He had seen the films. One minute the girl next door starts acting strangely. The next minute she whispers to the Antichrist and then slays fifteen innocent people.

But once outside the door such trickery was soon crushed beneath a singleness of purpose. He had secured a vital clue. He was hot on the trail.

Dexter drove down to Clapham. In the evening rush hour the traffic was horrendous. But as he queued at lights and other obstructions he felt unusually calm. It's only a matter of time. Only a matter of time. Other drivers swore at him, nudged him, cut him up, chopped him off. He bore it all bravely. Declined to belittle himself by responding in kind (except for one occasion when a kid in a sports car just had to be *told*).

He used his A-Z and located the street in question. It proved to be a main thoroughfare, which was a little disconcerting. All the same he parked the car and set off on foot, shuffling through the litter, reconnaissance patrol. Much of the area was swallowed by lowlife commerce. Grocers. Launderette. Takeaway. Off-licence. Key cut. Bargain store. At this hour the street was full of shopkeepers, putting up shutters, erecting barricades.

There were several blocks of domestic property, one of which looked the most obviously promising. A series of older houses clearly divided into flats. Youngish men and women returned wearily from the tube and slipped keys into locks. Others traipsed between front doors and black plastic bins and emptied endless sacks of assorted kitchen debris.

Brisk and businesslike, Dexter dropped into a grocer's shop to make a few enquiries. He was operating alone. He felt like a private eye. He didn't need Roy Bone. Who was Roy Bone?

He squeezed between stacked shelves, winced at a musty odour. The man behind the cash till was a spindly Asian in early middle age, street market threads, thinning crown. His wife stood beside him. She was small and plump and wore a hooded shawl. A circular red spot glistened on her forehead. Dexter wasn't sure if it was painted or pasted.

He described Nadene and asked the grocer if he knew her. The grocer said no no no, he didn't think so. Dexter persisted.

'She lives around here. Perhaps she shops for food?'

The man looked blank. Dexter was sure that he was hiding something. In his frustration he felt like wrecking the place. I'm not a racist, but ... It's just that these people don't go out of their way to help you. Roy Bone. And Silent Sam here. All I'm saying is this. We never had any of them at public school. And I was happy then. I had no problems.

Bottling his politics, he appealed to basic masculinity (which is surely uniform).

'A very attractive girl. Striking. I'm sure you would know her. Good breasts . . .'

He made the curving motions.

'Nice legs. Neat little ass . . .'

He patted his own bum. The Asian shook his head. Appeared to be embarrassed.

'No, no. Not interested at all. Happily married man.'

Yes, Dexter thought. But surely you look. Then he noticed that the Asian was doing odd things with his eyes. He seemed to be indicating the woman at his side, as if to say that while she was there he could not speak openly. Dexter glared at red spot. Wished he could take aim from ten short paces.

Just then a clamour of children from the back of

221

the shop took the woman away. The Asian now spoke quickly, as if fearful of a return.

'Oh yes. I know this girl. Tasty piece of meat. I would. I would. Over the road. Number twenty-seven. Flat one. Have a good time. Thank you.'

Roxanne Bliss was in the flat alone. She had left her old job. With holidays due she had been able to finish a few days early. Farewell drink with the girls and she was on her way.

Working from home was that much more civilised. Keep your own hours. No foolish etiquette, no petty vendettas. At the moment she was inputting addresses to her WP (she had acquired the machine at the weekend – it seemed a good investment). She would then send out letters to selected interview targets. The research project was shaping up nicely.

Nadene had returned only once since her night out with Royston, and that just to pick up some toiletries and clothing. Roxanne had seen her for barely ten minutes, but that was enough to be convinced of her well-being. Cheeks rosy, confidence flooding. She said that she was happy and contented and would be in touch soon.

Roxanne herself was contented too. She and Cordelia had talked for many hours. Cordelia felt much as Roxanne did. Both stressed a need for caution. For in personal terms they were breaking new ground. But the future was a challenge. They would work it out together.

The sound of the doorbell took Roxanne by surprise. Who would this be? Nadene perhaps?

She finished the address she was typing and headed into the hallway. With Royston no longer a threat the safety chain hung loose.

*

Dexter Humpage tapped his foot impatiently. Come on. Come on. Open the bleeding door.

It didn't once occur to him that there might be no one home. Anticlimax written out of the script. His destiny up for grabs. One way or the other. No half measures. No sir.

Waiting around outside he considered the emotional and physical buffeting he had suffered within twenty-four hours. The dull depression which followed Roy Bone's taped message. The visionary light which rescued him from that pit. The dire agonies of the working day at KCS. The dash across town to Bone's office building. The crushing chest pains that gripped him on the stairs. The interrogation of Sharon Cobb, and her spooky response. The dogged detective work by which he reached his destination.

And now the whole thing was hanging in the balance. A man or a mouse? He was soon to find out (hold that cheese!). He wanted to be calm and strong and decisive. But it really wasn't on. Not with so much at stake. At this hour of hours he felt wild and desperate and barely responsible for his actions.

Roxanne Bliss opened the door. Dexter stared at her. Tall slender black girl. (They get everywhere don't they?) Attractive, I must say. Eyes. Teeth. But this isn't what I want.

'Nadene Braxton,' he said, dumbly.

'Pardon.'

'Nadene? Is she in?'

'No. She isn't.'

Dexter didn't believe her. At the very least he had to verify the information. So he pushed past Roxanne and into the flat. Roxanne struggled to take it in. Who is this? A madman?

Dexter did his utmost to live up to her surmise. Dashing like a loon, he undertook a frantic search. Behind the sofa. Under both beds. In the kitchen cupboards. Around the bathroom door. Roxanne chased after him and asked him lots of questions. Who did he think he was? What did he imagine he was doing? Was he out of his mind? Dexter took not a blind bit of notice.

Finally Roxanne picked up the phone.

'Police please.'

Dexter heard these words and snapped to his senses. He snatched the phone from her and slammed it back down. Roxanne backed off, terror in her eyes. Dexter himself experienced an horrific vision. She would flee into the street, return with a posse of police officers or a tooled-up vigilante group. It was so unfair. So unfa-ha-ha-hair . . .

Dexter broke down. He lost it completely. Crumpled to his knees and bawled like a child. Unsure of how to react, Roxanne edged towards him. He grasped the knees of her jeans and began to sob into her thighs. Sticky wet puddles seeped through to the skin.

She wrenched herself free and tried to calm him down. Gentle mothering failed miserably. A stiff shot of whisky did the job a little better. In between blubs he poured out his plight. The whole thing. From the top. It wasn't quite coherent. But Roxanne picked up the gist.

She stopped to consider. They were in the kitchen now. Sitting on stools. He was in a bad way. His pride on the floor. He had put his faith in Nadene. But Nadene was with Royston. And happy where she was.

Roxanne expanded her conjectures to include her own situation. A life with Cordelia was the prospect she treasured. If things worked out then sexually at least men had had their day.

She bore them no grudges. For sure there were good times. With Royston and with others. Thinking this way she looked again at Dexter. She could, if she wished, construe it as a gesture. Of thanks and fare-well.

224

She took the ribbon from her hair, shook her black braided mane. Discarded her blouse. Unburdened her breasts. Stepped out of her jeans. Pulled her panties down.

Still sitting on his stool Dexter traced her movements. What is she doing? he thought, rather stupidly. Roxanne looked him over and recognised his fear. A case, she thought, for being cruel to be kind.

She slapped his face.

'Fuck me,' she said.

He jerked rigidly. She slapped him harder. This time his eyes blazed. Roxanne knew that look. She read him like an obscene publication. Black bitch. Black bitch. He kept repeating to himself.

Now, for Roxanne, it was a mammoth trial of strength. Not only would she help this dummy, she would educate him too. She was fighting for Nelson Mandela. Seducing for Steve Biko.

With these heroes in her mind she climbed him like a steeplejack, allowed her legs to straddle. With her hands on his shoulders she raised herself high and kissed his startled eyes. He squirmed to escape, fought to snatch some air. Found his mouth full of hair and bangles, and a licentious tongue rattling in his ear.

'Come on, white shit. What's your problem, white shit?'

Dexter jumped up off the stool. Roxanne clattered to the floor. Dexter hovered over her. Roxanne moved dazedly, as if requiring assistance. Dexter offered her his arm. Roxanne moved her own trembling hand towards it, then detoured violently, grabbing at the pouch of his pants and holding onto what was there. In this way she rose to full height. She tightened her grip and glared into his tear-filled eyes.

'Jesus, white shit. You still need instructions?'

She released him. He struggled for equilibrium.

225

Touched his toes. Then touched Roxanne. Rushed her through to the nearest bedroom (Nadene's), where they grappled energetically on the bed and on the carpet; Roxanne's body a seductive drug, a bullying master. Her skin (he thought, half crazily) like smooth dark chocolate. Bourneville perhaps. Or that new stuff from Rowntrees. He gnashed and devoured and wolfed a double ration.

Then, on the deck, with his trousers round his ankles, he gripped the backs of her thighs and formed her into a Y. This was it. Zero hour. His critical test of nerve.

Using the crudest of radars he located the target area. The first thrust was apologetic. The second tentative. The third probing. The fourth assertive. The fifth a genuine boomer.

On the sixth he exploded, shelled her with sperm. Roxanne luxuriated loudly.

'Oh lawdy! Oh lawdy! I's a good girl now! I's'll not be naughty no more! Thank you massah! Thank you sir!'

The mockery was lost on Dexter. Drunk with ecstasy, he didn't even realise that she was faking every spasm. He continued to drive, flogging his dead horse. Then he fell limp, and reluctantly withdrew.

'You angel! You angel!' he panted in her ear.

Roxanne slid from under him and darted for the bathroom. Dexter jumped up and chased her, but she had a crucial start.

Twenty minutes later she emerged, wrapped in a dressing gown. She peeped around the door, but it was quite safe now. Dexter had calmed down, made himself respectable. He didn't know how to thank her. He said he felt so humble. She told him it was nothing. He assured her it was not. His life back on the rails. A changed man. In every way. She said that she was pleased.

They parted as friends, a handshake and a peck. Roxanne went back inside to telephone Cordelia. Dexter skipped down the street, pausing occasionally to leap and click his heels. He saluted West Indians and smiled at Pakistanis. When he reached his car he found the window smashed and the stereo stolen.

When she emerged from her trance Sharon Cobb felt pretty groggy. It was weird, what had happened to her. The experience she had undergone. As if, just like Aunt Elma, she had drifted off onto another plane. It was odd. Peculiar. Wholly inexplicable. But at least it served a purpose. In ridding the office of that scary Dexter Humpage.

With this achieved Sharon refocused her attention on the main crisis in her life, and attempted a bridge from the hysterical to the rational.

ROYSTON HAS ANOTHER WOMAN! I WANT TO DIE!

Royston has another woman. What am I going to do about it?

Better, much better. Need to be clear-headed and composed. To formulate a plan and stick to it. Now what are the possibilities? There is always the simplest one of all. That, efficient as I am, I punched out the wrong number.

She punched it out again. Nadene answered. Sharon hung up. Of course, there are other people renting rooms in the house. Yeah, but I think I met them all in passing, and none of them sounded like this girl. She may be a visitor. She may have recently moved in. On the other hand SHE MAY BE WITH ROYSTON! IN WHICH CASE I'M DOOMED! DOOMED!

Clear-headedness. Composure. There was only one course of action open to her now. She would visit the house. Why had it not occurred to her before? Because, with no one answering the phone, she had naturally assumed that Royston was away. Now though it was a very different ball game.

She repaired to the women's room to mount a salvage operation. My, was she a mess! What with all that uncontrollable weeping and the roughing up from Humpage.

She washed her face, re-applied her make-up, combed out her hair. Then she fixed the mirror most defiantly. Hoped that she had managed to strike an appropriate balance between allurement and menace. Ah well. It will have to do. I venture forth to claim my man.

MY MAN!

MY MAN!

She locked the office, and took the lift down. Strode purposefully to the tube. There were empty seats on the train. Sharon declined them. Chose to stand all the way to Brixton. Knuckles white on the handrail.

Nadene was in the kitchen, preparing Royston's dinner. Royston was busy watching TV.

This was all new to Nadene. This intricate battle of wits with household technology. But she was doing OK. The pie was in the oven, out of harm's way. She had three separate pans heating up on rings. The peas were bubbling over, but the carrots and the sauce were quiet as mice. And she was happy to settle for two out of three.

The kettle was half filled, the tea bags in the cups. Plates and cutlery neatly arranged. She opened the oven door to peep at the pie. Pompous in its dish the pastry rose and fell, a caricature of healthy breathing. If the pie were an athlete you would back it for a medal.

Nadene thought that she would test the pastry to see if it was warm. She thrust a hand into the oven. Burned herself on the dish. Screamed loudly.

Slammed the oven door (stay in there, you bastard!). Skipped to the sink. Soothed her charred fingers beneath a cooling stream.

This was all new to Nadene. And painful too. But she was doing it for love.

Oh, Royston. Royston. Royston. Royston. Royston.

She turned off the tap and returned to the cooker, which was now rocking gently and beginning to hum. Nadene wasn't sure what this meant. Favoured a short-term policy of non-intervention. I'll give everything five more minutes and then have another look.

For some reason her thoughts drifted to Roxanne. Since meeting Royston she had only seen Roxanne the once. That when Nadene called around to pick up some of her things. In their few minutes of contact Nadene had formed the distinct impression that her friend had something to tell her. Probably connected with Cordelia, and the famous research project. Roxanne was clearly contented, happy in her new work. There was an almost serene quality about her, or so Nadene thought.

So what was on her mind? Maybe she was leaving the flat. Going abroad, perhaps. Nadene allowed her ten minutes in which to spill the beans. She didn't. Nadene left. And now stood here wondering. Oh, Roxanne will be all right. Anyway, I'll see her soon. Can't stay here forever. I'll go back tomorrow. Or the day after. Day after that.

Frothy white slime crept eerily from the pan containing the peas. It spilled over the side of the cooker and raced across the kitchen floor. The lid fell off the pan. Steam billowed. The sauce hiccuped. The oven belched. The carrots began to jive. The poor pie exploded. The gunge was visible on the oven door.

At that moment the doorbell rang. Nadene cursed. Maybe one of the others would answer it. No, no. They were all out. And Royston hated to be disturbed when he was watching TV.

The doorbell chimed again. Abandoning the kitchen, Nadene plodded down the hallway. Bloody hell. If it isn't bad enough having to answer the phone. Idiots who call you and then hang up. I wonder who this is?

Hmm, Sharon thought, as she regarded Nadene. Maybe. Maybe not. Honey flavoured bob. Very little make-up. Sweater. Apron. Jeans. Clearly ensconced in some domestic situation. But may be quite glamorous when she tarts herself up.

Hmm, Nadene thought, as she looked at Sharon. What we have here is a determined young lady. Looks as if she's come straight from work. Fairly attractive, I suppose, in a rather obvious way. A curious combination of allurement and menace.

The silence between them threatened to overstay its welcome. It was Nadene who broke it.

'Yes,' she said. 'Can I help you?'

Sharon didn't like Nadene's tone. She thought it rather gloating. Rather lady of the manor. Rather what I have I hold.

Clear-headedness. Composure. Keep that knuckle-duster concealed.

'Is Royston in?'

'Yes. He's upstairs.'

'May I see him?'

In Nadene's head alarm bells rang. Sharon looked at her expectantly.

'Er . . . Yes. I suppose so.'

Nadene stepped back. Sharon came inside. Nadene was about to indicate the way. But Sharon needed no directions. Marched up the stairs in a forthright manner. Straight to Royston's room. Rapped loudly. Disappeared.

Nadene followed her up the stairs and listened outside the door.

Inside the room Royston looked up from the TV

screen. He was clearly surprised to see his office receptionist.

'Hello Royston.'

He wondered what was up. He had a good idea. Began to waffle aimlessly. A bid to buy some time.

'Sharon. Baby. How are you? How's things at the office? I've been ill, you understand? But I'm coming in tomorrow. You needn't have called around. It's so far out of your way . . .'

Sharon seemed not to hear him.

'Who is she?' she said.

'Huh? Who is who?'

'That girl. Downstairs.'

Royston looked at Sharon. The efficient little teaser was in no mood to be trifled with. All the same he ran some trifling through his mind. Should he bluff her? Say that Nadene was a friend of one of the other tenants? Or a client, perhaps? A witness? An undercover police officer? (Damned shame he couldn't say his sister.) But by the look on Sharon's face he didn't think that it would work. She looked like a woman in search of pure truth. She looked like the Spanish Inquisition.

Royston weighed the rival merits of the two women in his home. Sharon was young, respectful, willing. An asset in the office. A slave in the sack. On the other hand he was forced to conclude that Nadene had class. Looked good on your arm. Made your brain tick. Contributed humour. Drank beer and smoked reefers. Took no shit from the forces of oppression.

And on the mattress where it counts she took the honours too. Nadene was outrageous. Blessed with heathen stamina and an instinct for the truly memorable. All those thwarted passions bottled up for Royston. Even the hottest baddest lover in town likes a challenge now and then.

'Who is she?' repeated Sharon. Her bottom lip began to tremble.

'She's . . . A friend.'

'A friend?'

'Yes.'

'A friend of yours?'

'A friend of mine.'

Sharon clenched her fists and stormed out of the room. She met Nadene on the landing. Nadene barely had time to recognise the battle signs in Sharon's eyes. Before she could even adopt a defensive posture Sharon caught her with a left and put her on the deck. Then dropped on top of her and began to pummel at her head.

Using her arms for protection Nadene quickly found her senses. The old fighting spirit pulsed in her veins. Sharon was tiring herself by throwing useless punches. They were striking Nadene's arms and doing her no damage. Then when Sharon paused for breath Nadene leapt up aggressively. Knocked Sharon off. Threw herself clear.

Both girls scrambled to their feet, then eyed each other fiercely, crouched in combative pose. Nadene's attire was more suited to rucking. Her sweater, jeans and trainers (shame about the apron). Sharon had a skirt to contend with, which was far from ideal. Not to mention high heels. And Nadene had done this sort of thing before. There was the night she KO'd Alice Graham in the car park of the Bled Pig. All of which served to bolster her confidence.

She rushed at Sharon, intent on a quick kill. But she reckoned without the tenacity of the youngster. Sharon deflected her blows, blocked her advances, even forced her back. Nadene dug in for a mean ugly contest. They tussled toe to toe, each swinging on the other's hair. Scratching with their free hands. Gouging when they could.

Nadene hooked her right foot behind Sharon's left and tried to trip her over. Sharon toppled, but did not loosen her grip. They crashed through the bannister and down onto the stairs. Nadene landed on Sharon, which left Sharon winded. Taking full advantage, Nadene grasped her by the collar and dragged her down to the hall. She bounced on every step. At the bottom Nadene stood over her, measuring her up for a conclusive strike.

But Sharon Cobb was not beaten yet. Bruised and shaken as she was she still recalled her guiding principles. Clear-headedness. Composure. Thinking this way she made an unexpected upward lunge and bit Nadene on the inside of the right knee. Her teeth ripped through the denim and cut into the flesh. A red hot jab of pain seemed to sever Nadene's nerve ends. She let out a piercing shriek and began to hobble awkwardly.

Sharon staggered to her feet. Seeing Nadene's discomfort, she sensed her time had come. Nadene backed off, one agonising step at a time, desperately searching for some feeling inside her injured leg. Sharon pursued her, throwing knuckles by the bunch. It took all Nadene's skill and know-how to bob and sway out of range.

Nadene backed into the kitchen. Sharon followed her in. The kitchen was in a mess. The kitchen looked like Armageddon. Pans and pan lids everywhere. Carrot juice and pea extract dripping from the walls and ceiling. Swamp effect on the floor. Cooker rocking vigorously. Oven glowing orange.

Such chaos and destruction was abhorrent to Sharon. Her mother had taught her how to keep a clean kitchen. On account of it was fairly essential once you got yourself married. Unable to prevent herself she broke her fighting stance and switched everything off. Nadene's initial instinct was to wade in unmercifully while her opponent's back was turned, but sportsmanship prevailed and she held a neutral corner. However, the brief truce did give her time to rest her wounded limb, and when hostilities recommenced she felt confident enough to put her best foot forward.

With the cooker becalmed Sharon raised her guard once more. Chancing the leg, Nadene first ducked low and then caught Sharon with a rising right cross. The ensuing left hook completed a classic manoeuvre. Sharon was stunned, and spun out of control. Her high heels collapsed and crucified her ankles. Her back struck the sink unit, her head swayed over the bowl.

Moving quickly Nadene forced Sharon's head under the cold tap and opened up the floodgates. The water matted her hair, filled her eyes and nose, made suction sounds in her ears. After a minute or so of this torture Nadene pulled her free. It was like talking to a drowned doll.

'You had enough?' she demanded, tough as you like.

Sharon's indefatigable spirit surfaced once again.

'Ugh!' she spat, defiantly.

Nadene shoved her back under the tap. This second ducking seemed to wash away her strength. Nadene counted out ten seconds, then renewed her offer of terms. This time with a hint of sympathy, a nudge in the right direction.

'You had enough? Baby? Huh?'

'Ugh,' she croaked, submissively.

The two girls embraced. Sharon cried. Nadene cried. They sat down together on the kitchen floor.

At this late juncture Royston made an entrance. He had followed the fracas from a very safe distance. When the girls were on the stairs he was on the landing. When the girls were in the kitchen he was in the hall. It was a boost to his ego to watch two such horny chicks fighting for possession. But all the time he harboured a sneaking suspicion that they might just recognise a common interest, in which case he was for it.

Now the violence was over he felt it safe to join in. But neither girl seemed to pay him much heed. In the end Nadene sent him out to fetch a takeaway for three. While he was gone she and Sharon made themselves respectable. For the second time within a few hours Sharon looked into a mirror and saw a ghastly distortion. This time she didn't even bother to correct it. Merely dried her hair with a towel and put cream on her bruises.

Eating in the kitchen the three of them talked things over. Sharon seemed resigned now to the fact that Royston was lost. Nadene recognised that the other girl was bearing up most bravely, and offered words of encouragement.

'Don't worry, kid. You're only young. You'll have plenty more chances. You'll benefit from this.'

Royston promised to meet Sharon at the office in the morning and pay her up to date. He would also write out a glowing reference to help her find a new job. He and Nadene said that they would walk her to the tube, but she declined the offer. She did accept a pair of dark glasses to mask her swollen eyes.

Good-byes were said at the door with handshakes and kisses. Royston and Nadene perched on the step until Sharon was out of view. Back inside the house Royston turned to Nadene.

'So,' he said. 'You fight to keep your Royston. Honey, I'm impressed.'

Nadene clenched her teeth and slugged him with a right. He staggered backwards. Rubbing a bruised beak.

'Hey! What was that for?'

'That was for Sharon. You treated her abominably.'

His lips quivered. His white teeth flashed. Before he could speak she unleashed a left which dug him in the ribcage. He let out an 'Oof!' and doubled up in pain.

'And what was that for? Huh?'

'That was for me. Just because I felt like it.'

Royston straightened up. Nadene smiled at him. He slowly flexed his muscles.

'Baby. I sure do love you.'

In a now familiar movement he whipped away her legs and held her like a sack. In this way he carried her up the stairs, kicking and punching for all she was worth. He took her into the bedroom. Closed the door.

In the next half hour the local police received several complaints about party noise. Later in the evening Nadene telephoned Roxanne.

'Roxanne? Guess what?'

'Nadene? What is it?'

'Darling, I'm engaged.'

Restored by his dusky darling Dexter Humpage sped happily towards the neon heartland of the cosmopolitan metropolis (he drove from Clapham back to the West End). In terms of strict physical comfort it was not the most pleasant journey he had ever undertaken. Arrowheads of cold air whistled in through the broken window and half-paralysed his right side. Rogue gusts breathed icily from the gaping mouth of the stereo mounting and shot him in the heart. But spiritually he was over the moons of Saturn.

When a man has kissed the depths his inclination is to soar. In the middle of the year Dexter adopted a Resolution. Do it now! Before you go home!

And there was one thing he would do tonight. Before he went home. He would call in at KCS and photocopy that client list. Then in the morning see his accountant. Set the wheels in motion. For his own operation. HOM. Humpage Office Machines. Hump Off Mac. Good. Eh?

He had no qualms whatsoever about sabotaging the livelihood of his current employer. His new found tendency towards goodwill and toleration did not

236

extend to Joe Krunt (that bastard). Nor to anyone else at KCS. Where were they when his need was greatest? Sniggering behind their hands. Plotting to steal his desk. So a man finds himself out on a window ledge once in a while. You want to make something of it?

Dexter parked in the courtyard behind KCS. Krunt's own motor sat not ten yards away. Thoroughly preoccupied, Dexter did not see it. He took out his keys and let himself in.

Up on the second floor Fran Lipp sat at her WP. She had volunteered to stay late and type some letters for Krunt. He was always happy to grant unpaid overtime.

The letters were easy. She had rattled them off inside half an hour. Now she was down to serious business. Applying for other jobs. Running off copies of her chequered CV.

She had an evening paper spread out on the desk. A well-thumbed Yellow Pages to keep it company. She was inputting addresses. A dreary task. But necessary. Click clack. Click clack. Whirr. Put-put.

With time on her hands she drifted into muse. Am I losing it? Are the boundaries redrawn? Or am I dogged by ill luck? And which evil spirit directed me here? To Krunt the disinclined (an old fag, I shouldn't wonder . . .). To Humpage the insane (never in all my born days . . .). The young lads all want me. That much is clear. But what would I want with them? Tuppenny wonders. I want instant class. And a high interest cheque account.

Working away she settled on a strategy. She would set up twenty interviews. Based on her career average she would be offered nineteen jobs. Of these she would draw up a shortlist of three or four. Based on seniority of interviewer, degree of eye contact, absence of wedding ring. Then she would make a careful selection. And aim for marriage within six months. By whatever means fell to her disposal. All's fair in love and war. And this is now war.

She ripped a sheet of A4 from the top of the machine. A shiver passed through her. Getting cold up here. A little spooky too. Creaks and moans and taps (you never hear them when the office is full). Occasionally she picked up distinctive shufflings and bangings coming from somewhere down below. Marked them down to distortion. Or a vivid imagination. For everyone had gone home.

Glancing out of the back window she saw Krunt's car still there. That's odd. Because he made a special point of saying goodnight. Perhaps he caught a cab. To some function in town. All the same I think I'll finish now. There's something about this building that gives me the creeps.

Dexter Humpage hurried up the stairs to the second floor. As he did so he became conscious of a raw itchy sensation, a rise and a rub which sparked simultaneously in his brain and in his loins, and caused him to adapt his stride accordingly.

Some ninety minutes had passed since his erotic resurrection. More than enough time for a full recuperation. The running rabbit in his pants was now a charging rhino. He considered the possibility of a quick detour via the gents, but dismissed this straightaway. His energies, now that he had found them, were not to be consumed by such schoolboy distractions.

Moving stealthily (just in case) he crept across the sales floor to his own office. The business at the photocopier was rapidly concluded. He slotted the list into his briefcase and switched off the light.

Fran Lipp turned around and saw the dull blur.

Gliding swiftly towards her like a monster from a bog. A million fears flashed through her mind. Stalk and slash videos suddenly made real. A classic set-up. Girl alone. Darkened building. No one to hear her scream.

Her limbs felt frozen, her movements deadly slow. In this manner she hopped agonisingly across the aisle and ducked down behind a desk. As she did so her retreating ankle struck a metal wastepaper bin. The sound rang out like a tolling bell.

Dexter heard it and jumped out of his skin. Where did it come from? So difficult to tell. He tried to move away from it but in fact moved closer. At the same time Fran rose hesitantly from her hiding place to spy out the land. Her head struck Dexter's bum. Her nose jabbed him sharply. The contact set them both off dancing and shrieking.

Dexter found the light. The shock of recognition. The prospect of instant sex. Dexter made the first move. Fran was taken by surprise. Then taken by the buttocks. Dexter was a crazy man. That was for sure. But she could have him certified any time. This was too good to miss.

They romped around the desks, slaves in a stolen galley. She led him. He chased. Caught up with her in her own lair. Fran's shoulder blades stabbing the WP (QWERTY ...). Dexter's right foot kicking hell out of the fax.

Dexter ripped and rummaged and poised himself to enter her. Then ten thousand pounds worth of machinery collapsed underneath them. Fran extricated herself from the remnants of a broken keyboard, a shattered screen. She was shaken but not stirred. Dexter now wore the fax machine like a shoe. Half naked, he clumped after Fran. Caught her by the arm, pulled her to him, swept her high.

Acting on a sudden whim he carried her out through the door and off down the stairs. Each sudden jolt juddered through him, and through him her. The fax machine disintegrated, bit by bit, step by step.

At ground level Dexter took a left, into the service department. Distorted shapes loomed eerily in this hospital for machines. Dexter clicked on the light and brought the benches and racks to life.

'Ooh,' said Fran. 'Is this where all the soap dodgers work?'

Dexter set her down and delivered a finger-wagging lecture on the evils of racism. He said that he for one would be forever indebted to a personage of dubious origin. Fran hung attentively to his every word and when he was done apologised profusely for her gross indiscretion. They then unwrapped each other's clothing, working fast, like kids on Christmas day.

Stark naked, they looked around for little toys to play with. Dexter found a miniature oilcan and threatened to lubricate her tubes. Fran found a pair of pliers and promised to tweak his nuts. Then Dexter wanted to do it. But Fran wasn't sure. All the surfaces so rough down here. Sharp splinters. Rusty nails. Scattered iron filings. Fran preferred to do it somewhere else.

Dexter knelt before her like a fairytale prince. He took her hand in his.

'Will you promise to accompany me wherever I lead?'

'I promise,' she said,

He leaned forward and indicated for her to mount him, piggyback style. Under his spell she climbed aboard.

'You promise?'

'Yes,' she said. 'Where to?'

He rose to full height His voice rang out.

'To . . . The cellar!'

He set off as best he could, supporting his burden manfully. For her part his burden let out a squeal.

Neither of them had been down to the basement before (Krunt etiquette specified that it was strictly out of bounds), but they had both heard wicked rumours.

'It's full of rats,' she cried. 'And spiders.'

'Yes,' he boomed. 'Big rats. Big spiders.'

He padded down the steps, his hands under her thighs, her arms around his neck, clinging on for dear life. Dexter hardly knew what he was doing. But after all that he had suffered it certainly felt like fun.

At the foot of the steps he thrust out a hand and pushed open the door. Joe Krunt sat in the grand inquisitor's chair. With five elderly gentlemen spaced evenly around him. Behind him stood X and Y. Plus A and B. P and Q.

It was clear that some sort of conference was in progress. However, the appearance of a naked couple played havoc with the agenda.

Early one morning Nuttall Mann awoke to find himself slumped at the roadside with a tramp picking his pocket. He rose quickly and shooed the vagabond away. Then dived back into the gutter, narrowly avoiding the menacing treads of a speeding car.

The fall bruised his knees and elbows and made him sick and giddy. For five minutes he lay prostrate, staring down a grid. Then he rose once more, gingerly touching up his limbs and torso, assuring himself that he was still intact. Over the knees, around the hips and up to the shoulders all went well. Then his enquiring fingers brushed the frazzled scar tissue just above the jawbone. Contact made him dance, and almost blew his head off. Like the River Euphrates it all came flooding back.

'One more thing.'

'What's that?'

'My mark.'

The heat of the moment scorched him once again.

He had clearly passed out. Down there in the cellar. And the two henchmen had dumped him here. He looked up at a roadsign. At least they had had the decency to abandon him somewhere fairly central.

He dusted himself down, and then cut a weary path back to Sparky's flat. Sparky had gone out to work. There was a note on the kitchen table.

> Where on earth have you been?
> I've been worried sick.
> What are you thinking of?
> Do I sound like your mother?
> (I'll have to spank your bottom.)

Nuttall passed a wry smile and then gathered his courage for a meeting with the mirror. It took him half an hour to walk five paces to the bathroom. He covered his eyes. Nervously peeped out. Instantly recoiled. Slowly reconciled himself. It wasn't so bad. (It wasn't brilliant, mind.) A ticklish red mouse imprinted on the skin. He could live with it. (He had to.)

Nuttall phoned the Gay Peacock and said that he was ill, would not be in that evening. Sparky came home around six. Nuttall told him the story. Sparky kissed the scar. Kissed it ever so lightly. (Not lightly enough, Nuttall thought, bottling the pain.) Sparky said it looked distinguished. Sexual. He also said that they should go to the police. Nuttall said no. Not the police. Sparky didn't argue. He knew the score.

And so he did all he could to make his lover comfy. Cooked dinner. Bought wine. Spoke of the future. Made love gently.

Sparky understood why Nuttall wouldn't go to the police. He felt that way himself. Most of the time.

But this was a case of brazen brutality. The man Krunt a danger to society. Something had to be done. So while publicly acknowledging Nuttall's obvious prerogative, Sparky privately resolved to sort it out himself.

In contemplating this he recalled an incident which took place shortly after his flight to London, some time before his reunion with Nuttall. A lonely Sparky stopped off for a drink inside a seedy gay bar, struck up idle conversation with a moustached barman. The barman indicated another fellow, fiftyish, unimposing, sat in a corner, drinking alone.

'See him? Scotland Yard officer, so they say. Pops in here maybe once a month. Married with kids. Likes boys though. Sniffs around. Usually leaves alone. Sad case, I should say.'

A little later the man sidled up to Sparky. Said his name was Norman. His chat was clumsy, his manner uncertain. Sparky found him unattractive, and made polite excuses. Then, months later, he saw him on TV. A news report covering the Lickie Loose case. There was Norman, expressing perfect confidence in established police procedure. Only he wasn't Norman now. He was Chief Inspector Todd. Tommy 'Cuffs' Todd, as the press would have it.

Well the Lickie Loose case was settled now. So maybe Tommy 'Cuffs' Todd would care to switch his attention to the mysterious Joe Krunt. Sparky planned to visit him at Scotland Yard and raise the suggestion. Todd, of course, was at liberty to decline. But Sparky thought it unlikely.

Joe Krunt wasn't really Joe Krunt. He was Joseph Kinder. Seventy-one years old. Hitler Youth. Nazi Party. SS officer. International fugitive.

In 1945 his chief concern was to escape from the Russians. He and a group of brother officers made a surreptitious exit from Berlin. Burned their damning uniforms, passed themselves off (sic) as deserters from the front. Before long, word filtered through that certain high ranking Americans were not unsympathetic to the plight of such renegades. An olive branch extended. Tense days in captivity. Singing like birds. A ride in a truck to a military airfield. Stepping off the plane in South America.

Kinder and his colleagues enjoyed a comfortable standard of living. At regular house parties they drank to the old days, and dreamed of new days to come. Once in a while they were visited by well-dressed men from Washington. These visits were usually followed by night-time excursions up or down the continent. Such missions were accepted with reluctance but accomplished with pride.

Kinder took regular holidays in Palm Beach and Miami. On two occasions he made month long visits to West Germany, travelling under the name of Joachim Kann, US citizen. In this manner, a black-clad figure alone in the churchyard, he laid a wreath on the grave of his father.

From his ranchhouse base he helped to establish The Chain – an organisation which enabled former Nazis and their acolytes to keep in contact via coded correspondence. His files listed names and addresses in countries throughout the world.

And all the time he kept himself sharp, kept himself fit. Rigorous exercise. Mental and physical. He knocked fifteen years off his age and no one disbelieved him. And life was not without its sensuous pleasures. Most of the old guard plumped for the girls from Buenos Aires. Kinder himself preferred the brown-skinned boys who seemed to drift in off the pampas.

By the late 1970s the fierce young Israelis were hot on his trail. Damn these Jews! Will they not let us be? If only we were more! If only we could fight! But the ranchhouse base was safe no more. The show trial loomed. Imprisonment. Execution. Eternity. The void.

At first it was regarded as a joke. The idea that the safest haven now was in the land of the old enemy.

But as viable alternatives failed to materialise the audacious logic assumed an irresistible appeal. Immigration easily arranged. No one looks for Nazis in London these days.

So Joseph Kinder became Joe Krunt, a supposed Czech migrant. And once he had found his feet he was quick to establish KCS as his base; a genuine commercial concern, staffed by unsuspecting outsiders; operated at a profit, but not allowed to outgrow certain set limitations.

The address was also used as the European headquarters of The Chain. Krunt organised collections from members and friends; the idea being to fund a new right-wing political party, a force which would operate first in Bavaria, then in Germany as a whole. He used the basement of his building to host fellow refugees. To train and encourage the limited numbers of virile young men still attracted to his cause.

Will Franks had hunted Nazis for twenty-five years. Rooted them out in South and Central America. Shipped them overseas to account for their atrocities.

The British connection was his very last assignment. When it was successfully concluded he would retire to Tel Aviv, and leave the fight to his sons and nephews. That is, if everything went according to plan . . .

For this time Will Franks had redrawn the rules of engagement. He was tired of watching killers unrepentant in the dock. Tired of watching justice commuted to appeasement. In France. In Germany. And even in Israel. Butchers sent to prison instead of to their deaths. To do what? Write their memoirs? Reminisce?

This time the judge and jury was Will Franks himself. He had with him three dependable men – ex Israeli commandos. They knew that Kinder and his cronies were holed up in the basement. The plan was simple. To park the van outside and then go in. The underground setting would muffle the gunfire. The cellar would serve as a temporary tomb.

The four avengers were already booked on a flight out of England. It was scheduled to leave Gatwick later in the evening. Once that flight was in the air a call would go through to the Special Branch in London.

It was then up to them to present it as they wished. Most likely (to avoid embarrassment all round) the truth would be concealed. The dead men buried under their assumed identities. If word got out at all it would be labelled a gangland killing. But it didn't really matter how they dressed it up. For Will Franks would be safe and justice would be done.

Dexter Humpage and Fran Lipp could not believe their eyes.

Fran thought: Oh heck, looks like Mr Krunt is holding some sort of meeting . . .

Dexter thought: What's the bastard doing? I'll bet he's selling out . . .

And then he thought: I'm stark naked! With a woman on my back!

While the Nazis thought: He's stark naked! With a woman on his back!

Krunt-Kinder was the first to react. He motioned to X and Y.

'Grab them! Schnell!'

Dexter loosened his grip and Fran slid down. Neither of them had time to seriously contemplate escape. X and Y took them by the shoulders and bustled them into the centre of the room. Krunt-Kinder barked out a further command.

'Against the wall! Facing the wall!'

X and Y moved towards the wall.

'Not you! The prisoners!'

They did as they were bid. Dexter caught only a passing glimpse of the others in the room. The seated veterans with their elongated skulls. The hovering henchmen, looking bent on brutality. Then he and Fran were lined up with their eyes to the wall. Arms and legs spread.

Krunt-Kinder indicated that X and Y should return to their original positions. Meanwhile he began to pace about the room. Took a pair of gloves from his pocket. Put them on. Took them off.

'Zo!' he said. 'Vot haf ve here?'

He knew of course that these two must be eliminated. They had seen too much already. What was teasing his evil mind was the possibility of some sort of sexual exploitation prior to execution.

The boys would doubtless relish an opportunity to stuff their wilting pokers into luscious Fran Lipp. But he himself was not overkeen on tackling the hairy bum of Dexter Humpage.

(Not half so smooth or firmly muscled as the dinky derriere of Nuttall Mann.)

Nor letting the boys know that he was that way inclined.

(Odd indiscretions in front of awe-struck acolytes quite permissible. But the boys would take the piss.)

And he certainly wasn't acting out any charade with a woman.

(Not after seventy-one years.)

Maybe it was best to press on with essential business.

(That was what Muttler, his old commanding officer, always used to say.)

Yes. That was it. What else was he thinking? Growing soft in his old age. He should have killed Roy Bone. And Nuttall Mann.

(Afterwards.)

At that moment the four Israelis burst into the

basement. Speed was essential to their plan of operation. Split second timing. They had to blow away the
Nazis before the Nazis had chance to move. With this
uppermost in their minds they fell into firing positions. But could not help noticing the naked couple
stood by the wall.

Eight eyes lingered fatally on the curvaceous de-
lights of Fran Lipp. A moment later four fingers
squeezed triggers. But by this time the ever alert
Nazis had pulled pistols from their pockets. The
crossfire screamed. The basement an echo chamber.
Fran threw herself on the floor. Dexter threw himself
on top of her. He truly thought that his number was
up. For certain nothing else was. For despite his
immediate proximity to Fran's nether regions, he
found it utterly impossible to maintain his recent
sexual resurgence.

Dexter and Fran stayed where they were, even
when the shooting stopped. Lost in prayer – convert-
ing, repenting – they did not see the sixteen bodies
on the floor. Dexter was scarcely aware of the sticky
presence of mixed blood on his back and legs. Even
the grisly stink of death did not penetrate his nostrils.
Until it caught him off guard and he could not hold
the sneeze. Which exploded like a cannon in poor
Fran's ear. She closed her eyes and called on Mother
Mary.

Lying on the floor, with searing pains in his chest,
Krunt-Kinder thought that he was the only one left
alive. And that even that situation would not persist
much longer. The life was draining out of him. His
body sick and weak. His brain cold and muggy,
drifting off to sleep. But there was one more thing he
had to do before he died. In his own office. On the
second floor. The master file containing the contact
addresses of the members of The Chain. He had to
destroy it. This was imperative. Otherwise the Father-
land might never rise again.

He gathered what little strength he had left and hauled himself to his feet. Moving slowly, suffering greatly, he laboured out of the basement and off up the stairs.

A few feet away Will Franks was aware of Kinder's departure. It surprised him somewhat. For he had previously been under the impression that he was the only one left alive. And that even that situation would not persist much longer. With his work done, and at least three bullets inside him, he was quite content to make peace with his God. But now one last great effort was called for. Kinder was probably heading upstairs to destroy some vital document. He had to be stopped.

Crawling on his hands and knees (like a sniffer dog) Will Franks followed the trail of fresh blood all the way to the second floor. He wheezed into sales reception. Put his hands on the desk to drag himself up. Accidentally pressed the 'Please ring for service' bell. Across the other side of the room Kinder looked around. Will Franks spotted him. Raised his automatic weapon.

The bullets flew over Kinder's head and speared the signs on the wall.

'LETS SELL COM UTERS'

'TIM   IS MONEY'

'THE ANSWER IS

Kinder disappeared into his own office. Will Franks cast aside his rifle and pulled a dagger from his belt. Reverting to all fours, he scampered as quickly as he could in pursuit of his foe. Outside Kinder's office he rose painfully to full height. Then kicked open the door. Kinder sat, half slumped, at the chair of his desk. He had a file of papers in one hand and a cigarette lighter in the other. He clicked the lighter. It wouldn't light. He clicked it again. Nothing.

'Himmel! Blitzen! Faulty British goods!'

Will Franks threw himself at Kinder. The dagger ripped through the Nazi's neck, almost severing his head. Joseph Kinder fell backwards off his chair and lay spread-eagled on the floor. Quite dead.

Will Franks picked up the file and looked inside. It was written in code. Which meant he couldn't understand it. No matter though. The code would be cracked. The names tracked down. Vengeance extracted. An eye for an eye. A tooth for a . . .

All of a sudden Will Franks had no use for teeth any more.

The Met, the Special Branch and the Anti-Terrorist Squad all arrived at KCS at exactly the same time. The Met alerted by Sparky's call on Todd. The Special Branch via a tip-off from an Israeli double agent. The Anti-Terrorist Squad following a report from a concerned citizen about a number of armed men seen entering a building in Central London.

The mingled officers exchanged angry banter.

'Who the blazes are you?'

'This one's ours, Jim!'

'Like hell it is!'

In a rough pecking order based on rank and muscle they scrambled down the stairs to the scene of the slaughter. One particularly alert young man noticed Dexter and Fran over by the wall. He grasped the arm of his commanding officer.

'Chief! Look! There's two left alive. And Chief! I do believe they're having it away . . .'

Dexter Humpage and Fran Lipp were not detained long in police custody.

At first, of course, it was difficult for them; their interrogators unsympathetic.

'I see sir, you just happened to select this particular evening for an erotic romp around the workplace with a woman you describe as "merely a colleague" . . .'

'Let me get this straight, Miss, you say you were not aware that the man in whose cellar you were found naked was in fact a notorious war criminal . . .?'

But both stood up admirably under pressure and by and by the validity of their protestations became increasingly apparent. Their stories were so unlikely they just had to be true.

As the heroic Will Franks had accurately supposed, attempts were made to hush up the extent and significance of the KCS killings. However, the canny Dexter Humpage was keen to raise capital for his new business venture, and immediately upon his release he telephoned Porky Waring and sold his story for cash.

The press had a field day. It was almost as big as the Lickie Loose affair. The Dinsdale Snape/Porky Waring end of the market raised the ghoulish spectre of rampant Nazism, and posed the crucial question: 'How many more of Hitler's evil monsters are living amongst us today, just waiting for the right opportunity to revive their despicable creed?'

Almost overnight elderly males living alone became a persecuted minority. Seasoned gentlemen who happened to walk rather stiffly, bark harsh commands at their domestic quadrupeds or accidentally mispronounce certain words of the mother tongue suddenly went in fear of their lives, and found themselves having to swear repeated allegiance to the Union flag.

The quality papers, quite naturally, did not succumb to such blatant sensationalism. Those of a more radical bent chose to explore the wider implications, and searched (high and low) for conclusive evidence of a South African conspiracy. Others, perhaps more inclined towards preserving the status quo, surrendered centre-spreads and supplements to the wartime memoirs of octogenarian generals and former private secretaries to the marginally famous. The rest-homes of England echoed to the clack of typewriter keys.

The government, as governments do, sought to play it all down. They first denied culpability, then announced the terms of a stringent inquiry – which, for reasons of national security, would be held behind closed doors. A select group of august patriots toasted the fact that for the foreseeable future lunch was on the taxpayer.

The opposition (if it did but know it) was in something of a quandary. How was it, the front-benchers screamed, that these heathen fascist butchers who tortured and murdered millions were allowed to exist in our society without fear of detection? And how was it, the backbenchers howled, that a force of paramilitary vigilantes was allowed to enter this country and infringe in so destructive a manner the basic civil liberties of these heathen fascist butchers? And how could we be sure, they both asked in unison, that this would not happen again?

In their homeland Will Franks and his colleagues were buried with full honours.

The Chain was disbanded. And replaced by The Link. An ever dwindling regiment of wrinkled Aryans managed to keep themselves a pace ahead of the law, only to be picked off one by one by committed young avengers or by the biggest killers of all. Old age and obsolescence.

Hump Off Mac was duly incorporated; and with a sound client base prospects appeared rosy. Dexter rented premises. His first employee was a certain Fran Lipp.

Outside office hours the Managing Director and his Personal Secretary strove to stir the embers of their frustrated passion (for nothing was ever consummated). Intent was firm on both sides but the deal was never settled. Fran pulled back from the brink. Time and again.

For her the sight of Dexter naked revived the horrors of the basement. She shuddered afresh with the fear of the moment. When he took off his trousers she heard the sound of gunfire. When he stepped out of his shorts she almost sniffed the blood. In such a state of turmoil she could not possibly perform. She hoped he understood.

He didn't. At first he was outraged, and cursed her loudly as he masturbated in the bathroom. Later though he came to take a twisted pleasure from the situation. It was, after all, a case of complete role reversal. It crossed his mind that, if he pursued her with sufficient vigour, he might force her out onto the window ledge.

In the event she secured an escape route via a written proposal from a former employer. The letter arrived quite unexpectedly (she had almost forgotten poor old Quentin Maugham).

The tone was distracted, the hand uneven.

Dearest Francesca,

How are you? I hope you are well. Incredible as it seems it is almost a year since we last met. Can it really be so long? Those times we shared, both in the strongroom and in the back of the Bentley, though tangled and hurried, rank amongst my fondest memories.

You will recall how at that time our relationship was hampered by my tiresome obligations. Well things have now changed. Nigella has left me, and taken Berenice and Hadley. When I say left me I mean kicked me out. I am living alone. In the company flat. I am lonely and distraught.

In short, Francesca, I am begging for a rescue. Nigella wants a quickie divorce. I will not stand in her way. How would you like to be the second Mrs Maugham?

Your ever loving,

Q-Q (kissey – kissey)

Fran played it cool. While Dexter was in a meeting she picked up the phone and ordered a company search – photocopied documents sent to her private address. Two days later they arrived. Executive Recruitment Limited. Last published accounts. Quentin's name at the foot of the Chairman's Report.

Fran flicked through to the additional information disclosed by way of note.

. . .The Chairman, who was the highest paid director, received remuneration of £125,000 (last year £110,000) . . .'

That settled it. She telephoned Q-Q and promised to wear white.

Epilogue

Dexter Humpage needed a new secretary. The agency suggested an ambitious young girl named Sharon Cobb. She had an excellent reference from her previous employer, and was currently temping, but anxious to secure a permanent position. Dexter said to send her round.

When she pushed open the door he almost fell off his chair. Roy Bone's hysterical receptionist – the girl with the disturbing gift. For her part Sharon almost turned around and fled. Roy Bone's unpredictable client – the man with the volatile temper.

Between them they overcame these initial reservations and acted out a formal interview. Sharon was just what Dexter was looking for. She had to admit that she fancied the challenge. They talked across the desk for an hour and then adjourned to the pub. The circumstance of their earlier acquaintance made it easier for them to exchange confidences. Before the evening was out Dexter knew all about the hottest baddest lover in town, and Sharon was thoroughly versed in the activities of both spunky vixen and dusky darling.

Dexter offered Sharon the job. Sharon took it, and played an important part in the rapid development of Hump Off Mac. Outside working hours Dexter and Sharon dated, then became lovers; an honest, sincere and monogamous relationship. Sharon was a frequent overnight visitor to the flat in Fulham. Later, with the first set of accounts boasting a healthy profit, Dexter bought a bigger place and she moved in.

For the most part the sex was highly satisfactory. Just occasionally Dexter found himself haunted by the ghost of his impotence. At such times Sharon soothed him skilfully (lauded his libido, praised his prowess) and nursed him back to fitness. In the normal run of things she accomplished her task with relative ease. Only once did she find herself struggling (Dexter heavily depressed, and as outwardly forlorn as a rodent in a rainstorm).

They lay naked on the bed.

'You're the best,' Sharon insisted, her fingers working on his disinclination.

'No I'm not,' he replied glumly, arms folded on his belly.

She stopped what she was doing. He didn't even notice.

'I never told you this,' she said. 'But when you're on form you're much better than Royston.'

'You don't mean that. You're just saying it.'

'No I'm not. I wouldn't tell a lie. It's just that . . . Well. I ought to know.'

Dexter sat up, anxious to be convinced.

'You really think so?'

'Yes,' she said, convincingly. But even as she spoke she found herself faintly troubled by an echo of the Ecstasy Express, whistling eerily in her head.

'Dexter, I love you,' she said, and meant it.

'Royston, I miss you,' she thought, and meant that too.

Royston and Nadene were married at a registry office. No members of either family attended the ceremony. The local free press listed the guests in the following manner:

'. . . Ms Roxanne Bliss, Ms Cordelia Welch, Mr Dexter Humpage, Ms Sharon Cobb, and four young gentlemen (believed to be friends of the bridegroom) who refused to give their names or addresses . . .'

Mr and Mrs Bone lived together in Royston's room in Brixton. They had no problems except one. What to do for money. The alternatives were stark.

On the one hand they could take demeaning jobs,

grab a slice of the property action; thereafter struggle by, their monthly instalments helping to boost the expansionist corporate strategies of our beloved financial institutions. By the time they were fifty they would be out of debt.

On the other hand they could drink and drug and fuck themselves stupid; sacrificing jam tomorrow for honey today, burning final demands on a bonfire of indulgence. By this method, if they were lucky, they would hold out for three months before they were evicted.

It was really no contest. Royston and Nadene bought in the booze and went to bed for a long time. The first batch of letters lay quietly on the mat. The next batch coughed politely. The third batch climbed the stairs and peeped through the keyhole. The telephone was cut off. Then the electricity. Fortunately what the happy couple were doing could be accomplished in the dark. Then something rare happened. They enjoyed a lucky break.

Nadene didn't even remember submitting the manuscript. The publishers had held it for over eighteen months. To give them their due they apologised profusely for the delay in getting back to her. Said that this was due to staff sabbaticals and two festive seasons.

However, none of this mattered now, for the bottom line was that they liked her style. She was invited to lunch with a commissioning editor; a raunchy forty-two year-old chain-smoker who called herself Moll Flinn. Moll took Nadene to a vegetarian restaurant. The crunch came over dessert.

'The way we see it,' Moll said, dripping ash over the tablecloth. 'You may just be the last great writer of the century. The first of the next. We'd like to sign you up. We'd like to give you money.'

They did. A sizeable advance. A five book deal.

Nadene and Royston took a late honeymoon in Jamaica. Stayed with Royston's grandparents. Had a lovely time. Weather beautiful. Food good.

And Nadene learned something about the nature of inheritance. For though he was eighty-four, Royston's grandfather remained sprightly and agile and very highly sexed. One sunny afternoon he lured Nadene into his hammock and promised to teach her a few of the old songs. The hammock sagged heavily, severely straining two palm trees. Only the distant hollering of Royston's grandmother ('Zebedee! Where is you? Where is that girl?') prevented a mutual explosion.

Royston, meanwhile, enjoyed a measure of celebrity. The local girls milled around him and eyed with intent. They had heard so much about him. Proud tales of distant lands. Was he really worth a million? Legend said he was.

One evening, down on the beach, a little drunk on rum, he whispered to a winsome sixteen year old about the Ecstasy Express. Picking his pockets for bank notes, she whispered back that she would like to ride that train. He backed it out of the siding. Finding no cash, she laughed aloud and kicked sand in his face. Underlined the fact that in certain other parts of the world even the highest standards set by British Rail appear very mediocre.

Back in London Nadene started work on a blockbusting novel. Decided that for the time being she would set art aside and give the public what it wants. Lots and lots of sex.

She worked to a punishing schedule, typing ten hours a day. For a week or so Royston moped around, feeling fairly redundant. Then, during an afternoon break, Nadene hit on the perfect role for him. With a nod to Cordelia she appointed him her research assistant. To liase with the author (and only the author) on certain specific scenes.

Accordingly she showed him a synopsis of the novel. He thought it over for ten seconds, then made a few suggestions. Determined to demonstrate that she was in earnest, Nadene demanded an immediate expansion. Royston obliged. Nadene resolved to make it a very long book.

Cordelia and Roxanne decided to go public. Or had it decided for them. Porky Waring fastened onto trade gossip and the shit hit the fan mail.

FEMINIST WRITER AND HER BLACK FE-MALE LOVER!
Research assistant quits Fulham flatshare for love nest in South Ken.

But in truth only one letter in ten was derogatory or abusive. The rest supportive and congratulatory. Denying nothing, Cordelia and Roxanne emerged as heroines of the resistance. All future works, they announced, would be genuine collaborations.

One evening they dressed in black combat gear. Jeans and sweaters and woolly balaclavas. In such disguise they trailed Dinsdale Snape and Porky Waring from a West End club. On a lonely side-street they leapt from the shadows and struck the press baron and his hired gun some heavy blows with baseball bats.

Trixie and Pepper backed up the car. Opened the boot. Took out the vat of tar, the sack of feathers. Made the phone call to the press agency. The biters bit.

Steven Sparks and Nuttall Mann acquired their sports shop and lived happily for quite some time.

The Lickie Loose kidnap trial was a(nother) media event. From the headline scam in the tabloids to the artist's impressions on News At Ten. Lawyers cast in robes and curls. Gallery agape. Sagacious old hound resplendent on the bench.

Called to the witness stand Tommy 'Cuffs' Todd cut a reassuring figure. He delivered his evidence unswervingly, reading from his notebook in the time honoured manner. Indeed, his only moment of perturbation came when a mackintoshed figure in the public gallery rose unannounced and cried out 'Wotcher Norman!' No one understood the cryptic reference, and the mackintoshed figure was soon bundled away, but Tommy 'Cuffs' Todd remained somewhat ruffled for ten minutes or more.

There is no tradition in English Law by which a son may not offer damning testimony against his father. Charlie Hammer rued this fact. For, despite the unnerving experience of having to clutch a bible and swear to tell the truth, young Johnny related all too faithfully the climactic events in Epping Forest; beaming proudly when the Crown brief asked him to confirm that he had received an official commendation for bravery.

'That's right,' he said. 'Good innit?'

Judge and learned counsel frowned at the coarse vernacular; retreated from it as one would from a very bad smell. But the battered nation took him to its heart. The press ran features. 'Johnny Hammerspeak – a guide to interpretation.' A high profile current affairs programme commissioned an expert in linguistics. Johnny himself didn't know what the fuss was all about. Did he? Eh?

Charlie, Eddie and Fast Mits offered little credible defence. (At a very late stage, acting on medical advice, Fast Mits changed his plea to one of diminished responsibility. It made no difference.) Each was sentenced to ten years' imprisonment. On the way to the cells they grinned for posterity and exchanged time-scarred platitudes.

'If you can't do the time don't do the crime.'

'Sit tight. Do your porridge.'

'Keep your head down. Do your bird.'

Then, when finally alone, each one of them sat down and wept. But to a man they maintained the traditional code of honour. Which meant that, to his great chagrin, Tommy 'Norman' Todd was unable to nail Albie 'Lucky Bastard' Alibi.

Albie took advantage of this by marrying Lickie, and then transferring both wife and business operation across to California. One morning, after consuming a garnished hog for breakfast, he suffered a series of violent convulsions and very quickly died.

For a while Lickie wore black. But she soon reverted to whatever colour the lensman asked for. Her career ebbed and flowed. A couple of minor hits, two or three obscure film roles. Then she married an ageing English rocker, a forty-nine year old wild child who resided in Beverly Hills.

The divorce settlement, two years later, left her financially secure. She returned to England where she was commissioned to write a column ('Loose Talk') for a Sunday newspaper. As a publicity stunt to launch her new career she was persuaded to visit Fast Mits Finnegan in Parkhurst. Her mother called around once a week and left seven frozen dinners and seven frozen breakfasts.

For the duration of the trial Babs Hammer played the dutiful wife. She shaved her legs each evening and wore a different skirt each day. The flashbulbs popped as she tripped from the taxi to the courthouse steps. It was the happiest time of her life.

After Charlie was sentenced Babs listened to offers. The best one came from a lady named Flinn. The ghost-written autobiography was rushed to the shops. Serialisation rights sold by telephone auction. Babs banked the advance and took a lunchtime job in a pub. Dug out her old address book. Never had an evening free.

Every now and then she left a bowl of chopped juicy rabbit heads outside the kitchen door. Stray cats came a-picking. Robin never returned. But once in a while, as Babs lay in bed, beside Eric or Stanley or Milko or Clive, she would hear a distant barking carried on the wind. When this happened she smiled to herself. It was silly, she knew. But she felt that Mummy's Big Boy was sending his regards.

Johnny Hammer felt let down by Lickie. He caught her eye across the courtroom, caught red-handed courting favour. For a while, on the witness stand, it all seemed so natural. With his medal around his neck and his name in the papers – how could she possibly refuse?

Quite easily, it seemed. Making the best, smiling through, Johnny went down the pub. Got drunk. Had a curry. Had a fight. Felt better. Lickie Loosh is jusht a fantashy, he shlurred to himshelf. She in, inhab, lives in a different world. She may be rich and famous but I bet she's insecure. You, Johnny Hammer, have a much more solid platform. A closeknit family unit (Dad may be out in five, Mum looks better than ever), a bunch of loyal mates (Keef stood up for me like a fucking Trojan), a whole bleeding culture.

Wussell Maycock found wejection impossible to bear. His Wickie, it was cwear, was wost to another. Following her ordeal she wetweated into the arms of her manager (who Wussell didn't twust). Wussell wote her. She didn't weply. He called her up. She wouldn't come to the phone. He knocked on the door. Was wefused admission. In the end the despicable bwackguard (Albert) sent awound two heavies who thweatened to bweak Wussell's wegs.

A few days water his worst fears were confirmed. There it was in the papers. They said she made a beautiful bwide.

Wussell went for wong wonely walks. He hung awound under iwon bwidges and stared into murky canals. He bwoke down on the air, burst into tears on pwime time wadio. Which was more than enough for the pwogwamme contwoller. Wussell was dismissed. Wussell didn't care.

In a distwacted fwame of mind he decided to end his torment. Lay down on the twacks. On the day of a national wail stwike. Wept from a motorway bwidge. Wanded on the back of a twuck fewying stwaw to the Midlands. Bowowed a pistol. Bewied the bawel in his temple. This is surely it. Good-bye cwuel world.

Being a vewy poor shot Wussell Maycock missed. Succeeded only in cwipping his weft ear. A fwend said that he was wike Vincent Van Gogh. Wussell said:

'You what?

And:

'Half past five!'

He meditated awhile on his failed self destwuction. Wondered if perhaps it was a sign fwom on High. Sought the advice of his old family pwiest. As a wesult of which he took vows and entered a monastewy. Soon settled in to a new way of wife. The man once timed at a hundred and forty-five words per minute (fifty-thwee of them pwonounced wong) now spent the bulk of his waking hours in siwent pwayer or subwime contempwation.

Indeed, he made but a single concession to his former mode of existence. A few of the bwothers organised a petition which wequested his participation in one of their more wadical schemes. Wussell thought it over and weluctantly agweed. Thereafter became installed as wegular pwesenter of Fwiar's Favowites on the in-house piwate wadio. The show bwoadcast one hour a week (fwom a wofty tuwet) and pwayed a vawied sewection of wock and wole cwassics.

*

Robin the Rottweiler headed north, alongside the M1. Eagle-eyed motorists spied a spectral hound framed against the rising/setting sun. Others swerved to avoid a dashing beast as it careered across the carriageway. Robin skipped along slip roads and bounded on the hard shoulder. Hovered on overhead bridges, haunted the central reservation. He blew with the wind. His eyes glowed at night.

After a while he grew tired of travelling and hung out instead in fields and forests. Living rough, he stole chickens and screwed sheep. Nothing in the farmyard was immune from his appetites.

As the carcass count mounted and the tracks led nowhere stories began to surface about a phantom predator. The trail of destruction totted and valued in the regional press. Disgruntled farmers interviewed on local radio. An investigative report on North East Today.

Then Robin fell in love. It began as a chance meeting. A Doberman bitch bolting south from Scotland. Contesting right of way, they fought most savagely on a bridge across a stream. Then moved in together in a thicket outside Ossett. The relationship was stormy. The sex incredible. Robin leapt on his baby's back and pumped like a frenzied piston. His baby took it standing and still howled for more.

The stealing and killing continued. Twofold. Life was a gas. Dodging buckshot. Confounding the enemy. One afternoon, hurtling down a country lane, Robin collided head on with a 2CV. The car disintegrated on impact. Robin slunk away with a buzzing in his ears.

But such outrageous fortune was of its nature short-lived. A couple of weeks later he collided with a Volvo. The end was mercifully swift and as he would have wanted it. Robin died as he had lived. Robin went out blazing.

jessica likes it

....

tiffany quin

**"Jessica has a quality that men admire and women
fear – an overt and shameless sexuality."**

Jessica is a sexual chameleon; she can be anything to anyone. For Jessica
is a prostitute. She may not walk the streets; she may only take payment
in kind, but sex is Jessica's game and, in this game, everyone pays.

When asked to join Jon and Sophie in their luxurious London flat Jessica
is only too happy to oblige but soon discovers that, for some people,
love lies on the other side of affection.

This is a novel of graphic, angry eroticism.

In this, her first novel and a stunning debut, Tiffany Quin slashes open the
sexual psyche to expose the trials of a damaged woman in a world where
there is no one left to trust.

IBSN 1 898051 10 0 Available: *Sept 1994* **£8.99**

Ringpull

Ringpull

Ringpull Order Form

All Ringpull books are available from good bookshops but may also be purchased by mail-order.

ISBN	TITLE	AUTHOR	PRICE	NO REQ'D	£ TOTAL
1 898051 02 X	Come Again	Ed Jones	£5.99		
1 898051 00 3	The Baby War	Peter Whalley	£5.99		
1 898051 01 1	Death Duties	Julian Roach	£11.99		
1 898051 18 6	The Allegation	Peter Whalley	£14.99		
1 898051 06 2	A Matter of Chance	Sheila S Thompson	£13.99		
1 898051 04 6	Robbers Bandits Villains	Peter Whalley	£7.99		
1 898051 03 8	Vurt	Jeff Noon	£7.99		
1 898051 05 4	Bitches & Bastards, Angels & Saints	Michael Robinson	£8.99		
1 898051 12 7	Beautiful Soup	Harvey Jacobs	£8.99		
1 898051 14 3	Technicolour Pulp	Arty Nelson	£8.99		
1 898051 13 5	Every Mother for Himself	Ed Jones	£8.99		
1 898051 10 0	Jessica Likes It	Tiffany Quin	£8.99		
1 898051 08 9	Without Consent	P Mantle & C Nagaitis	£16.99		
1 898051 11 9	Pollen	Jeff Noon	£14.99		
1 898051 09 7	Purely Decorative	Michael Montrose	£13.99		
1 898051 16 X	The B Book	Brian Randall	£16.99		
1 898051 19 4	Mythtaken Belief	Graeme & Sue Donald	£15.99		
1 898051 07 0	Manly Stanley & the Killer Whale	Ed Jones & R Jeffers	£9.99		
1 898051 17 8	The Story of Ax	John Perkins	£9.99		
			TOTAL:		

PLEASE SEND THE BOOKS I HAVE MARKED ABOVE.
I enclose £............... PLEASE SEND CHEQUE ONLY, NO CASH to: Ringpull Press, Queensway House, London Road South, Poynton, SK12 1NJ, UNITED KINGDOM. Tel 0625 850037. All prices and publication dates are correct at time of going to press but are subject to change without notice. All orders are supplied at price on receipt.

NAME: ....
ADDRESS: ....
....
....
....
SIGNED: ....